the sorrow of archaeology

The Sorrow
of Archaeology

A NOVEL

RUSSELL MARTIN

University of New Mexico Press
Albuquerque

10 09 08 07 06 05   1 2 3 4 5 6 7

Library of Congress Cataloging-in-Publication Data

Martin, Russell.
  The sorrow of archaeology : a novel / Russell Martin.
      p. cm.
  Includes bibliographical references and index.
  ISBN 0-8263-3725-2 (alk. paper)
  1. Mesa Verde National Park (Colo.)—Fiction. 2. Multiple sclerosis—
Patients—Fiction. 3. Pueblo Indians—Antiquities—Fiction.
4. Excavations (Archaeology)—Fiction. 5. Archaeologists' spouses—
Fiction. 6. Women physicians—Fiction. 7. Archaeologists—Fiction.
8. Colorado—Fiction. I. Title.
  PS3563.A7285S67 2005
  813'.54—dc22

                                            2005014577

Body type is Utopia 10/14.
Display is Tempus Sans.

for my mother,
Jean Rutherford Martin,

my daughter,
Megan Joy Nibley,

and in memory of my grandmother,
Roxie Elizabeth Lewis Rutherford

The past is still, for us, a place that is not safely settled.

MICHAEL ONDAATJE

It was the story she had been telling herself night after night ...

her perfectly secret story, delivered back to her....

Believing that such a thing could happen made her feel

weightless and distinct and glowing, like a fish lit up in the water.

ALICE MUNRO

one

away from the surrounding ground

SCRAPING EARTH AWAY from the short, gray femur, exposing it to the air with a bamboo tool after seven hundred years of entombment, I can't help but keep thinking: these canyons and crop-striped mesas mothered us both. This child and I are siblings surely, sisters of stone and bone and the curious accident of birth. Although I still can't see enough of her pelvis to be sure, I've imagined she was a girl during the two days since I first probed the midden's ashen soil with a trowel and unexpectedly bumped it against her skull. And in that time it's seemed certain to me that she was as rooted here as I am, strangely captive at the lips of these sandstone bluffs. Perhaps she lived long enough to be desperate to get away, much as I often have been, determined to see if life could be better lived in other landscapes, to fasten herself to fresher country, or even to become a kind of nomad, mercifully free from belonging somewhere.

In the dry early summer of 1992, I am nominally still a physician, but I dig in the dirt these days instead of taking stock of my patients' bodies, attending only to bones stripped of muscle, blood, and brain for almost a millennium by now. I sit in the shade of a juniper tree near the cliff-carved head of Tse Canyon in far southwestern Colorado, and part of a human skeleton is exposed in a meter-square hole beside me. Fragments of what once was a turkey-feather blanket lie among the vertebrae and finger bones, a tooth-tiered mandible and the small and delicate ribs. Beside them, and just now coming into view as I pick at the hard red soil with the blunted point of my trowel, is the dome of an overturned gray bowl, an intricate geometric pattern painted in black on its underside.

Working alone through the rising heat of the morning, then the blanched and baking hours of the afternoon, I expose the bowl, photograph it, and at last lift it and the mound of earth inside it away from the surrounding ground, then work to bare more bones to the light and the late twentieth century until I encounter something arresting: this second femur is much smaller than the first, seemingly stunted, and the tibia to which it once was attached also is atrophied, the child undoubtedly crippled by the misshapen leg. The defect must have been congenital, and it is easy to imagine that it also could have caused her death: the girl might have fallen from a rocky ledge, might have stumbled and struck her head. I'm eager to examine the skull as well now, but before I dislodge it I want Harry, my husband, and his crew to have a look at the remains of this poor Puebloan child, to ensure that my initial excavation doesn't destroy important information, to hear what they separately will make of a prehistoric girl who surely had to struggle to walk, who died in Tse Canyon and was buried beside this bowl.

"Me too," I mumble out loud, speaking to no one but the twisted skeleton as I labor to get to my feet, bracing myself with my cane as I stand, waiting before I start to be sure I have my balance, then walking with wide and measured steps along the powdered-dirt path to the place nearby where Harry too is digging into my homeland.

rabbit hunters on chestnut street

WHEN I WAS almost as old as this skeletal child must have been at the time she died, it seemed to me to be particularly good fortune to have been born right in the center of things—an ocean on either side of us; the twisting spine of the Rockies sending rivers both east and west; four separate state capitals—each one so big that *buses* plied its streets—only a long day's drive away. Over a bare brown hill from the bank of the San Juan River, you could stand on a cement slab and touch four states at once: Colorado, New Mexico, Utah, and Arizona. The slow-witted tourists assumed you had to stick an appendage into each state to perform the feat, but we shrewder locals realized that all you had to do to truly center yourself was to plant an instep right where the incised lines intersected. The Colorado history text opened with the story of the people who first began to inhabit Montezuma County back when Jesus was growing up in similarly arid circumstances, and it ended with a brief mention of the oil boom of the early fifties that had turned little Cortez into a tacky version of modern times. It was hard for a twelve-year-old to imagine that any other place could matter more.

We lived on the north end of Chestnut Street, my parents and my sister Barbara and me, right where an unnamed arroyo curled into Hartman Canyon, the shallow, sage-filled little depression encompassing all the magic of the Wild West as far as the kids in the neighborhood were concerned. Unlike my father, who was vice-principal of the high school, or my mother, who made mosaic-tile serving trays and appliquéd barbecue aprons and who dreamed of a far bigger life, my grandparents actually seemed connected to the country. They raised hay and red-hided cattle, had a garden so they could can food for the winter, and their last name, Lewis, was the same as the name of the farming community in which they lived, twelve miles north of town—both names supplied by my great-grandfather, who in 1897 had abandoned his Kansas City hardware store for "space," his appellation for the empty expanse of land that spread northwest from the settlements in Montezuma Valley toward scattered Mormon outposts in southeastern Utah. The fact that Hiram W. Lewis had established the still-extant post office called Lewis, Colorado, seemed to me to be further proof that I belonged to a line of people who were right in the thick of things. By the time I was in junior high, the region's earliest settlers—whom my grandparents had always called *Moquis*—began to be referred to as *Anasazi*, a Navajo word the archaeologists took a liking to for a time, one that was supposed to mean "the Ancient Ones," but which actually meant something more like "old strangers who were our enemies," according to Benson Yazzie, a Navajo kid in my science class.

All I really knew about the Ancient Puebloan people in those days was that they were the reason a national park now covered much of Mesa Verde, a high, canyon-cut island of land that rose just south of Cortez. Somehow Mesa Verde never lost its exotic luster, even after a lifetime of Memorial Day–weekend excursions—my father always delighting in the way the masonry ruins seemed exquisitely at home in the cool and arching sandstone overhangs, my younger sister never quite so enthusiastic, sometimes so bored she would stay in the Corvair with *Meet the Beatles* or another favorite book rather than trek with us into secreted, spellbinding Balcony House, suspended in a shallow cave hundreds of feet above the canyon floor. For my father, the Mesa Verde architecture was everything—the precisely shaped stones, walls as straight and true as transits and T-squares could have made them, balconies cantilevered on bark-stripped juniper beams, circular kivas dug into the hard-packed earth. My mother, not surprisingly, took far more interest in the crafts—beautiful baskets, some woven so tightly they held water, sandals and satchels, bracelets and beaded necklaces, fine pottery that looked as if it might have been painted by twentieth-century abstractionists.

I was a dozen years away from entering medical school, and bones still seemed creepy, but I remember being fascinated, even then, by the remains of the people themselves—skeletons of short and stocky people who were prone to suffer from bad teeth, bad backs, and osteoarthritis; the hard cradleboards that flattened the backs of children's skulls; primitive menstrual pads made of woven barks and fibers; mummified bodies brazenly displayed in glass cases, the leathered skin on their faces drawn into expressions of quiet anguish. Yet more than anything else, I think I was intrigued by the Puebloans' surprising numbers: on Mesa Verde and throughout the tilting valley to the north, as many as thirty thousand people once had been at home here, three times the number who lived here now—early farmers tending land at Lewis, potters shaping clay from the banks of Hartman Creek, rabbit hunters on Chestnut Street, kids in breech cloths at play in the arroyo that later was ours.

extraordinary acts

MY HUSBAND HARRY wears a cowboy hat so bent into submission, so sweat- and soil-stained and indispensably part of his everyday field apparel that it has achieved true notoriety by now. His jeans are torn in the knees and crotch; the steel toes of his work shoes shine through holes in the leather, his forearms and broad, expressive face so sun-darkened they nearly match the shoes. He is sifting soil through a frame-mounted screen—stopping occasionally to examine pebbles and ceramic sherds that are caught by the wire mesh—when he sees me walking toward him through the trees.

"Well, did you get her out?" he asks, vigorously shaking the last of the earth through the screen before laying it aside, the disarming smile he always uses to such easy advantage spreading across his face.

"She *is* a female, I'm pretty sure," I say. "I've got the pelvis now, and the sciatic notches sure look female to me. But I want you to come look. The right leg is deformed, stunted. I'm a little surprised she lived as long as she did."

"How old?"

"Ten or twelve maybe. I want to check the skull for signs of trauma, but you'd better lift it out. I don't want to screw anything up. Can you come now?"

"Okay," Harry surrenders. "Let me touch base with Alice and Charlie and then I'll be right behind you. You love it when I'm behind you."

This time I manage half a smile, pleased that, given the circumstances, Harry still can make a sexual jest, aware too that the love-making that for years so often confounded us with a kind of aching disconnection and Harry's pouting disappointment now is little more than memory. "I'll be the one stumbling down the trail," I tell him.

Henry David Donagan MacLeish, forty years old come the first of July and fully six years younger me, was raised in Cherry Hills, an affluent Denver suburb, his father an esteemed anesthesiologist who had made himself genuinely wealthy, his mother a lawyer who specialized in contentious divorces. Gregarious, engaging, his intellect quick and effortless, Harry first was captivated by the obscure science of archaeology during a summer in his teens when a group of students from Denver Country Day School lived in tents for ten weeks, at work on Tom John Brown's long-term excavation of the large Puebloan settlement called Cow Canyon Ruin in northwestern Montezuma County.

Something about the slow and measured methodology of this academic digging in the dirt attracted the kid who otherwise couldn't sit still; something about the rooting for information in stones and bones, in scraps of material that till now had escaped decay, seemed to challenge him, to goad his curiosity. And there was even something about the feel of the land in this dirt-poor, rock-crested corner of Colorado that had an indefinable kind of appeal. Rough roads and scattered ramshackle towns, dryland farms that seemed to cling to the back of the neck of the world, ranches where the fences were eternally falling down—all seemed oddly compelling during the long, sweltering, sun-drenched days of that summer.

When—in Boulder, nearly a decade later—I met him as he passed me a joint at a mutual friend's annual May Day party, he had seemed astonished to discover that the family-practice resident who didn't know quite how to take him had grown up in Cortez—the town and the country surrounding it still possessing a compelling kind of magic as far as he was concerned. "What a wonderful place to be a kid in," Harry had said, seemingly eager to sustain our conversation, infatuated by my hometown, I presumed, and certainly not by a rather unassuming looking woman who clearly was several years his senior.

"And a great place to get away from," I had assured him. "By the time you're a teenager, you're absolutely desperate for someplace hip."

The child buried at the head of Tse Canyon probably didn't live far into her teens, Harry agrees, as he and I compare the leg bones. Then he takes my bamboo pick and begins to free the skull from the dirt packed tightly around it. "Look at this," he says before long. The girl had suffered a severe blow; the skull's arching parietal dome is marred by a ragged hole.

"She must have fallen quite a distance," I say as Harry helps me get down on my knees for a closer examination.

"But look at the hole. If she fell, she must have fallen on something hard and pointed. Maybe this happened when something hit her."

"Like...?"

"Like an ax. A rock held in somebody's hand..."

"She was killed?"

"Could have been. You'd think that if she had fallen, the skull would be crushed. This looks like the blow was limited to the area where the hole is."

"Would they have...? No. No one would have killed her because..." I can feel the blood drain from my face.

"The people in the lab will be able to do a better job of describing what penetrated the skull, but that won't explain anybody's motivation."

"Sometimes I wonder what all your collected minutia is worth when it doesn't end up explaining anything," I say, my mood suddenly soured by his too-brief explanation.

"What fields do you know where they answer everything to everyone's satisfaction?" It's Harry's classic kind of response, an attempt to remind me that life isn't perfect anywhere. But then there's a shift in him, and now his attention to me seems laced with concern. "You okay? I should get back, but I could come finish this at the end of the day if you want to head home." He tips my hat forward into my face and massages the nape of my neck, and in doing so announces that it's far too hot for a fight.

"No. I'm okay." I reach into the hole and rub at the skull's brown-stained bone with my thumb. "This is my little project. She is." And as I go back to work, scraping, photographing, mapping the square, separating the last of the bones from the soil, wrapping each one in paper and laying each bone in a box, my thoughts drift away from my swelling miscommunications with Harry and back to the circumstances of this child's death—to what, or who, brought her short life to a stop. Surely her deformity was responsible, but how so? Was her death someone's horrible and brutal responsibility, a father's or mother's awful decision meant to save her from more suffering? I can imagine that: I have no children of my own, but I have been a physician long enough to know that simply staying alive isn't always—not every time— worth the terrible trial. And in the year since my own limbs have begun to betray me, I have discovered what this child too must have understood—that effortless movement is magic, sleight of hand or foot or thigh, proof, if we need it, that each one of us performs extraordinary acts a thousand times a day.

noms de cowboy

I WAS GENE Autry for a time, racing across the lawn on Center Street with a stick-horse between my legs, making the middle years of the fifties safe for decent folk with the help of Bobby Magneson, my next-door neighbor, who called himself Roy Rogers, the two of us insisting on the *noms de cowboy* despite my mother's growing dismay at the specter of raising a tomboy. I owned a red felt hat with a drawstring, which I could wear flipped onto my back à la Annie Oakley when I was feeling feminine; I had a fringed jacket and a six-shooter on each hip, and for reasons I really don't understand, I was absolutely enthralled by that shoot-'em-up western myth until at ten or so I finally fell in love. With a horse.

Bill was a bay gelding with hoofs the size of pie pans and a commensurately sizable penis. I know I was put off by that strange and slightly disgusting appendage of his on the occasions when I saw it fully extended, and I simply don't accept the psychologizing that suggests that horse cocks are the reasons for most girls' equine infatuations. The reason I loved Bill—a sedate seventeen-year-old cow horse my grandfather had bought with a nod of his head and a fifty dollar bill at the Cortez Livestock Auction—was simply that Bill seemed to be a gentleman. I could scrape his teeth inserting a curb bit, poke him in the eye as I struggled to lift the bridle over his ear, send the saddle spinning between his legs when I forgot to tighten the cinch, and he remained a model of measured composure. I would ride him for hours, round and round in the south pasture where he otherwise would be grazing, and he never gave the slightest signal that ferrying me wasn't a fine way to spend the day.

My grandfather, Win Lewis—the source of my red hair and an inveterate teller of tales—had tried to convince me that Bill once had worked at a racetrack in California, that he had run in huge ovals so much in his younger days that walking in similar fashion was simply second nature for him. But Granddad was careful to make it clear that Bill was his horse, that he didn't belong to Barbara or me or our cousins from Colorado Springs, who rode him (mercilessly it seemed to me) for a week each year in early August. We were merely Bill's "partners," as my grandfather put it. I remember him telling me, just before a pneumonia sent him to the hospital and kept him there till he died, "Sarah, old Bill's a better person than most people are. Horses like him don't come around too often."

Mourners said similar kinds of things about Winton Albert Lewis on the blustery April day he was buried, and I like to think that their comments were genuine. True, he had disappeared on week-long drinking binges a half-dozen times in his married life; he could scold you so severely on occasion that you were sure you could never again look him in the eye; but he loved his own patch of ground with a sweet pastoral passion, and for forty-eight years he loved my grandmother with something akin to a schoolboy's crush. He revered FDR as a kind of secular saint and occasionally would aver that Ike should have stuck to soldiering. He complained continually—sometimes cussing a blue streak as he did so—about the stupidity of domestic cattle, yet on cold spring nights he would readily surrender his sleep to help bring new and bawling calves safely into the world. He told me once, offhandedly, that I could do anything I wanted to with my life, and that assurance, however subtle, supported me like a stanchion in the years after they laid his body in the small community cemetery a half-mile east of the house where he had been born.

I don't think Oma cried on the day of my grandfather's funeral. What I noticed on her face instead of tears was that beatific expression that has always seemed to substantiate her rare and precious wisdom, my grandmother greeting her neighbors and kin that day with an unspoken acknowledgment that all of them were sharing something elemental, a death that was hard to bear but that somehow had to be. Oma worked in the kitchen in the early afternoon, helping ready the casseroles that women from nearby farms and ranches had dropped off a few hours earlier, cutting the ham, heating the fat, green King's Banquet beans she canned with bacon and onion each autumn, and which long had been her signature dish, working with a daughter, daughters-in-law, and friends to prepare the luncheon that has always seemed to me to be the only burial ritual that really has much meaning. She hugged everyone in her house as, group by group, people got up to go home late in the afternoon, assuring them that she would let them know if she needed anything, thanking them for something she left specifically undescribed. She hugged me too when I told her I'd be back in a little while, a fourteen-year-old with her grandfather's hair explaining that it seemed like a good idea to go curry his horse.

a life like that

I'M BOILING PASTA when my mother calls from Santa Fe wanting to know how I'm feeling, eager to warn me again that working in the sun all day is something I shouldn't be doing.

"We've talked about this before, you know," I say into the telephone as I walk out onto the porch to wave Harry in to dinner. "I appreciate your concern...Yes...I know...But I'm not going to stay home and make myself crazy. Thank you for reading up on this, and yes, I know heat can make symptoms worse. It makes mine worse. But I haven't had an exacerbation in six months. I feel good. I'm happy, and I'm going to pretend I'm an archaeologist for as long as I can. I'm sure it does me more good than harm."

Harry mimes a cheer as he comes onto the porch, hearing my half of the conversation, assuming he knows to whom I'm speaking by the familiar filial strain in my voice. My mother and I long have tended to argue about which one has the clearer understanding of dozens of topics, far from the least of which is my struggle with disease and my mother's ongoing concern. As I listen to her, I motion for Harry to attend to the pasta, and I'm still silent when he opens the screen door again and sits beside me on the railing.

"Mother! No, for Christ's sake," I say at last, shaking my head, then whispering to Harry that I'll be off the phone in a moment.

But Harry surely isn't surprised when he eats alone. Although I seldom see my mother these days, the two of us talk regularly, my mother calling simply to inquire about how I'm feeling, calling with the splendid good news that barley syrup or mud-bathing or cold-water enemas have just been proven—beyond any doubt—to be an effective treatment for multiple sclerosis. Mother calls to remind me that Wednesday is the summer solstice, to inquire about whether my cookware is that awful aluminum stuff, to share the blissful information that she has begun to date the dentist who is treating her TMJ.

My parents divorced when I was ten, my father leaving Cortez with an English teacher ten years his junior, my mother reeling in angry disbelief for a long time afterward and somehow blaming Barbara and me for his disappearance, it always seemed. None of the three of us understood how he could leave us. My mother hoped for too long that he would be back, and I did my best to fill in for him in ways that I thought she would welcome, not under-standing that lawn-mowing and the regular trash detail weren't his contributions to our little family that she missed the most. Then, my junior year in high school, he did return—with Fran, the English teacher who was now his wife—and that event ulti-mately spurred my mother into leaving the town she never really had been at home in during nineteen years of residence, going first to Denver, where she grew up, then on to New Mexico when Santa Fe began to seem the place she was meant to be. And in Santa Fe, Louise Lewis became Luisa, a weaver and a woman of many metaphysical interests, a great believer in the medical efficacy of crystals and a smorgasbord of cathartic diets, a woman who has become equally sure that astrology uncannily explains the human condition. Although neither of her daughters seem to be similarly seeking enlightenment, my sister Barbara and I have been pleased in recent years by how secure our mother has grown, the literal terror and sustained sadness that followed her divorce finally replaced by brimming self-confidence, if also by an adher-ence to what seem to us to be some formidably odd ideas.

"She says she's sure that if I came to Santa Fe for six months and had therapy from this friend of hers," I say when I come into the kitchen at the end of the long conversation, "I could throw my cane away, at the least, and probably get cured. She's full of all these miracle stories, but they just sound like remissions to me."

"You want to go?" Harry is opening the bottle of beer he plans to attend to while I begin to eat.

"You want to get rid of me?"

"You are kind of in the way of some major scandal I'm planning."

I try to remain lighthearted, but his joke has touched on a subject that's much on my mind. "That's going to happen." I look at him and offer a smile. "You're going to get tired of having less than major-league sex with somebody who can't feel anything, who's about as lithe as a baseball bat."

Harry doesn't respond for a moment, trying to find an easy way out of a conversation he does not want to have. "Then you better go get that cure, hadn't you? Your health is one thing, but when my sexual needs are on the line, well, we're talking about something serious here." Joking is always his first line of defense, his first choice for an ally when I want him to be open with me, when I seem to understand too well who he really is.

"Listen to me for a second," I say, reaching across the table for his hand. "I just ... The worst thing would be to ignore it, or for us to pretend that it isn't a problem."

"Sarah ... I can't talk about it as if ... not now anyway."

"Okay."

"I'll try to figure out a way to say what I want to say."

"Do," I tell him.

At twilight, the two of us and the border collie we call Teddy walk through the grass pasture and down to the edge of the pond. I use my cane to maneuver across the uneven ground; as he walks, Harry repeatedly throws a stick for the insistent, jubilant dog. Beyond the tall cattails that ring the glassy surface of the water, a green and newly mowed meadow stretches away to the south, its fragrance sweet and wet and thick with the pleasures of a summer evening. In the distance, the high northern escarpment of Mesa Verde rises up abruptly, its sandstone cliffs still orange in the last of the light.

"I don't want to make plans," Harry says as we sit on the wooden pier that reaches out over the water, its surface now roiled by Teddy's determined paddles. "I'll try to talk about this now, but I don't want to assume we already know what's going to happen to the two of us."

"The Santa Fe shamans notwithstanding, I think we know I'm not going to get better."

"But maybe not any worse. And this idea that you're waiting for the day I walk out the door..."

Harry's wounded tone triggers my sympathy, triggers something in me that is quick to try to relieve his pain. "No. It's just... If you were in my position you'd... I want you to know that I understand that this isn't easy for you. Any of it."

"And don't you see? What makes me feel like such a fucking shit is talking about what *I* have to deal with when you're the one with..."

"With the legs that don't work."

Harry doesn't respond, can't respond except to throw Teddy's stick and watch for its distant splash. I reach down, dipping my cane in the pond, cutting the water, splashing Harry's feet as if to say never mind.

"It isn't just this, just the MS," I add after a time. "From the moment I realized all those years ago that somehow you were attracted to me, I've known too that I wouldn't always be enough for you." His face is blank when he turns to look at me. "It's always seemed to me that you could love me enormously if I could turn into someone else."

"I've wanted us *both* to be different people, to change every day—to remake ourselves a million times. I mean, why would anyone want inertia?" He emphasizes his question by heaving the stick far out into the water.

"I've never been...I don't know, complicated enough for you," I say. "You want a whore and a mommy and somebody who can drink even you under the table all rolled into one. You get this ridiculously easy-to-spot crush on about every woman you meet. But *me*, plain-Jane Sarah Lewis from little Scratch Ankle, Colorado...of all the zillion things you're passionate about, I'm not sure you've ever felt truly passionate about me."

"What I've felt... what I've hoped is that we both really let go, soar with our lives," Harry says, defensively, "to believe anything's possible and make exactly what we want out of them."

"But this *is* what I want. You are. A life with you. And that scares the shit out of you, doesn't it?"

"Jesus, Sarah," Harry says, but then he says nothing more.

"The skeleton. That girl," I finally say to end the silence. "What are the chances of coming up with something substantive about how she died?"

"You're curious about whether she was killed because of the deformity." Harry lightens. I can feel him begin to relax with the change of subject.

"I don't know. Yeah. I mean, if it wasn't an accident, why would someone have struck her?"

"At an abandonment-era site like that, I suppose it's possible that her people all were heading south and she simply couldn't make the trip. But... depending on what we find, we might be able to tell whether the site was inhabited for very long after her death. Maybe somebody in the lab will come up with something interesting. Shall we hire some hotshot forensic pathologist?"

"Do you find things like this very often—evidence of violence, if that's what it is?"

"Yeah. Well, not every day, but... It couldn't have been an easy life in the best of circumstances. Maybe half the kids survived to ten years old. People got sick, broke their arms and legs, got infections, pneumonias, got arthritis early, and probably never had enough to eat. Death had to have been almost constant. At Tse Canyon we've found several skeletons with trauma that makes it look like they were just dumped, not buried. Your girl at least had a burial."

"They might have been desperate enough to leave that they killed her and left her behind?"

"I would guess she died a good while before that site was abandoned," Harry says, acquiescing to Teddy's demands, throwing the stick yet another time. "Maybe she did fall. I'll be honest, Sar. I doubt that we have much chance of ever telling you something conclusive."

"Imagine a life like that..." I say.

an ungenerous geography

IN THE YEARS since the Puebloan people had become "The Ancient Ones," a tourist-tailored notion of a hearty and happy primitive culture, it increasingly had seemed to me that their society was held together far more by hardship and stingy landscape than by anything else, that witches and powers evil enough to create constant havoc must have seemed as real to them as moonlight. Spirits, deities, all kinds of unaccountable forces must have been held responsible for ruined corn crops, for killing frosts and droughts that refused to surrender, for infertility and the deformities that often accompanied births. Gods must have been to blame when, in the end, their collective lives here seemed too difficult to bear any longer and the people wandered away.

The pamphlets at Mesa Verde and the feature stories in the travel magazines tended to focus on the great "mystery" of the Anasazi's disappearance. Where had the people gone? Had they simply vanished? But those questions ignored the available answers: At the end of the twelfth century, the Ancient Puebloan people had made their way toward places now called Zuni and Walpi and Acoma, to Frijoles Canyon, Pecos, and Santo Domingo, south into terrain that was warmer, if drier, than that encompassing and surrounding the Montezuma Valley, southeast into the more receptive region that flanked the Rio Grande.

Since early in this century, archaeologists had understood that the contemporary Hopi and Pueblo peoples were the Puebloans' descendants, and that generational connection seemed anything but mysterious. What remained unexplained to Harry and his colleagues in tattered field clothes was the complex mix of reasons why the Puebloan culture had survived intact and in place for a thousand years, then had fallen apart. Still no one could say conclusively why these arid uplands of the Colorado Plateau had been a good home for so long, then, very quickly it seemed, had become a place from which to flee—villages, possessions, a whole history abandoned.

I had known what it felt like to be certain you had to get away. Often in earlier years I had imagined driving over the crest of Mancos Hill and never returning, not even glancing in the mirror as the valley became a tangled memory. What I hadn't understood, and perhaps never would, was the decision to come here in the first place, to stay, to build shelters and clear fields and huddle by winter fires when so many other places must have seemed more hospitable. Why did those Old Strangers lay claim to such an ungenerous geography? What did Hiram Lewis encounter here that he felt was missing in Missouri? How did Oma endure here in her nineties?

the effects of child-rearing

BARBARA HAS DRIVEN me out to Lewis and, as usual, is reeling from the effects of child-rearing—her twelve- and ten-year-old boys (as well as the husband I've barely tolerated during the dozen-plus years of their marriage) assuming, she claims, that her sole purpose in life is to keep them in clean underwear, cold Pepsi, and mashed potatoes.

"If I killed myself," she says, glancing across the seat at me, "the boys would have a ball game and wouldn't be able to make the funeral. Rudy'd be there, but in the middle of the service he'd get the hots for the woman who was singing 'Ave Maria.'"

I laugh and my sister shakes her head, aware that I enjoy her comic descriptions of her domestic turmoil, the life she contends has taken such a wrong turn. At the end of the 1960s, soon after I headed off to Bryn Mawr, Barbara—the comelier, shapelier, and always rather more outgoing sister—enrolled at Fort Lewis College in nearby Durango, struggling with the rigors of higher education only until Rudy Matlock of Alamosa had his way with her and pretty well ensured that her big dreams, whatever they were, would not be realized. Barbara miscarried the first baby well into her second trimester, miscarried a second child before any of us knew she was pregnant again, then carried both Jason and Ryan to term during Rudy's marathon years at the Owl Tavern in Cortez, an era during which he shot eight-ball at the back of the bar every night instead of trying his hand at fatherhood. By the time he finally landed a succession of jobs operating a backhoe and somehow decided to assume a bit of responsibility, the boys were well on their way to becoming teenagers, and I think they hardly knew this guy who could so easily make their mother cry.

As I really got to know the boys—once Harry and I moved back to Cortez in the spring of 1983—I discovered that I adored the little characters, excusing their antics as they grew older, defending them in the face of their mother's exasperation, and bestowing gifts with only the vaguest excuse. I think Barbara appreciates the attention Harry and I continue to lavish on her children, and I know it's a kind of pleasant counterpoint to the sororal discord that still is far too common between Barbara and me. But somehow, in addition to continually insisting to me that my marriage is a secure and genuinely good one in comparison with hers, Barbara occasionally seems to begrudge the appearance that I have nothing but fun with her kids while she—and she alone really—has to shoulder the realities of raising them.

"I could keep the boys for a few days, you know," I tell her. "I'd love to. It's not like my presence is actually required out at the site. You and Rudy could go to Lake Powell or something. Or to Santa Fe—let Mom entertain you."

"Do you know how long Rudy would last at her house? The first time somebody came over for ginseng tea and deep discussion, he'd be history."

"So go to Ouray. Stay at the St. Elmo. No kids, no TV. A big brass bed."

"Jesus, Sarah," she says, "this thing's going to require a little more than a passionate weekend to patch it up. Besides, sex for Rudy is sort of like eating supper. You do it because if you don't you'll be hungry in the morning, not because it has a thing to do with anything else, and it sure as hell doesn't *mean* anything."

"It was just a thought."

"I stand all day at that teller window at the bank and I think, God, *this* is the life I got?"

"You should hang out with Harry more often," I tell her. "You'd love his stirring pep talks about how anything's—*every-thing's* possible."

"What would you and Harry know about real life?" Barbara wants to know.

"You want to trade?" I ask her icily.

"No, I don't want to trade, and I don't mean to sound like an insensitive bitch, but sometimes..." She stops the car as she pulls off the county road into Oma's driveway, the towering old cotton-woods that line it forming a kind of canopy. "That was a rotten thing for me to say. Your life's pretty real, I do realize that."

"Forget it."

"I'm trying to apologize."

"I know you are," I tell her.

this purported paradise

YOU COULD TAKE the train as far as Dolores in the years after
the turn of the century, but then your only options were to ride a
buckboard or the back of a Navajo pony as you headed out into
space. President Lincoln's Homestead Act had opened much of
the surveyed West to settlement, and by the turn of the century
even Montezuma Valley was receiving a rush of immigrants.
Hubbard and Margaret Spencer and their four children had left
Texas in the summer of 1909, stepping off the train at the Dolores
depot to discover that this purported paradise looked every bit as
miserable as did the mesquite-choked prairies they'd just abandoned, no one in my ancestral family feeling a bit better when, six
hours and thirteen miles later, a hired teamster pulled his wagon
to a halt and pointed to the sorry acreage a mile west of the Lewis
post office that would become the Spencer homestead.

Hubbard Spencer and the oldest boy finally had grubbed the
last of the stubborn sagebrush out of the ground with hoes and had
planted a pasture and fields of oats and feed corn when Margaret,
barely pregnant again, contracted phlebitis and died. It fell to Mary
Margaret, at thirteen the elder of the two girls, to try to take her
mother's place—preparing meals and keeping the primitive house
in order, tending to the washing and the garden that had to flourish
if the family was to survive the distant winter, patching britches

and telling bedtime stories, surrendering her own adolescence to the needs of her siblings and the father who, more and more, responded to hardship with cold and stony silence.

Five years later, however, Hubbard and his children had succeeded well enough to take title to their 160 acres. Both boys had quit school and were working the place alongside their taciturn father; little Blanche had turned fourteen and had become as capable as her older sister, and Mary Margaret had fallen in love with a redheaded suitor named Winton Lewis. Seven years her senior, Win Lewis was in the process of finishing his house— already something of a local showplace, complete with dormers in the second story and a front porch graced by Doric columns— when Mary Margaret agreed to marry him. Three days after her nineteenth birthday, on her wedding day, she moved into the house and never moved out.

Win and Mary Margaret Lewis's house didn't have electricity for the first thirty years; a cistern by the back door had to be filled with water out of an irrigation ditch; the outhouse was down by the calving shed; and the two bedrooms soon were too few. Twin boys were born in the spring of 1915; a girl, then a boy—my father—then another girl followed in successive summers. A child was stillborn in the early years of the twenties, then influenza took two of the children in 1926. Three survived into their teens—one of the twins and the youngest girl and boy—each one in turn leaving home to go to high school in Cortez, twelve miles away, the distance deemed too great to allow more than a couple of weekend visits each term back to the place that shared their surname.

It was Aunt Ruth's second child, my cousin Jimmy, who first called his grandmother Oma—the name "Grandma" too much for him—and Mary Margaret had been Oma ever since, through the lean war years that dragged out the Depression like a story that wouldn't end, through the births and nascent lives of nine grandchildren in the hopeful era of the fifties, during which time the cattle business finally flourished but Win's health began to fail. And she was Oma still once she was widowed in 1963, living alone in the simple house her husband had built for her until, two decades later, at age eighty-seven, her children decided she should move to town. My father, who by now lived in Boise, Idaho, returned briefly to help arrange his mother's move into an apartment in a retirement center in Cortez only to hear her inform him and his anxious sister that, as long as she was the one who was living her life, she'd make her own decisions. It had been sixty-eight years since Oma last had emptied her mahogany dresser, since pictures of family members and a painting of Jesus had come down from the walls and precious possessions had gone into boxes. She saw no point at this late stage, she told her children and grandchildren, in getting to know new surroundings. Besides, she said, she had a home and didn't have need of another.

In the years since she had determined to live out her life at Lewis, Oma had grown frail, and arthritic knees now necessitated the use of an aluminum walker, yet she still read large-print books each morning and afternoon and watched television late into each night; she continued to crochet blankets for infant great-grandchildren, still canned quarts of King's Banquet beans each autumn to give as gifts at Christmas. She still could recount wonderful stories about the summer she and my grandfather had spent without children—that first summer they were married—at his cow camp on Wild Horse Mesa, and she still was full of questions and bright-eyed curiosities about a world into which she virtually had never ventured. She loved to ask me about medicine—about basic anatomy and what seemed to her to be the divine mysteries of healing, and about how you possibly went about telling someone she was dying. She often queried Barbara about the bank, full of wonder at how they moved all that money around like magic. To Harry went occasional and always slightly troubled questions about why the Moquis had chosen to leave this place.

nine decades absent answers

OMA'S EYES ARE moist as she listens to me describe the skeleton I have unearthed at the ruins of Tse Canyon Pueblo. She sits still and straight, and her rust-colored lounger seems to envelop her. Once, like many of the farm wives who were her friends, she was dramatically overweight. But now her forearms are gaunt and fragile and her narrow face is deeply etched by her ninety-three years. "The precious little thing," she says to Barbara and me, seated on a sofa adjacent to her rocking chair in the small, book-piled, picture-lined living room. "How old was she when she died?"

"Harry and I think about twelve or so," I say. "Couldn't have been much more than that."

"You know, how we used to live here on the home place, how rough it was sometimes, it's surprising a little crippled child could live that long back in those days when things had to be so much harder still. Do you think she might have caught polio?"

"Well, I'm no pathologist, but from the looks of the leg bones, I think probably she was born with some sort of deformity. But it's hard to be sure. Harry's bemused by all this, of course. Finding human remains isn't particularly novel for him, and he keeps reminding me that even seemingly healthy children must have died all the time."

"Oh, but losing your little ones..." Oma stops to reach for the words. "Indian people wouldn't be any different. I thought I'd ache forevermore—truly hurt all over the same way my heart was broken—when Granddad and I lost Edwin. Then Dorothy died six days later. People said someday the Lord would let the hurt pass, but I thought they were such fools."

"Did it ever?" Barbara asks.

"Not really, honey. Not really. Oh, something happens. Time does something to it, dulls it, I suppose, but your babies are the best thing you ever do, and you never know why they had to die."

"You mean getting to be more than ninety years old doesn't answer all the questions?" I attempt to kid her.

"Oh, gracious. It doesn't even begin to. It's like your little Moqui girl. Reasons why things happen, well..." There is a look of acquiescence on her face, one of nine decades absent of answers, before she turns to Barbara. "And how're my boys, by the way?"

"The monsters? The maniacs? They're fine, Oma. Just fine. I'll bring them with me next time, but you'd better brace yourself. Jason shaved the sides of his head and the top's coal black all of a sudden."

"Why on earth...?"

"Fashion statement. Proof that no mother bosses that boy around. Evidence that he is way cool, and cool is everything."

Oma seems tickled by the image. "Bless his heart," she says.

carry a big lightbulb

THE ONLY THING worse than being an acne-plagued freshman in high school is being a freshman whose father is the principal of the place. Teachers tend to coddle you shamelessly; either that or they can't seem to look at you without remembering that the bastard sired you in addition to all his other crimes. Your friends assume your grades are good for reasons that are primarily nepotistic, and those who get sent to Mr. Lewis's office to suffer the oak stick henceforth plot your assassination as a means of giving the man a taste of his own kind of medicine.

When he returned to Cortez to take a job as principal of the high school—and to try to rebuild a relationship with his daughters, I suppose—I think my father did try to understand the difficult position his job put Barbara and me in. He did his best to ignore us at school and, when we had dinner with him, to inquire about our academic progress without sounding like a principal on patrol. But about the time I began to wear a 60-watt bulb on a leather string as a necklace (because Bob Dylan had exhorted us to walk softly and carry a big lightbulb), about the time I began to reek of patchouli oil and to persuade Barbara to iron my hair, my father's dual role increasingly seemed to greatly distress him. I had become a common topic of conversation in the teachers' lounge, the sympathetic members of the staff agreeing that the principal's daughter couldn't help but act out a bit, others opining, I'm sure, that if they were David Lewis, that young woman would toe the line. My father tried to convince himself at first that this stage of mine would quickly give way to something else, but it wasn't long before he was trying to convince me that the hippie lifestyle that he and *Life* magazine were becoming so concerned about could ruin an otherwise promising adolescence.

My mother, to her credit, seemed to realize that something more than just inevitable generational discord was abroad in the land in those days, and I think she relished the fact that her daughter and a few of her daughter's friends had brought a touch of currency to provincial Montezuma County, but the big issues— like the fact that I refused to shave my legs or to wear the touch of eyeliner that she assured me would make me look pretty despite all the angry pimples—somehow seemed to stymie her. By the time in my senior year when I was caught smoking a cigarette in the science-wing rest room, both my parents were beside themselves with concern. Then my father found the roach of a joint in the ashtray of his new Impala (I could be truly stupid sometimes) and the family fell into a kind of crisis. Mr. Rhodes, the school's longest tenured guidance counselor, was enlisted to try to convince me that my behavior jeopardized my chances of being accepted by the colleges to which I had applied; Reverend Rosebrough, the Methodist minister, tried to explain that while, yes, there was much that deserved legitimate protest in America in those days, I was becoming unduly influenced by a group of young people bent on destroying not only the nation but themselves. This Jimi Hendrix, I can remember him telling me—and he had it on the good authority of an article published in the national Methodist magazine—was trying to use drugs and maniacal music to ignite a racial civil war.

For my part, I couldn't figure out what all the fuss was about. If I wore nothing but long skirts, hiking boots, and men's sport coats procured from the thrift store, it was simply because I liked those kinds of clothes. If I smoked a little pot with my close circle of friends, if I adored The Doors and was passionate about *Soul On Ice* and *Siddhartha*, it was only because somehow I had been lucky enough to escape the mind-numbing complacency that afflicted the rest of the citizenry of Cortez, Colorado—the "Town Without Hope" to those of us who would remain captive only until the semester was out and a grindingly slow summer job had come and gone.

My father was furious when the school board refused to allow me to graduate because I had quit the marching band in midyear and now lacked all the required activity credits—furious with the board for the de facto slap in his face, disgusted with me for the way my cavalier action had resulted in his public embarrassment. I remember sitting in the bleachers at the football stadium on a warm morning at the end of that May, hearing my father announce the names of my classmates, watching them file toward the dais as their parents in the seats surrounding us fairly burst with parochial pride. Sometime in the midst of the proceedings, Tom Turner, a history teacher who had become an important ally, quietly presented me with my letter of acceptance to Bryn Mawr—it was a private ceremony of sorts—and my mother hugged me as if to say she was proud of me in spite of it all. I remember staring at the mesa during an interminable valedictory address, seeing the shadows shift along the cliff line, seeing the low, flat-topped buildings on Main Street that stretched east toward the snowy peaks of the La Platas. From high in the stands, I looked down on my long-suffering father, who had participated in a dozen of these commencements by now, and who was undeniably wounded that his daughter wasn't participating in this one with him. I tried to find the few friends who were such close and vital accomplices beneath a sea of mortarboards, and I remember that I was giddy with the thought that the group of us had succeeded in getting away.

middle age among the ruins

"DID HARRY TELL you?"

"Tell me what?"

"Oh, I assumed you'd heard," says Alice. "Kay in the lab's been spending some time with your skeleton. She's pretty sure the girl's skull was broken by something stone, probably an ax head. Plus, I guess in addition to her leg, there are signs of an early onset of arthritis. Not a lucky kid." Alice is sitting with her back against the trunk of a tree as she eats her lunch.

"So she was killed." I try to sound nonchalant.

"Could have been an accident. Or who knows what. Or yeah, I suppose she could have been murdered, but that's probably a bit of a reach. Harry says she's really captured your attention." Alice, Harry's colleague and regular partner in alcohol-fortified crime, wears her snap-button shirt liberally unsnapped, exposing the swell of her breasts in a way that would be unimaginable for me to do, in a way that announces a kind of sexuality I suspect I simply never possessed. The cuffs of her tight jeans are tucked into weathered Wellingtons; her dark hair is pinned high on her head.

"You guys are so lame. Weren't the first human remains you came across sort of a big deal?"

"They were. No, I understand that. I think he meant the fact that she had that handicap, and that..."

"You two have put your heads together and decided that, since I'm in the same boat now...Please."

"We haven't decided anything." Alice sounds defensive. "I only brought it...forget it."

"Listen." I try to be conciliatory now. "I know what you mean. But the thing that actually interests me is the thought that some nasty things must have gone on among those people. I used to have this rather rosy, Ozzie-and-Harriet image of the Anasazi, one that didn't include executions."

"Or mercy killing."

"Maybe that's what it was. I'd just like to know."

"The whole abandonment question is like this. Here we are trying to figure out why the culture failed in the end, but maybe we're all blind to the fact that it wasn't a failure. Deciding to leave, getting the hell out of here, may have been absolutely brilliant. It could have been the best possible thing to do."

Alice Adelman has been my friend for more than a decade now, since Harry and I returned to live in the valley and Alice, seeing the region for the first time following the completion of her doctoral work, arrived hard on our heels. Married and divorced twice—and adamant that a third time would not be a charm—Alice spent most of the seventies in southern Mexico and Central America, the dissertation she had struggled with and finally finished at the University of Pennsylvania examining the evolution of Mayan ceremonial architecture. The prehistory of the American Southwest never interested her much until, in 1978, she floated through the canyons of the San Juan River with a National Geographic group and was entranced by the extraordinary petroglyph panels at the mouth of Butler Wash—a wonderful array of otherworldly figures, fetishes, and recurring geometric shapes pecked into massive, dark-stained walls of sandstone—evidence, Alice immediately was certain, that the Ancient Puebloans not only had been master builders but were enterprising shapers of symbol as well. Subsequent visits to what archaeologists believe once was a solar observatory at the Holly ruins at Hovenweep and to enigmatic Sun Temple at Mesa Verde convinced her that these people who had been potters, farmers, and masons also had strived to come to terms with the meaning and magic of the universe and convinced her as well to stay in the

Southwest a while. She found a stucco house on Elm Street in Cortez, found Harry MacLeish at the lip of Tse Canyon and talked herself into a job, and, a decade later, Alice, Harry, and I have become something of a storied threesome—sharing meals and movies and weekend get-aways, working side by side at the Tse Canyon excavation Harry supervises for the Bureau of Land Management, plotting protracted holidays in Spain, short flights from winter on the shores of Baja California, and peaceful middle age among the ruins of an earlier people.

During the ten years she has lived in backwater Montezuma County, Alice has become notorious for her scattershot liaisons with college-age archaeologists, as well as with men of more prosaic professions who are similarly young and comparably comely. But none of her relationships ever seems to last more than a month or two, and none, she has confided to me on numerous occasions, has made her hope that sometime she might truly live in concert with someone again. "I'm getting to be a pretty great date," Alice says when Harry infrequently presses her about her love life. "I really don't aspire to more."

"You're going to make me go back to work in a minute, aren't you?" I ask her. I'm lying now on a mat of piñon needles, my big-brimmed hat resting on my stomach.

"At the wages you're getting paid, I don't have the heart to be too demanding." Alice's tone becomes a bit concerned. "Is this getting to be too much for you?"

"Occasionally it is. But I've tried to convince my husband and my hovering mother that what would not be good for me would be to stay home and simply watch the soaps."

"Harry says the heat though..."

"Yeah, the heat can be a problem. But I'm interested. When Harry suggested I begin to dig out here, I thought, okay, sure. And I'm enjoying it, and, well, here I am for a while." I awkwardly hike myself onto an elbow before I add, smiling, "But I still think it's a very weird choice for an occupation."

"Our futures lying in ruins and all that?"

"Nothing to go on but bits and pieces that haven't decayed. Bones and sherds and weird little bits of information."

Alice says, "Sounds like medicine to me."

fireworks

TOM JOHN HAS joined Alice and me at Nero's, the dinner my treat since Harry is out of town for two days and our ostensible purpose is to plan a party for his fortieth birthday, one of the few times I've made much of the impending first of July, and the only such surprise for him in which I've ever conspired. Tom John is lobbying for something theatrical—fireworks or maybe a stripper, perhaps some sort of skit—and Alice keeps saying that what he'd really enjoy is just having all his friends get roaring drunk with him. My opinion falls somewhere between the two: if we're going to go to the trouble, I think we might as well make the celebration memorable, yet I know too that friendly, funny, hail-fellow Harry is also entirely capable of abandoning his own celebration—announcing that he has to finish writing some mythical report by eight the following morning—if the tenor of the merrymaking somehow makes him uncomfortable.

"Well, the ingrate can walk right out the door if he wants to; he won't spoil my evening in the slightest." Tom John's lush and rather sumptuous Arkansas accent hasn't diminished much in the four decades since he left little Gum Springs for good, an eighteen-year-old already painfully aware that his sexual orientation would make adulthood difficult even in relatively urbane and tolerant Little Rock and render it downright impossible anywhere else in his native state. He spent a year or two driving a bread truck in Chicago before he managed an acceptance into Northwestern University and a calculated detour around the Korean War. By the time he was teaching anthropology at Illinois State at the end of the 1950s, he had made several sojourns west into Anasazi country and had staked a kind of personal academic claim to the large and apparently important ruins in Montezuma County's Cow Canyon. His university minimally funded an annual field season; Tom John headed the excavation without a salary, and by 1968 (when a gangly kid named Harry MacLeish came to work for him) he had become a kind of summertime celebrity on the streets of Cortez—his hair worn long and wrapped at the back in a Navajo-style chignon, his floral-print cowboy shirts and heavy turquoise jewelry, plus a disarming frankness and the sense he quickly gave people that he had known them since they were babies, all combined to render him something special. If people sometimes whispered about his particular brand of bachelorhood, it didn't seem to bother them. I think in retrospect that Tom John Brown became a kind of local legend in large part because he was an obvious outsider who deigned to spend several months of each year among the sagebrush yokels, and there weren't too many people who did so in those days.

Although he was Harry's mentor, and probably more of a father than Harry Senior ever had been—the two men shared not just a profession but also avocations and prodigious gifts of gab—Tom John loves to tease Harry, to needle him in his presence and to pretend to defame him when he is absent, and tonight I find myself laughing again at his suggestion that living with Harry has been an eternal trial. "He's a great cook. That's all I can say," is my reply.

"Well, he'd better be, dear. He'd better be good for something besides . . . no, let's leave that topic alone."

"No sex talk," Alice demands. "It'll stir me up and I won't get any sleep."

We decide in the end that a boozy barbecue at our house is probably the sensible party to plan, and Tom John offers to pit-roast a pig, Alice screwing her face up in disgust at the thought but agreeing to take charge of inviting people. "Is this going to be everybody he knows, or just everybody he likes?" she wants to know.

"Invite everyone you can think of."

"God, I'll need a big hog." Tom John is having second thoughts. "Plus, the nuts-and-berries kids'll need some sustenance. Let's just forget all the work and somebody can make a run to Kentucky Fried Colonel."

"No," I say, "let's make this memorable. Alice, you might even need to buy a new come-hither outfit for the occasion."

"Well, then maybe I should rent one of those awful pastel tuxedos that all the Hispanic kids get married in. Wouldn't I cut quite a swath in one of those?" asks Tom John.

"I will not be wearing a dress or a tuxedo," Alice announces, "but you're right. If there are going to be a lot of people there, I may have to look requisitely hot. It may be time to do some trolling."

"Oh, kind sir..." Tom John pretends to swoon, then wonders, "You know, if hitting on everything with a penis in his pants is so vital to you, why in the wide world do you stick around this place?"

"I could ask you the same question," Alice retorts.

"And I'd tell you I've finally learned a thing or two late in this old life."

"Like what?"

"Like the fact that it isn't sex that makes you happy."

"It kind of perks me up," Alice says, and I laugh.

"No, sex is just our animal nature rearing its...well, we all know what rears, don't we? Happy is something else all together, sweetheart. Isn't that right, Sarah?"

"Do I have to get involved in this?"

"You have to give us your wise and considered counsel, yes."

"Well, as a learned physician..." I say before I find a new subject.

as ludicrous as cortez was

AMONG THE MANY hardwood trees and progressive thinkers in Pennsylvania, away from family and the tyranny of home for the first time, I marveled at how alive I seemed to be—terrified of my freedom and my isolation among strangers, euphoric for the same reasons, depressed and manic in almost equal measure. There was a kind of confidence among the people I met that I hadn't encountered before, a sense that they knew who they were and that their identities were nothing for which they had to apologize. I, on the other hand, came from a place whose very name—Cortez, Colorado—sounded as if it had been borrowed from a John Ford movie, a frontier berg where horses likely still stood tied to hitching posts and where the sheriff still ambled down wood-plank sidewalks. I came from a part of America that never crossed anyone's mind, I discovered, and I spoke with an embarrassing "western" accent that theretofore I hadn't known I had.

Among my friends—young women with whom I began to share the vibrant and passionate comradeship that, I now understand, makes coming of age so splendid—I became a kind of curiosity, the girl with the bright red hair and pathetically pockmarked face whose Rs sounded a little sticky. But by the autumn of my sophomore year, I think I had begun to take a certain pride in the fact that I didn't hail from Darien, Connecticut, or Newton,

Massachusetts. I began to brag about my part of the American outback, yet instead of falsely lauding how hip we were out West, the thing that I could be legitimately proud of was the landscape, the glorious emptiness. The photographs on the Sierra Club posters were images of home—"Here, this is the place, that's what it's like," I'd say with a kind of clutching nostalgia—and I knew without telling myself so that I'd live in the Rockies again. I wouldn't, couldn't return to Cortez, but Boulder or Bozeman or Santa Fe would be my home someday.

When Jill Frampton pressed into my hands a book called *Desert Solitaire* by some guy neither of us had ever heard of and told me I had to read it that instant, I acquiesced and was quickly transfixed. This Edward Abbey guy had eloquently and lovingly portrayed the environs of Moab, Utah, for heaven's sake, a place at least as forlorn and ludicrous as Cortez was and only two counties away. "This is the most beautiful place on earth," he had written, admitting that you could say the same of hundreds of other locales, but I wore his affirmation of the frowzy Four Corners country like a badge of honor as the book became required reading in the ensuing years.

By the time I was a senior biology major with adequate grades and a desire to go to medical school—for reasons I still couldn't succinctly explain—I knew without doubt that it was time to head home. I didn't apply to the University of Massachusetts, to Johns Hopkins or Columbia or to any of the dozens of schools where, so the word went, one would be soundly and successfully trained. Instead, I ended up in Albuquerque at a medical school with no real reputation and at a university with little to recommend it except that the ground was familiarly bare and brown in that part of the world, and it was cut by canyons underneath a dry and dramatic sky.

its rat-ass complacency

HARRY IS ALWAYS bemused by the border crossing. The moment the car jolts across the cattle guard and the WELCOME TO THE LAND OF ENCHANTMENT sign appears by the roadside everything seems suddenly altered: the highway's shoulder vanishes and the striping invariably fades; potholes pop open like craters and ancient pickups sit stalled at blind curves; in winter, if the road has been scraped down to a thin and thawing sheet of snow on the Colorado side of the cattle guard, you can count on six inches of slush in New Mexico.

As far as Harry is concerned, New Mexico remains the best of the Four Corners states. Much of Colorado once was a knotty-pine kind of place—"cowboy Bavarian" is the way he likes to describe it—but by now the scourge known as "resortism" has taken its dreary toll and holiday homes—so often strangely referred to as "ranches"—have brought their own sort of blight. Utah encompasses perhaps the single most astonishing chunk of geography on the planet, and its towns are tidy, but they are bland as a butter sandwich—a little like those in Iowa but absent all the excitement. Arizona has become little more than a place where people put themselves out to pasture—plump women in jogging suits, bald-headed men in bolo ties. But *New Mexico*. New Mexico is the Third World, and Harry relishes its rat-ass complacency. As a matter of fact, except for the capriciousness of the lines of latitude, Cortez rightfully would be part of the state to the south. It looks like a New Mexican town, feels like one, and the border is only forty miles away by the highway that cuts straight to Shiprock. As a native Coloradan, one possessed of its peculiar kind of chauvinism, Harry is rather proud that his home state also contains a strain of that wonderfully weird and disheveled town-building you only find in the true Southwest.

But the problem with New Mexico these days is that Santa Fe chic is threatening to devour the place, to turn it into an awful kind of caricature of itself. Crossing the border at Chromo, and driving south through Chama and Tierra Amarilla, Harry remarks to me that at least the lovely, impoverished mountain country still seems spared the onslaught of rapt attention. Abiquiu does show signs of becoming the principal stop on the Georgia O'Keeffe Memorial Tour, but the little city of Española remains wonderfully out of sync with the close of the twentieth century— pawn brokers and burger stands, body shops and roadside chile vendors, adobe and decades-old neon all in casual and comfortable disarray. It isn't until the hillsides grow thick with trophy homes and the highway begins to get crowded that Harry begins to bemoan the changes.

"Remember when we really used to love this place?" He sounds surprisingly nostalgic.

"The years I lived in Albuquerque, I thought having a practice here would be perfect."

"I'd never even been here till you brought me that first time. After the drive down from Denver, seeing this funky, quiet, brown little town that smelled like piñon smoke, I thought, if this woman can take me to these kinds of places..."

"You were wonderfully behaved, my dear. You did everything just right. Even meeting my mom that trip, you couldn't have been sweeter."

"I thought her boyfriend was a twit."

"Yes, but you're good with twits." I smile, reaching over to touch the denim stretched across his thigh. "No telling what this dentist of hers will be like."

"He'll be very... intense. And he'll want to talk shop with you, to prove that just because he's a DDS doesn't mean he's a dipshit."

"Stop. I don't want to think about it. I just want to be in a good mood and make this nice and simple. Nothing's going to faze me."

"You're right. I'll keep quiet about how all the Dallas matrons in pleated skirts and squash blossom necklaces have utterly fucking ruined this place!" His quick tantrum over, Harry heaves a deep breath.

"Don't worry. Cortez will never be trendy."

"I wish you could promise me that. I love it that you can drink good coffee there nowadays, but it's also a very bad sign."

"Your problem is that these backwaters you love so dearly are also poor as hell and they are dead ends for most of the people who live in them, Cortez included."

"If you can convince me that skyrocketing land prices and jobs as maids and kitchen help are a good solution, I'll promise to pray for prosperity."

"I know."

"Maybe we should move to... San Francisco," Harry says, full of sudden enthusiasm, as if we maybe we should move there tomorrow. "Wouldn't it be nice not to have to worry about everything surrounding you getting ruined by assholes?"

"People in cities have the same worries. They're different issues, but..."

"How do people have children in the face of all the world going to total hell?"

"Promise me, Henry, that we're not going to get into children this trip." I try to shape a steely smile, one meant to prove that I will broach no compromise. "That subject remains a distinct disaster with her."

"Maybe I'd better just drop you off." He sounds hopeful that I'll take him up on the suggestion.

"Maybe you should just show them your pretty teeth for two days," I offer instead.

something i have to hope is love

LIONEL IS A Leo, Luisa a Sagittarius, and the two signs are a propitious combination, or so it seems. I haven't seen my mother so lighthearted, so effervescent in a very long time. And Lionel Miller does seem like a nice enough man—his thick hair the color of cotton, his darker mustache perfectly trimmed, his eyes bright and (Harry has guessed correctly) somehow very intense. Lionel has made margaritas with Mexican Controy, key limes, and sea salt— they are his specialty, he avers—and we sit in the shade of a cottonwood on my mother's brick-cobbled patio.

"I'd love to see your digging sometime," Lionel says after Harry has done his best to explain the scope of the Tse Canyon project and the long-term goals of the research, something he does with a kind of clever élan when people visit the site, but a chore he normally goes to great lengths to avoid in the context of cocktails.

"Any time. We'd be glad to have you."

"We should go up sometime this summer." Mother is enthusiastic. "It's not exactly a trip to Scottsdale, I suppose I've told you, but you'd be amazed by the work these kids are doing. Sarah too— although I'm not at all sure she should be out there every day."

"Why such a large community that far from Mesa Verde?" Lionel wants to know, impressing me with the way in which he cuts off the other topic.

"Well, we're not at all certain that the villages on Mesa Verde were focal in terms of the population of the region. In fact, they may have been pretty remote. Some people speculate that the Mesa Verdeans were hillbillies, in effect, rubes up in the high country, and that the cultural centers actually were down in the valley at places like Tse Canyon."

"Really?"

"It's hard for me to imagine that particular valley was ever the center of anything," my mother interjects.

"Mother, spare us. It drives me crazy too, but it's where your daughters live, and your ex-mother-in-law—who wanted me to give you a hug for her, by the way."

"I know what you mean," says Lionel, a born mediator by the appearance of things. "I couldn't bear to live in Wichita again, but I have a son and grandkids there, and honestly, it's really the closest thing I have to home. Santa Fe's just where I get to play." He reaches for Mother's hand as they share a private glance, one that further goads me in the process.

"I'm too excited to finally have you three meet each other to get stuck on this." She is magnanimous now. "The important thing is that you two are happy, wherever you are."

"We are," offers Harry from the bottom of his margarita glass. He has opted to drink his way through the stickier moments of this evening's tête-à-tête. "And you are too, by the looks of things."

Mother's smile is radiant. "I'm surrounded by such terrific energy these days. And by such beautiful people."

"Take a bow, Lionel," Harry instructs. Lionel blushes and I'm afraid I visibly cringe. "I assume one of you is going to move in with the other one of these days." I can't believe what my husband is up to now; Mother's smile is a nervous one and she adjusts the pleats of her skirt.

"Well, that might come to pass, I think," Lionel responds carefully. "You've caught us a little off guard, to be honest, but we have..."

"And it's none of our—"

"Yes, I'm sorry, I didn't mean to pry," Harry says, fibbing about what he has meant to do.

"That's all right," she says, composed now. "I guess we've just demonstrated that people our age still aren't quite as comfortable with all this as you kids are."

"Fair enough."

"But that doesn't mean we don't have every bit as much fun," Lionel says, and I want to crawl into the cracks in the brick.

"Can we talk about repression in China or something?" I ask. "I'd even prefer the issue of whether I ought to go out in the sun."

Lionel laughs, Harry grins in a kind of agreement, and Mother says, "We'll eat, that's what we'll do. I'll serve you a wonderful dinner."

The city smells like piñon smoke in the still of the night, although the June weather hasn't warranted the fires. Curled on my mother's futon, my husband's knees pressed against the backs of my thighs, I lie awake listening to the incessant bark of a neighborhood dog and the occasional thunder of a muffler-less car. The evening with Mother and Lionel has gone as well as it could have, it seems to me now, and I have to admit that she might have allied herself with hundreds of men more objectionable than this dentist, yet there is something in the subtle switching of roles—me a partner in a marriage weighed down by the habits of two decades, she, in comparison, now full of youthful exhilaration and flush with romantic promise—that is strange and a little unsettling. I revel in her happiness, of course I do, and perhaps what I feel is a kind of jealousy, I decide, a longing on my part for my life, for our lives, to be as full of possibility as my mother's now is—giddy and healthy and unencumbered by time.

"I couldn't believe you asked them about living together," I whisper into the darkness. Harry sleeps so lightly I know he will answer.

"What?"

"I hope this isn't another flash in the pan. I don't want her to get hurt. She's so entranced at the moment."

"I don't think you need to try to protect her." Harry is groggy, but he's awake.

"It's weird to have the tables turned, worrying about your mother and her new young man," I tell him.

"I like him. I think he's fine."

"No...I'm just feeling a little maternal myself. I want her to be happy, but I suppose most of all I want her to be safe."

"Most of all I want to sleep."

"But we're on holiday." I'm animated now.

"But it's probably three in the morning."

"You're getting old, you know that?" I reach behind me and persuade him by making him hard, and Harry responds as I know without question he will, and we do our best to be quiet in my mother's living room. Although it's a desire I seldom have any-more, suddenly I'm eager to have my husband inside me. I want to be literally joined to him, to be reminded that there was a time when having sex with Harry was wonderful for me, regardless of what so often was missing for him. Nowadays, it's so different and very strange—the physical sensation that Harry is there but also not there, a man making love only with the parts of me I can feel, my beaten-up body bridging those spaces with memory, impuls-es arcing between damaged neurons with something I have to hope is love.

to buy some time

IT WAS THE beautiful efficiency of the human body that attracted me to medicine, I'm sure. I wasn't one of those students who opt for medical school simply because she's been told she's bright for twenty years, nor did I approach the profession with a kind of altruistic fervor, intent on saving lives. I did want to do something that mattered, that showed some tangible evidence of its value, but much besides medicine could have accomplished that. Instead, it was the wonderful wizardry of the corpus—first introduced to me in an anatomy class at Bryn Mawr—that led me to think, my God, this is something I could pay attention to for a lifetime.

There were moments—whole days and weeks really—in my first year of medical school at UNM during which I was certain I didn't actually have the intellectual stuff to become a physician, but I survived basic physiology and hematology and somehow maneuvered through the minefield of microbiology, and at some point late in the year I knew that if I could only make it out of the classrooms and into the clinics I wouldn't wash out of the place in shame.

During the course of those months, I had long discussions about my self-doubts with my cadaver, an ancient Hispanic woman who couldn't have been more than five feet tall, a woman who had borne many children once upon a time, who had died of bacterial pneumonia, and who, I liked to think, had been happy at the end of a fruitful life. Getting to know her body in ways even she hadn't known it, I couldn't help but be reminded of the stories I'd heard about tribal peoples thanking their prey for allowing themselves to be killed. Maria, after her death, had allowed me to come to know her in an incredibly intimate way, and it seemed that, at the very least, I owed her some conversation—a sense of who I was in return and of the great and complex challenge that was my present occupation. And I often thought of Oma during the hours I spent with Maria's atrophied body, sometimes thinking, oh, Oma's breasts have come to this too, as mine will someday as well if I get to have children; other times being reminded of a bargain I thought I would be very willing to make—my own body inevitably growing old and weak in exchange for the certain wisdom that motherhood and family and the aggregation of time had brought to Oma and, I hoped, to my Maria, and perhaps one day even to me.

Like lots of medical students, in the beginning I tended to contract every disease I studied. A case of diarrhea meant I had Crohn's Disease; a stiff neck and a bit of a headache meant meningitis; any new spot on my freckle-infested skin was a sure sign of melanoma. Ironically, I don't remember being terrified by symptoms of multiple sclerosis, but I did have to face the sorrowful fact that I was dying on several occasions. I had pancreatic cancer, I once was certain, and no doubt it had metastasized to my lungs and liver as well, and my prognosis was decidedly poor. My reaction—in addition to a stunning, almost incapacitating kind of fear—was to try to strike a deal. If I could live, I'd practice medicine on Indian reservations for the rest of my life; if I could live, I'd devote my career to researching cystic fibrosis or spina bifida; if I somehow survived, I'd become the best doctor this side of Sloan-Kettering. I wasn't religious, seldom pondered the existence of God, and I didn't really consider with whom I was desperate to reach this agreement, but I had to buy some time. I could die; I didn't have to grow as old as Oma was or Maria had been, but first I had to have lived, to have passed from child-student-apprentice into tangled adulthood. I had to make a life for myself in which I was secure and completely at peace; surely my life couldn't yet come to a close.

the brief life of the girl

THE CHILD WHOSE life had ended early and who had been buried near the intermittent creek that cut Tse Canyon belonged to a cultural progression of people who had lived in the American Southwest for perhaps ten thousand years. Nomadic hunters and gatherers, their home country encompassing the dry quadrant of the continent that reached from the Gulf of California east and north to the Rockies, from the short-grass southern prairies west to the bald peaks of the Great Basin. Their society evolved slowly, changing little until maize—the preeminent crop of the Americas—was introduced, traded northward from the region in southern Mexico where it was native, beginning about 1000 B.C. With the advent of agriculture in the north, a kind of cultural revolution ensued. Groups of hunter-gatherers who were already at least partially sedentary—storing foodstuffs in secure locations—became anchored by the demands of the growing season, developing new tools, fashioning clothing, building shelters as they awaited the autumn harvest.

As groups discovered good growing regions and chose to stay and lay claim to them, adapting themselves to the particular demands of a place, distinct cultures had begun to emerge—among them a large and already influential people in what we now call the Four Corners region who wove increasingly sophisticated baskets, who had begun to devote their attention to architecture, and who somehow could make do in country characterized by short, dry summers, cold and snowy winters, and far more rock than tillable soil.

It's a rather meaningless coincidence, of course, that the identifiable Ancient Puebloan tradition got under way at roughly the same time the Christian era commenced, but I know I've always attached some significance to it—not for religious reasons (not because a resurrected Jesus visited these parts, as the wildly imaginative Mormons would have us believe)—but because the comparative time-scales are intriguing. During the course of the subsequent centuries in Europe and the eastern Mediterranean, the Celts fell to the marauding Romans, the Romans succumbed to the Goths, the Byzantine and Holy Roman empires had their heydays and declines, the Normans stormed Britain, and three times Crusaders marched on the Muslims. It was a turbulent, pivotal epoch in Europe, during which time on this continent the Puebloans lived in relative peace, their prosperity increasing with their growing proficiency as farmers, their pottery and architecture reaching aesthetic heights, their communal lives flourishing in an austere and difficult sort of way.

While the first Christian millennium affected perhaps half the earth's population, the Ancient Puebloan era touched a paltry number of people. Yet the stability of that society—the degree to which the lives of one generation were a clear continuation of the lives of their ancestral kin—still seems stunning to me. That kind of cultural equilibrium was already strained in medieval Europe; it was rendered almost impossible by the Industrial Revolution, and at the end of the twentieth century, it has become literally hard to imagine.

The brief life of the girl I disturbed at Tse Canyon would have been almost identical to her grandmother's childhood, to her grandmother's early years. Yet the world had thoroughly changed in the fifty-four years between Oma's birth and my own, and even Montezuma County had undergone an acute kind of transformation. "It doesn't feel like the same place," Oma had told me. "The memories I have, some of them, are so sharp and clear. But it's like they belong to another place I must have lived, except, of course, that this is the only one."

When I was in Colorado at Christmas during my last year in Albuquerque, I remember too that when I remarked at how quickly medical school and an internship seemed to have gone, Oma cautioned me that everything would pass far too quickly from now on. "It seems like it could have been yesterday that that fella from Dolores hitched his team and drove us out to the home place for the first time, Papa saying the land looked awfully sorry to him, and the teamster saying 'Well, sir, looks like it's your name on the papers.' Old as I am," she said, "you still feel like life is over hardly before you know it."

how to pit-roast pig

I FEIGN A touch of the flu on Friday morning in order to ready the farm for Harry's birthday barbecue. As far as any of us can tell, he still doesn't suspect a thing, and Alice is under orders to delay him out at the canyon this evening, or to entice him into town for drinks if need be, in hopes that everyone can get to the house before he does. Convivial Harry is invariably keen on the cocktail hour, of course, and in the summertime Alice is always eager to ward off the threat of malaria with as many gin and tonics as she can manage, so it seems certain that she can detain him.

Within minutes after Harry leaves for work, Tom John arrives bearing the late pig, a secret barbecue sauce that he's been concocting for several days, and the kind of manic early-morning enthusiasm I've always envied. After spending perhaps thirty seconds with me on pleasantries, he is off to dig a pit down near the pond, to gather wood for a blazing fire, then to wrap the creature in foil while the fire in the pit burns itself down to glowing coals. "If nine hours isn't enough, we're going to have some pretty unhappy partiers on our hands," he says when I slowly make my way down to check on his progress an hour and a half later, seeing Teddy sitting nearby him in rapt and begging attention. "Rare pork's a hard sell out west. Back home, a lot of old boys liked it that way. Course some of them tended to die soon after a hearty meal."

Tom John's hair is pulled back and tied at the nape of his neck, and in the bright light I'm surprised to see how shot through with gray it has grown. His broad hands and bare arms are a blur of motion as he shovels dirt over the coals and foil-wrapped mound of meat.

"This is awfully sweet of you," I say. "I couldn't have got something like this together by myself."

"Well, of course you couldn't have, dear thing. That's why I'm here. Besides, I'd a lot rather eat my own cooking, all things being the same. That way you know where what you put in your mouth has been."

"You don't trust my cooking?"

"I'd trust you with my life, you know I would. In fact, I believe I recall letting you cut me open on one occasion."

"It was just a sebaceous cyst, Tom John. Not quite open-heart surgery."

"But it was my neck you were slicing, and my jugular vein was probably an inch away, and I'm surprised I didn't faint."

"You were a brave soldier."

Tom John laughs, then stops and turns toward me. "You miss it, don't you?"

"Being a doc? Yeah, I do," I say, a bit surprised at my willingness to answer so unguardedly. "I guess I'm still a doctor, but I don't feel much like one anymore. What I miss, I suppose, is feeling like I'm useful. You complain bitterly about getting phoned in the middle of the night, and being on call on holidays, and all the endless hassles—and you do get sick of it—but people telling you they need your help, that's what I thrived on, I think."

"If somebody told me I had to quit digging in the dirt, which is all I've done for a million years, I don't know what I'd do."

"Nobody actually told me I had to quit. I just finally had to face the music. My energy was shot so much of the time, and then once movement in my arms and hands started to get erratic, well... the one thing I wasn't going to do was to let my pride end up hurting somebody."

Tom John dusts off his hands on his pants, then walks over and hugs me tightly. "Girl, girl," he says, his face pressed into my hair, "why can't the rotten things happen to the rotten people? I could make a long list of folks I'd wish some things on, but you ... not you."

"Thank you," I tell him, wishing I could say more. He, more than anyone else I know, makes me feel that who I am is exactly who I should be. "You're wise and wonderful and you matter a ton to me," I say.

"No, I'm just somebody who's going to be sixty-two years old one of these days, and you know, I don't think I'm one bit smarter than I ever was."

"They say you make a fine barbecue." I pull away to see his face, and I hope my smile tells him that when I'm in his company, my life makes perfect sense.

Tom John shrugs and smiles broadly back at me, but for some reason he needs to convince me that he is less capable of things than I am. "You know how to deliver babies, and keep that drunken Harry under control, and cut out salacious cysts, and do a thousand things. I'm just a dumb old southern boy what knows how to pit-roast pig."

general practice

FAMILY MEDICINE HAD seemed like the logical specialty for me, even while I was still in Albuquerque. Cardiology had captured my attention early on; the oncology classes were interesting; I liked obstetrics and, although I wasn't fascinated, I could put up with orthopedics. And it seemed obvious that I wasn't meant to sub-specialize; a career spent solely with lungs or brains or bowels sounded gruesome; radiology was just for the ardent capitalists among us, anesthesiology for the social misfits, surgery for the egomaniacs who would save the world with their scalpels.

By the time I entered the medical world, the general practice of the first half of the twentieth century had become "family practice"—a Jill-of-all-trades jumble of obstetrics and gynecology, internal medicine, pediatrics, and orthopedics, plus a lot more day-to-day dermatology than I ever would have wanted—and somehow it seemed to suit me. I enjoyed working with women— with apprehensive teenagers who wanted to believe they were ready to go on the pill but who knew in their hearts that they were still children, with expectant mothers who were so wonderfully healthy and hopeful, with new mothers now overwhelmed by the work and the worry, and I was often struck by women for whom menopause was a disquieting reminder of their mortality despite the fact that most of them would live for forty more years. The first time I delivered a baby entirely on my own—it was early in my residency in Denver and he was a black-eyed boy whose young mother gave him the name Socorro, I still remember—I was giddy with satisfaction, delighted that all had gone well, that I hadn't done something stupid, and aware in a way I hadn't been before that this sole arena of medicine in which your patients aren't necessarily sick or suffering was one I was fortunate to be a part of.

The medical folklore had it that the reason residencies were so demanding, so exhausting, so stripped of sleep and any sort of social life, was that the doctors who ran the programs had been slave labor once themselves and now were determined to exact similar suffering on their protégés. As far I could tell, it was folklore founded in fact. Following a full day in the well-baby clinic at Denver General, or seeing adult patients at one of the hospital's neighborhood health centers, I could count on—depending on my rotation—a wild night's work in the trauma center, a couple of hours of sleep on a cot in obstetrics during a protracted labor, no sleep at all when the babies were popping out as if we were having a party, none as well when I had to scrub and assist on a C-section. Two nights a week I was off—gloriously alone and undemanded—my phone disconnected, my bathtub filled for a change, my flannel nightgown pressed into service, then sleeping the sleep of the dead for eight hours before the cruel morning came and it was time to go back to work.

I survived my residency, as virtually everyone does, by acknowledging that I was learning an amazing amount, that I finally was beginning to feel like a doctor—increasingly confident of my skills and critical perceptions—and by reminding myself that, in the long run, I was going to be rewarded with money. Doctors who tell you they never consider the financial end of the profession are lying through their teeth—not that everyone who becomes a plastic surgeon or a pediatrician, a pathologist or a family practitioner, for that matter, does so solely to build her investment portfolio, but the frank fact is that after seemingly endless years of study and apprenticeship, of sacrifice and sleep deprivation, of making less than the minimum wage while you cover for staff physicians taking the afternoon off for golf, you become convinced that, when your turn finally comes, you damn well deserve some dollars.

During the first year of my family practice residency—before I encountered one Harry MacLeish and my life made a different turn—I was so unattached as to consider the eventual likelihood of mating and marriage pretty improbable. I was going solo, it appeared, and it would be up to me alone to pay off my education loans and join a practice somewhere and find a house and finally replace my battered Honda and maybe even buy a dress for those occasions when I simply had to wear one. I wanted to practice medicine—good medicine, and by now my aspiration had become a real commitment—but oh, I was eager to escape that imposed professional poverty, and, after thirty years, at last to be on my own.

the final hundred yards home

WITH THE PORK provided by Tom John, and with salads, breads, desserts, and booze coming from several quarters, I don't have to spend the day cooking. I do prepare a large dish of "Oma's beans," and in the afternoon I mow the tiny patch of lawn that reaches away to the orchard before the sun and exertion make me retreat indoors to rest. Even this much work is too taxing, it angers me to admit, and if I'm going to last till the end of the evening, I know I'll need a cool bath and more than a bit of a nap.

Tom John, wearing a blood-red velveteen shirt cut in the classic Navajo style instead of the tuxedo he threatened to rent, has returned and is unloading chairs from his truck when I come outside again. I've simply pulled on a linen tunic and still wear the black cotton pants I put on this morning, but Tom John indeed has decided to make a bold sartorial statement. "You look grand," I tell him because, in point of fact, he does.

"Well, I have to go so far as to look like Manuelito because *somebody* around here must show a little style. You just watch. The rest of this bunch will all arrive wearing T-shirts that say I'M WITH ASSHOLE."

I laugh and try to help Tom John arrange the chairs on the grass under the cottonwoods that shelter the pond, but he refuses to let me, sliding a chair underneath me and telling me to sit still, reminding me that when guests arrive a hostess has a duty to appear as if she hasn't done a lick of work all day. And by a few minutes past five o'clock, I'm doing my duty, greeting people as they pull into the farmyard—their cars impossible to hide and certain to tip Harry off when he gets home in an hour or so. I hug former colleagues from the hospital, young archaeologists I know best by reputation, friends who are teachers and builders and even a farmer or two. Barbara arrives with Rudy, something that seldom happens, and I'm genuinely happy as I embrace them both to have an excuse to do so.

"So the old man's forty, is he?" Rudy says, full of bluster, looking beyond me as he speaks in an attempt to scout for familiar faces. "You know what they say. He'll conk out just about the time you finally get interested in getting some."

I laugh a little too enthusiastically to try to ease Barbara's embarrassment at her husband's remark. "Aren't you glad you invited him?" she asks. "Can I lock him in a closet?"

An hour later, people are still arriving—some bringing babies and children with them, dragging diaper bags and playpens, hauling plastic tricycles and wooden carpenter sets. Toddlers are tripping over the tall grass, their parents trailing them as they try to carry on conversations, trying to ascertain how old friends are faring, how a small-site survey is coming, whether the alfalfa is ready to cut. A group of teenagers, eager to shed their parents' attentions, has discovered the volleyball net, and down at the pond, Jason and Ryan—who have raced past me without so much as stopping to say hello—now are lunging at terrified frogs.

Plates of food are spread across folding tables, dozens of bottles of beer are cupped in people's cold palms, dozens more have been stuffed into a tub filled with ice, and Tom John—his spirits high as he holds his accustomed court—is ready to peel back the dirt from the top of his pit, the pork at last surely ready to cut and eat. "How long do you want to wait for that fool man before we feed these people?" he asks me, my cane hooked on the arm of my chair near the serving tables now, a sweater I brought out from the house wrapped around my shoulders.

"Do you think people are getting hungry? I told Alice not to get him here before seven. I bet they'll be along in a minute. But why don't you get the meat ready. We might as well get this feast under way."

Just then, Teddy darts away from the edge of the pond, where he has been hoping a stick might make its way into the water, winds his way through the crowd like a running back, then races down the path he has worn beside the fence that faces the county road; Harry's pickup is approaching and it is Teddy's duty and delight to escort him on the final hundred yards home.

"Here's Harry," I call out to everyone, the dog's dash all the information I need. "He may act at first like he's not too thrilled about this, but if he does, just get a beer into each of his hands and be patient a drink or two."

remarkable children of our own

HARRY SEEMED SO supremely confident, so utterly at ease with himself when I met him those many years ago that I was surprised I was drawn to him. I tend to be suspicious of people who are boldly at home in the world, and I'm sure I also assume they'll want nothing to do with me. But Harry's spectacular smile and infectious sense of humor, coupled with the conspicuous interest he aimed in my direction, was quickly disarming, and that day on which we met was one of those afternoons in early May when the weather tries to persuade you that we live in a perfect world. He was doing the final course work for his Ph.D. in anthropology; I was delivering babies and prescribing antibiotics and otherwise leading no sort of social life. Harry recently had ended a long and complex relationship that he seemed to need to talk about regularly, to my chagrin. I, on the other hand, remained a virgin, something about which I was privately embarrassed and had grown increasingly eager to do something about.

When Harry began to wax poetic about Cortez that day we met, my opinion of him momentarily soured, but by the time we left the party and drove up to Flagstaff House for a dinner that neither of us could afford, he almost had me convinced that there was something in the Town Without Hope that I had overlooked. I didn't see him again for three weeks, but we did find time for a couple of telephone conversations that lasted an hour or more. Then we spent a Saturday in Denver browsing—and buying nothing—in the furniture shops on South Broadway, and afterward I invited him to my dank little apartment for dinner. Four days before, I had gritted my teeth and punctured my hymen in the hope of keeping my secret secure, and on that Saturday night I gave up my virginity, such as I still could claim it, to the only man I've ever slept with, to the man I already suspected I could love far more deeply than he might ever love me in partnered return.

In the chaotic midst of my residency, my days and evenings off were maddeningly sporadic, but before many more weeks had passed, any time I was away from the hospitals or the clinics, I was with Harry MacLeish. We made it our special mission to find the best Mexican food in metro Denver; we climbed Long's Peak and canoed the abused South Platte; there was a rainy and wonderful weekend at his parents' elegant "cabin" outside of Tabernash, and there was the awkward evening in Cherry Hills when I met Harry Senior and Eleanor and so obviously disappointed them. Medicine was an acceptable profession, of course, but family practice seemed a little demeaning, and Harry's effusive comments about my red hair unfortunately had led them to suppose I was something special to look at, rather than the acne-scarred girl from the boondocks who now sat so uncomfortably on their coffee-colored Roche-Bobois sofa. Dr. and Mrs. MacLeish barely responded when I described my parents and their occupations, but they did remember Cortez quite well, to my regret—they had visited Harry during that long-ago summer—and their memories (unlike their son's) definitely did not support my cause.

Despite his parents' misgivings about me, Harry was always ebullient and often wild with mischief when we were together that summer, and I responded to his caring and sometimes crazy attention by falling truly in love with him—a turn of events I attempted to conceal from friends and colleagues, my mother and Barbara, Oma and everyone else, yet a circumstance that made my remaining year in Denver a dizzy blur of constant work and unwieldy emotion, the headiest sorts of dreams, and every kind of exhaustion.

On weekend afternoons in the winter—when Harry had no
classes and I was temporarily on leave from attending to Denver's
diseased and infirm—we would drive the county roads north and
east out of Boulder, keeping an eye out for FOR SALE signs, imagining ourselves living on a small farmstead somewhere out in the
valley—Harry finishing his doctoral work then teaching and writing to wide renown, me practicing medicine out of a little old
house on Boulder's Pine Street and bringing babies into the world
at Community Hospital, the two of us raising remarkable children
of our own before finally growing old.

sparkling in the last of the light

TO MY PLEASURE and relief, Harry immediately seems to welcome the celebration, in large part because his birthday already has been toasted a few times in town, and he arrives home lubricated enough to be at his social best. After he has made a quick round of our guests, sharing enveloping hugs, laughing with his particular kind of abandon, and enduring dozens of jests—Teddy dancing at his heels all the while—Harry excuses himself to shower and change his clothes, then returns in a white oxford shirt, a silk tie, and an ancient pair of bib overalls that belonged to my grandfather. Oma offered them to Harry a few years ago—after twenty-some years she was ready to go through Granddad's closet—and he accepted them gratefully, although until this evening I've never seen him wear them.

Alice, of course, bests Harry, bests everyone else, and would win the style award hands-down if one were part of the evening's program. A minute or two after Harry's reappearance, she arrives wearing peg-legged black-leather pants, black heels that will be hellish to walk in, a burgundy silk shirt that draws direct and immediate attention to her bra-less nipples, and a silver Navajo choker that I've always much admired. "How'd I do?" she asks as she twirls away from my hug.

"With Harry or with this outfit?"

"Both," she answers, spreading her arms a bit as if to say, "Am I not a fine sight indeed?"

"Spectacular job. And you're well watered too, I can tell."

"I had to join him for three gin and tonics before I finally got him headed home. Don't let me have anything else or I'll be in serious trouble."

"Doctor's orders," I say as she moves away in the throes of a new conversation.

Tom John's pork has been unanimously declared delicious. He notices that Harry is telling stories and hasn't drifted near the serving tables, so Tom John delivers a plate to him and instructs him to shut up for a minute and eat. Then, finding a chair that will support his weight, Tom John mounts it and calls for everyone's attention, the sweet southern strains of his voice never more pronounced than when he's addressing a crowd.

"Now y'all are probably wondering why we invited you here this evening," he begins, an impish grin spread across his sun-darkened face. "Well, the reasons are many and varied, of course, but principal among them is the fact that Farmer MacLeish, here to my left, has grown so old that he won't be with us much longer and we thought we'd better throw him a wing-ding before he departs. As most of y'all know, the old fella has spent the better part of his life scratching around in ruins, and so consequently he doesn't have much to show for himself in the way of a career, and he hasn't sired any children—at least there are none to speak of—and he's been a great disappointment to his parents, and his friends are few in number, so I thought that maybe instead of just singing him 'Happy Birthday,' we might do like the Quakers do in place of preaching. Anybody who has anything to say to this man, or to say about him, can just say it out loud, share it with us all. I need a cold can of beer, so I'm going to get down from here, but I'll start off by saying, Harry, in all the years I've lived in this country, you are, without a doubt, one of the people I've known."

People applaud and whistle and Harry throws his head back with pleasure, shouting thank you, shouting to Tom John that he's never been so touched. Others follow Tom John's lead—Barbara telling him that he is the best brother-in-law she's ever had, her breathless voice implying sexual secrets; Alice saying she doesn't care what everyone says about him setting southwestern archaeology back by decades, his eye for fine places to pot-hunt is nonetheless uncanny; Harry's old buddy Charlie Roseberry saying the one thing he can never forget about Harry is that he owes him twenty bucks.

Several times, I laugh so hard I ache, but I haven't said anything yet. Finally, people begin to shout that I have to offer something in the way of a speech, so I get out of my chair and steady myself and survey the clustered multitude while I try to think of appropriate words. "You've all just about captured him, I have to admit. You've left out the nastier details—the toothpaste tube, the toilet seat, the armed robberies, but over all, well, that's our Harry. He's all we've got, I'm afraid." I hold out my hand and Harry takes it, his face beaming, his eyes sparkling in the last of the light, his overalls making him look like a forty-year-old Dennis the Menace. "Your turn," I whisper as I kiss his whisker-stubbled cheek.

"Well." He sips the beer he holds in his hand and waits like a comedian who is eager to get his timing right. "Despite the fact that I actually had planned to celebrate with a bottle of single-malt scotch and a rented porn tape, and despite the fact that Tom John's obviously trying to give me trichinosis because he wants my record collection, and despite the fact that I've been defamed here tonight and seriously slandered and that my lawyer will be contacting each of you within the week, I guess I'd just like to say that I appreciate it and that... fuck, I love you all a lot."

forevermore

IT HAD BEEN the rainy season in the Caribbean lowlands, and I remember the summer of 1977 as a kind of steamy, misty, muddy dream. During one week in July, as much rain had fallen onto the village of Mariscos as Cortez could count on in a year; a fungus sprouted in the insides of Harry's rubber boots, and everywhere odors were dank and fetid and strong. This sea-level land beside the indented Gulf of Honduras was a Guatemala seldom visited by outsiders—a rain forest of rosewood and mahogany trees, a rotting savanna where agriculture was cursed by too much moisture, where the beautiful collecting basin called the Lago de Izabal shimmered in hazy sunlight, and the slow, sweet river, the Rio Dulce, emptied the lake into the nearby sea.

My family-practice residency was finished; I had taken the boards and passed them despite my apprehensions; and Harry, halfway through a dissertation that was driving him crazy—one attempting to plot and interpret increasing population densities among the pre-abandonment Puebloans—had been more than happy to surrender his typewriter for a season. The plan had been for Harry to spend some time as a tourist, exploring Mayan ruins at Copán, Quirigua, Tikal, and Uaxactún while I spent a busman's holiday in tiny Mariscos at work in a medical mission operated by the Sisters of Mercy and staffed in cycles by vacationing American doctors, dentists, and optometrists. But Harry too had been pressed into service, first working as a carpenter's helper on an addition to the antiquated clinic, then trying his hand at translating for medical volunteers whose Spanish didn't go beyond *gracias*, and for the first time he had been able to understand emotionally what I had poorly described to him—the lure and the literal pleasure of being able to offer assistance.

Reaching scattered fishing and farming villages on the lake's periphery via an old and rusting flat-bottomed *lancha*, we and a few other physicians and assistants would set up makeshift clinics, then spend fourteen-hour days inside huts that often did little to shed the rain, sometimes seeing a hundred patients in a single day, seemingly every *campesino* within walking distance queuing up for hours for a ten-minute consultation, their complaints as simple as common gastritis, as complicated as gangrene or what I suspected was liver cancer. Surprisingly few mothers reported serious problems with pregnancies, but it seemed as if every child suffered from dysentery, as if every little belly was bloated by malnutrition. The work often was frustrating—no way to treat intractable problems, too few pharmaceuticals, too little luck convincing people that shoes could prevent invasions by worms. Yet sometimes the assistance we could offer was straightforward and efficacious, and at follow-up consultations patients would beam with pleasure, others shaking their heads in grateful disbelief. They would offer us fresh tortillas wrapped in palm leaves, a kind of sugarcane candy, an occasional bottle of sun-warmed Gallo beer, and they also would wish for us God's abundant blessings.

During the three months we spent on the shores of Izabal, we never did find time to travel up to the highlands, to visit colonial Antigua or the renowned market at Chichicastenango, and Harry opted in August to stay at the clinic instead of joining a friend from Denver on a trek north to Tikal, telling him he would love to see the storied site but begging off because his help was needed at the mission. But on Sundays when it wasn't raining, we would borrow the sisters' wooden *cayuco* and steal away to the ruins of the old buccaneer fortress at San Felipe, to a black-pebbled beach where we could lie in the sporadic but welcome sunlight, to a grove of coconut palms where we would laugh at our inept attempts to wield machetes, dozens of coconuts hacked to pieces in the process. Evenings after work we would eat eggs and rice, wonderful soupy black beans, and tortillas made from white maize, then invariably adjourn to the plank-floored Miramar down on the water, where the beer was refrigerated, the jukebox was full of *cumbia* songs, and the proprietress was full of good cheer.

At the beginning of September, two weeks before we were scheduled to fly back to the States, Sister Joan Marie insisted that we take a weekend journey down the Rio Dulce to the port town of Livingston. The *lancha* was ours, she said, she didn't want any arguments, and we happily acquiesced, the two of us by now familiar with the eccentricities of the boat's diesel engine, with navigating the glistening lake and the dark, tannin-stained waters in its lagoons and coves. Chugging, smoking, bellowing our way down the river, the thick jungle bounding the smooth water on either side, we joked that we were reliving *The African Queen*, and we marveled at how we seemed more than a world away from Colorado.

Livingston, just a few kilometers from the Belize border and accessible only by boat, was a collection of buildings built on stilts that the Caribbean winds had done their best to weather away, a community whose residents were black and whose language was lilting Caribe, a twentieth-century town without cars or sewers or cares, so it seemed, a place where the nightly Kung Fu feature at the Paradise Theatre was shown in English and where Saturday dinner at the Pensión Rio Dulce was normally roasted armadillo—an end-of-the-earth locale that enchanted Harry almost at once.

I wasn't sure I was game to try armadillo but we booked a room in the pensión, paid a boy at the docks to keep a vigilant eye on the *lancha*, then began the long walk northward along the beach toward the waterfall at Altares that Sister Joan Marie had told us was one of God's glories—a clear, cool stream cascading off a mossy cliff and into a rocky pool, then spilling out and cutting its way across the sand and into the Caribbean. Sister was right, we agreed, as we sat alone in the pool, the water spraying us as it tumbled down, the gentle surf slapping the shore just beyond, the view unobstructed all the way to Cuba.

We made awkward love on a makeshift mat of ferns hidden away in the trees; we walked to the far northern end of the long beach in the steady, splendid sun of the early afternoon, then, back in the pool again, Harry decided that we should marry, and that today would be a fine day to join our lives. I acquiesced, of course, because even though I doubt I would have been brave enough to make a similar suggestion to him, it was a plan that had instant magic in it for me. It was a decision, I realize now, that had at least as much to do with the exotic luster of that low-land Guatemalan day as it did with a carefully considered decision to spend our lives together. For my part, I knew even then that Harry loved me precisely as much as he could, as much as I was capable of drawing love out of him. Although our separate kinds of love already seemed a bit mismatched and strangely mute, I resolved silently that day that what love he had for me always would be enough.

Back at the pensión, the innkeeper explained that, yes, there was a minister in town, a priest of the Church of England called Father Abraham—an elderly man with coal-black skin and tight-ly curled white hair who came out onto his porch in his T-shirt and assured us that his wife would be pleased to serve as our wit-ness. Suitable rings did pose a problem until Father Abraham's round and merry wife remembered a cigar box full of jewelry she had tucked away for a junk sale. For twenty American dollars—five dollars for each of the rings and ten dollars for his ecclesiastical services—Father Abraham stood beneath a banana tree as a light rain began to fall and pronounced us married forevermore.

this body that will not work

IT IS ONE of those celebrations that doesn't want to come to a close. As darkness drapes the mesa and the mountains, then slowly settles onto the broad sweep of the valley, Tom John builds a big fire in the hole where he has roasted his pig, and although the night is warm, people huddle around it for hours, laughing loudly, talking in little groups, telling stories embellished by memory and animated by alcohol, spreading sweet and savory gossip. By eleven, people with children asleep on their shoulders begin to gather themselves to go, but others announce that they will refuse to leave till the beer is gone, or at least until Tom John agrees to recite some Robert Service—his rendition of "The Creation of Sam McGee" having become a much celebrated cultural event over the years, performed by now at his excavation camp at Cow Canyon more times than he can count.

"There are strange things done in the midnight sun," he begins, succumbing to the demand, his Arkansas-styled enunciation stretching out the poem's syllables, shining its rhymes, bringing them to delightful life. Harry, boozy and blissful, listens raptly, knowing the poem almost as well as his friend and mentor does; he wraps his arm around me, standing close to the chair I haven't left since the sky surrendered the day. Tom John takes a deep bow as he concludes amid hoots and applause and a shout or two of *bravo!*, then announces that he is too old to stay to see the sun rise, and his farewell to me and the birthday boy triggers a second wave of departures.

I can't believe it is one o'clock in the morning when at last I look at my watch; it has been a wonderful evening—Harry responding to the surprise with warmth and real appreciation, the food plentiful and popular, old friends in comfortable sync for a few hours as they too seldom are these days—but now I'm absolutely exhausted. Alice offers to help me get to the house, but I decline, giving her a hug as I get to my feet, telling her to stay by the fireside, telling everyone who is left that Harry and I have plenty of room, that they all should stay the night and keep safely away from their cars.

Sometime in the still of the night, I awake with a start. The house is silent and the moon is down and even the frogs are quiet, but something I've been dreaming has jolted me into consciousness and now I'm wide awake. Harry isn't in bed with me, and I doubt too that there are bodies spread across the living room rug. I try to relax myself back to sleep, try to think about nothing, then finally surrender and fumble for my robe and find the cane where I keep it by the beside table.

No one is in the living room, and the rest of the house is dark, but I can see through the kitchen windows that the fire is still burning bright down by the pond. It takes me an awkward moment to pull on my rubber boots, and I'm careful as I descend the steps and make my way across the grass. The air is cool and still and moist, and as I negotiate the sloping ground beyond the outbuildings, I note how seldom it is that I witnesses this fine, fragile, crystalline time of the night. Then I trip, lose my balance as I try to command the cane, and fall.

I'm okay, I can tell—I'm a stupid idiot, and I can't believe I'm sprawled in a clump of rabbit brush in the middle of the night, for Christ's sake, with my nightgown up to my armpits—but getting back on my feet is going to be problematic. I can't pull my ankle out from under me, can't lift myself, can't quite reach a piece of brush for leverage, and I'm sure I'll have to call for help when I hear squeals of laughter, the splash of water, and Teddy's attendant barks.

The orange glow from the campfire creates a dome of light that spreads out onto the surface of the pond, and from where I lie, I can see bodies flailing to get back out of the too-cold water, two bodies struggling to escape the mud that rings the pond, Alice's and Harry's bodies moving toward the warmth of the fire now, the two of them embracing, pressing their naked bodies together to fight the cold, Harry sweeping his broad arm across Alice's back, patting her reddened butt, laughing out loud, kissing Alice's neck as they move out of the light and into the darkness again.

I do not want to see this—whatever it is—and I feel faint, suddenly sick, trapped, hating my clumsy limbs and my helplessness now even more than I did the moment before. I don't know who else, if anyone, is still with Harry and Alice down by the fire. However innocent it is or is not doesn't matter to me in this wretched moment. I don't care, cannot think about it. All I know is that I'm desperate to get up, to get away from this fucking predicament, this horrible place, this body that will not work. I struggle until I know once more that the struggle is futile, until Teddy somehow is standing beside me, licking my face, his tail twirling to evidence his delight at having discovered me.

"Teddy, go on, get, get out of here!" I try to command in a hoarse whisper, afraid that he will draw Harry's attention. "Get out of here!" I shout just as I'm able to free my ankle at last. But Teddy remains disobedient, his tongue dangling from his grinning mouth as I struggle to get to my feet, as the cool air stiffens me and chills me and the still night makes me feel like a perfect fool.

the clarifying power of a
cruising pickup truck

I LEAVE A message on Tom John's machine, asking him to call me, explaining nothing except to say I need to talk. Harry stays in bed until eleven this morning, then showers, swallows a piece of toast, and jumps into his truck—his hangover not quite brutal enough to detour him from a softball game his crew has scheduled for noon. He asks on his way out the door if I want to go along to cheerlead. His demeanor is amiable and unsuspecting—although subdued by many more beers and whiskeys than hours of sleep—and when I tell him I can't think of anything less interesting than his softball game, something my voice betrays makes him ask if I am okay.

"Just tired," I tell him. "And I'm not looking forward to dealing with this mess."

"Don't do a thing. Promise. I'll get it all cleaned up when I get back." He stops as he steps out onto the porch. "It was great, Sarah. It really was." He flashes me his smile, that smile I love so much and which sometimes makes me insane, and I know that if I had an arm with any coordination at all, I would have thrown my coffee cup at his head.

Tom John hasn't heard my message when he drives into the yard at noon; Teddy twirls with pleasure at his appearance, and I'm equally glad to see him. I'm not sure I can tell him anything, but I need to be with him, need him nearby when my version of last night's lurid conclusion begins to spill out. But for now, I say even less than I normally do, I'm sure. I make another pot of coffee, a couple of pork-roast sandwiches, and we've settled ourselves out on the deck when I inform him he absolutely isn't allowed to help with the cleanup. "Mr. MacLeish is in charge of that detail," I explain.

"Oh, Mr. MacLeish is, is he?"

"I think the smell of stale beer will be good for him. Too bad he couldn't have gotten on the job the first thing this morning."

"Did he get terribly drunk and say something ugly after I left?"

"I don't know what he did—except act like a fucking idiot."

"Okay, dear thing," Tom John says, setting his sandwich down, calling an end to my practiced vagueness. "You're going to have to spell this out. I'm brilliant, it's true, but I don't do mind-readings. What did the dipshit do?"

I get teary before I answer him, and I'm sure Tom John takes the tears as an unexpected sign that we're circling something more substantial than Harry waking up in an insensitive mood. "Jesus, Tom John, I feel so ridiculous...and I can't believe I'm going to tell you this. I'm forty-seven years old and I've never ever dealt with anything remotely like this."

"Like what, girl?" Tom John's concern is focused now.

"Like...oh, shit, I might as well just tell you. In the middle of the night last night—I don't know what time it was—I couldn't sleep, and the fire was still blazing, and as I was walking back down to see how the party was proceeding, I saw Harry...I saw Harry and Alice getting out of the pond. They'd gone for a swim, I guess, and they didn't have any clothes on, and then they came back up by the fire, and I don't know if he ended up fucking her or what, and I don't want to know." I'm startled by how suddenly I spill the story, but at least tears haven't turned me into a maudlin, crying mess. "I felt so stupid. I still do—the poor crippled lady who doesn't have any idea what's going on."

"You saw enough that you think something's going on?"

"Enough that I...I just feel disgusted, with myself, with him. I didn't even think about Alice—bless her horny goddamn fucking heart—until I finally got back into the house and tried to go to sleep again, which was a joke."

Tom John sighs. "Lord, Lord. I could have gone all day without hearing this."

"I'm sorry. I know it isn't fair to—"

"No, no. Of course I wanted to know. I can tell you from personal experience that when you try to keep secrets you run a good risk of driving yourself insane." He tries to smile at me as he says it, then wants to know, "What was he like this morning?"

"I think his head hurt. I think he felt pretty hung over. But he acted fine. Perfectly normal. He turns forty and he fucks our best friend—no big deal."

"Should we assume that this fucking actually took place?"

"Does it matter?"

"Well, I think it does. If they went skinny-dipping and played grab-ass and just horsed around in their drunken stupors, well, that isn't quite the same thing, is it?"

"The idiotic thing is that I've been trying to be so mature about this. I've tried to talk to Harry about the fact that with me in this sorry state, he's inevitably going to want to... I've tried to convince myself that I can accept it. But now here it happens, and I feel like I want to die."

Tom John stares up at the cloudless sky. "I don't know, sweet thing. I don't know how it looked, what you saw. I want to think no, but—"

"Why do I even care what happened? Am I going to confront him? Her? 'Harry, dear, do you mind if I ask you a little question? Did you fuck Alice last night?'"

"I suppose it's a legitimate question."

"Is it?"

"Yes, you probably ought to talk to him. But I'll tell you, I've got no earthly idea what you ought to say."

I don't really expect Tom John to proffer prompt and tidy answers, but it isn't until he admits he doesn't know what I ought to do that I realize I really can't do anything. I can't confront Harry about something I'm not sure happened. And how hypocritical would it be to hammer away at him with accusations after my previous speechmaking about how something exactly like this is bound to happen sometime? I don't want to approach Alice with wounded indignation, warning her to stay away from my man with the threat of wounded-bitch consequences. But neither will I quietly acquiesce to something neither of them have the courage to tell me about. I'm not going to be some pathetic victim—the cheated-on housewife enduring the dread disease—and all I really can do, for the moment at least, is get away, out of that cloying house and away from that hideous husband, and this time Tom John does seem to read my mind.

"You know, the one thing we can do, dear heart, is to take a drive—hop in that pickup and set the tires spinning. For forty years, I've sworn by the clarifying power of a cruising pickup truck."

"Where do you want to go?" I ask, my tone making it obvious I'll agree to just about any destination. "I'd love not to be here when he gets home."

"I actually need to go out to Hovenweep. I stabilized a wall for the park service a few weeks ago, and I've still got some stuff out there. Sound appealing?"

"Could we stop by my grandmother's on our way? I really should, just for a bit."

"Fine," he says, full of enthusiasm now. "You get ready and I'll make more sandwiches in case we linger into supper time."

Teddy is crestfallen when he realizes a few minutes later that he has to stay behind, and Tom John hollers to hurry me up as I'm explaining to him that Harry will be back before long, as I'm writing a note to Harry telling him I've run away.

two

a casual bit of information

I HAD GONE to a conference in San Francisco, and the ring at the bottom of the tube endorsed my uneasy suspicions. There on a marble countertop in my room at the St. Francis Hotel, the little orange donut was unmistakable. I would have a lab confirm it, of course, and that would wait until I got back to Boulder, but these new self-test kits were remarkably reliable and my suspicions were confirmed and now I knew I was pregnant.

I wasn't sure a moment or two later whether I could eat my room-service breakfast. I had been hungry, but suddenly I felt almost faint, and my queasy stomach churned both with elation and terrible apprehension. We wanted children. I did hugely and Harry assured me, at least, that he wanted them as well. But parenthood would come later, we had decided, after we had anchored ourselves a bit, done our best to establish our professional lives, once we finally felt like adults; and I had dutifully greased a diaphragm so many times by now that I almost had stopped resenting the chore. Neither of us had dared yet to suggest that perhaps we were ready for children, and as I sat in my robe in San Francisco and considered the matter, I immediately worried that the time was wrong in every respect. Yet by now I was sharing a good practice with three other physicians; Harry was filling in for a year for an anthropology professor on sabbatical, and it looked as though a more permanent job offer at the University of Colorado might be in the offing; we hadn't found our longed-for little farm yet, but we lived in a lovely old house on Mapleton Hill, and even Harry's parents had begun to grow cordial, showing signs at last that they approved of their daughter-in-law and showing a symptom or two of the onset of grandparents' disease. The idea of giving birth and raising a child did seem glorious, I privately admitted to myself that morning, and for a while I sat in my robe and pondered how in the world I would break this news to Harry.

The conference on infectious diseases I was attending was scheduled to end at noon that Friday, and our plan had been for Harry to fly in and join me. We were going to spend some of Saturday at Stanford, Harry giving me a guided tour of the alma mater he remembered with a complex mix of waning emotions, then drive south to Big Sur. But when he hugged me at the airport—ebullient and blustery and plainly delighted to be back in California for a bit—he also informed me that he had decided he didn't want to revisit the campus, simply didn't want to take his years there out of the comfortable closet of memory. So we went north instead of south, spending the night at the old Altamira Hotel in Sausalito, sitting in sweaters on the verandah in the cool early-September air and looking out at the gloaming light on Angel Island, Harry drinking scotch while I began to teetotal for a stretch of time, the two of us talking at animated length about the world being fat with wonderful places, conspiring ways to live in the lion's share of them, me telling him in turn about the conference and the events of the past days, but not telling him what truly was on my mind.

It wasn't until we had hiked across Inverness Ridge at Point Reyes on Saturday—through thick laurels and elegant live oaks and finally a mat of wind-buffeted firs where the trail crested the ridge—that I resolved to tell Harry what I wasn't sure he would be happy to hear, to tell him I knew for a fact that he was about to become a father. I'd jokingly let the news drop, I told myself—tell him offhandedly, as if all I had for him was a casual bit of information. But as the fog crawled into Drake's Bay from the open ocean, shrouding the white cliffs in mist, obscuring Arch Rock and covering like a blanket the seals asleep on the beach, Harry was enchanted by the poised and untroubled beauty of the place, and somehow I couldn't be flippant.

"Let's stay," he said, standing behind me, his arms around my shoulders, the two of us staring into the Pacific we couldn't see. "Fuck archaeology. I'll raise those spotted milk cows. You can become Olema's local doctor."

"Can we earn a living off milk cows?"

"I doubt it. But surely these hippies around here are still having babies; you'll make lots of money."

The surf scudded across the sand, and I watched it rather than turn to look at him. "I do know one old hippie who is. I haven't known how to tell you. I'm pretty sure it's true."

Harry needed to see my face, to decipher what I'd said by my expression, to see in my eyes what I meant. I shrugged. I nodded my head. I began to smile as he said, "Sarah ... seriously?"

"I'm afraid so. Please don't freak out."

"How long have ... how do you know?"

"I'm a woman. I'm a doctor. It isn't a complicated diagnosis."

He walked a few steps away, then marched back to me, taking my hands. "Wow. I'm a little shocked," he confessed, and it was the first time I'd ever seen him truly taken aback by anything.

"Me too."

"But I ... ?"

"What do you think?" I asked. A bull seal had begun to holler.

"We'll have to go home," he said, creasing his forehead, suddenly alive with energy, a thousand thoughts already racing beneath his brow. "I don't think we ought to raise kids in California. Colorado's definitely the better place for kids. God, Sarah, really, is this *true*?"

ever since there were people

I'M SURPRISED AND a little perturbed at myself when I realize that in all the years I've known him, Oma never has met Tom John. But she's heard many times about this ebullient character from Arkansas, of course, and she tells him how pleased she finally is to make his acquaintance. Tom John, in turn, takes her frail hand in both of his, tells her he knows now why I'm so pretty.

"You didn't prepare me for such a flirt," Oma says, turning to me, obviously enjoying the flattery.

"Madam," Tom John protests and I laugh, telling my grand-mother to be careful with this guy.

Oma wants to hear that Harry's party has been a success, wants to be sure that I held up under the strain, but soon she turns to Tom John to make several inquiries. Do his people still live down in Arkansas? Is it lovely and green there with all the rain? Has he always been single?

"Always." He winks at me. "Except that I've got my eye on this girl. As soon as Harry lets down a moment's guard, I'm going to steal her away."

"Don't tell her our secrets," I caution.

"Oh, it's safe with me," Oma answers, a little smitten herself by this man and obviously delighted to have the company.

When Tom John asks her how long she's lived here on her farm, she needs a moment to calculate. "Well, come August, it'll be seventy-four years, can you imagine? I'm afraid I'm old as Moses."

"Seventy-four years..."

Hearing him repeat the number makes Oma pause. "Funny I hadn't thought about it. Dad and I would have been married seventy-four years next month. He built this house—with help from his brothers—and we moved in when it was so new the paint was wet. We didn't have any money at all in those days, and couldn't really go anywhere for a wedding trip, you know. We spent our first night here, and I've been here ever since."

"Amazing."

"Is it? Well, maybe it is anymore. Course I wasn't born here. I was born in Garland, Texas—just outside there—and we homesteaded up here when I was a little girl."

"Were there obvious ruins here when your family started to work the land?" Unlike a few of his colleagues, Tom John is far from single-minded, but once a conversation becomes couched in the past, his professional interest nonetheless is always easy to pique.

"Now, this place is part of the old Lewis homestead," Oma explains. "My family's home place was a mile south and a half-mile west—over where Olive Tomlinson lives, if you know Olive. I don't think there were ruins over there. Here, though, there was a big ruin down by the draw, what we called the south pasture. It's still there; Dad wouldn't ever let anybody pot it. He said how would we like somebody digging up our graves just to get at our pocket watches."

"He was right." Tom John is serious now. "And I'm afraid I have to confess that I do that kind of thing on a fairly regular basis."

Oma worries that she's said something she shouldn't have. "Oh, no, no it's a different thing when you're studying it. When you're trying to learn something, well that's..." She turns to me as if to ask permission to tell a story. "It's the same as when Sarah was in medical school. She told me one time about how each student had a dead person's body that they studied. At first I couldn't imagine sweet little Sarah doing what she had to do, but the more I thought about it, I thought, well, now that's something useful you can do when you die. How else are doctors going to learn what people's bodies are really like?"

"I wish I thought we were learning as much," Tom John tells her, a bit surprised at where the conversation has taken us. "Sometimes I get discouraged about how little we really understand."

"Do you suppose it really matters in the end how people lived here a thousand years ago?" I ask the question I've often asked in other settings, one I'm sure Tom John has a ready answer for.

But Oma speaks first, her small voice rising with quick conviction before it subsides again. "It's the same as why people should read the Bible. Otherwise you never realize that people have had the same problems you have ever since there were people."

Tom John nods his head, the smile that slips onto his face affirming that he is keeping remarkable company at the moment. I say nothing more, but something swells inside as I look at my grandmother's deep-set and watery eyes.

all we get are potsherds

SMALL PINTO BEAN plants stand in straight, corduroyed rows and the alfalfa fields lately have been mowed to stubble where the valley rolls and sweeps upward in the west. The washboard road that cuts through the farmland jolts the pickup as it aims at the Utah border, then a dusty wake trails the truck when the road cuts into a ragged piñon-juniper forest and curls round the head of Hovenweep Canyon. The trees give way to sagebrush and Colorado gives way to its western neighbor without even a cattle guard to mark the sudden transition.

"I'd live out here," Tom John says to me. "I'd be a hermit if it wasn't for the problem of being all by myself." He smiles at me across the blue vinyl seat that is liberally patched with duct tape. "I'd live like the aboriginals for a couple of weeks at a stretch, then hightail it to town for a night, fairly begging for civilization."

"I don't think I could do it," I tell him in response. "Not sure why. What I like out here is how empty everything is, clean I mean. None of the junked cars or oil-patch hovels that give Cortez its special appeal. What I wouldn't like is having no one for company except myself. It'd be too easy to concentrate solely on my pitiful self."

"But we'd each have a boyfriend," Tom John explains. "Yours would be better than Harry by far. Mine would look like Robert Redford."

"So would mine." I grin at him, then the grin goes flat. "God, Tom John, with this neurological mess I'm in, I can't even fantasize about trading for somebody better. I'll be stuck in a chair by the time I finally encounter that perfect man who was always meant for me."

Tom John waits before he speaks. "It pains me to say this, but I have a hunch that our Harry is, in fact, the man you're meant to be with." He turns the truck off the sand-dusted road and onto the rutted track that leads to Round Castle Ruin, where massive sandstone walls stand at the head of a narrow and twisting canyon, and where a circular stone tower—miraculously still intact—climbs out of the canyon and into the dry blue sky. Tom John stops the truck where boulders block the way, and he sits with his door open as he completes his thought. "What I mean is, I have a hunch that, last night notwithstanding, Harry MacLeish remains a decent human being."

I try to smile. "You're not playing fair if you're attempting to soften me up on the son of a bitch."

"No, no. I am simply suggesting that, in the end, you may not have to find this other fellow."

"I wouldn't even try, Tom John. He wouldn't want what he would encounter. I'm a pretty awful specimen, I'm afraid."

"Praise God that you don't talk like this all the time," he scolds, then helps me out of the truck and makes sure I can stand comfortably before he moves through the sage and saltbush to the place where he has cached a wheelbarrow and tools beneath a cantilevered slab of rock.

Alone now, I negotiate the narrow trail that leads to the canyon rim, then stand in the bright, color-bleaching light while I marvel again at the slim, symmetrical tower shaped out of buff blocks of sandstone. The Ancient Puebloans built many of these towers in the Hovenweep area, some D-shaped, some square, most near seep springs at the heads of little canyons, others perched on the bald-rock canyon rims. A few contained windows that admitted shafts of sunlight; most had low, ground-level door-ways; some were connected to subterranean kivas by tunnels so small that people would have had to crawl on their knees to get through them. But the Round Castle tower appears never to have had an entry. Lithe young men might have been able to climb its exterior walls then descend inside by a ladder, but otherwise its interior must have been inaccessible, and now archaeologists can only guess at the reasons for its construction. Was it some sort of phallic shrine, an insurer of fertility? Did it store grain or water or something equally precious? Was it a lookout or even a simple observatory? It's hard to imagine that it was built solely to be beautiful, yet at this moment I have to think that maybe it's best simply to consider it sculpture.

"I suppose you belong to the ceremonial school," I say to Tom John when he finds me near the rim.

"Ceremonial...?" His breath still heaves a bit from the effort of loading the heavy wheelbarrow into the truck.

"These towers. You, no doubt, decided long ago that they were built as part of some sort of devout religious endeavor."

"The truth is, dear thing, that I have always taken great pride in the fact that I don't have a clue why they were built. I'll nod my head appropriately at any number of plausible explanations, but when it comes to issues like this, I really prefer not knowing. Honestly. You want to sit down for a bit?" He hooks my cane on his forearm, then takes both my hands as I lower myself to the rock. Once he's seated beside me, Tom John says, "I think we ought to be searching for truths about these people, but I don't mind a bit when some specific question doesn't seem to have an answer. I like it, in fact."

"All you guys have is the literal stuff—the architecture, the tools, human remains. Your only peek at the big picture comes via all these minute little details."

"It's the ugly irony, isn't it? We crave great understanding and all we get are potsherds."

"Alice—who I didn't want to think about today—tried to make the case to me that medicine's in a similar predicament."

"Oh, I suppose any investigative enterprise is. Nothing's ever laid out all nice for you like a buffet supper. By the way, that skeletal girl you excavated? I had another thought about her."

"Yes?"

"Oh, it isn't much. It just crossed my mind that it might be worth wondering whether she had had a child. If she was thirteen or fourteen, she could have, and there are osteology people who claim they can tell by marks and colorations on a pelvis if someone has given birth. My thought was that maybe her death and her deformed leg were unrelated. Maybe she was bleeding to death and in terrible pain and the midwives knew there wasn't any hope for her. Bashing her in the head might have seemed like the merciful thing to do."

"Isn't that a little far-fetched?"

"I'm just trying..."

"They can examine a pelvis and determine whether that person ever had a baby?"

"They claim they can. I certainly couldn't do it, and I know that plenty of people scoff at the idea, but I don't know."

I need to think about this for a moment, to reconsider the life of the girl as I've tried to construct it so far. Till now, I've never imagined the girl as a mother—she was hardly more than a child—and I'm quite confident that, in one way or another, her leg was her undoing. But this is intriguing, even if it is more than a little far-fetched. "If that was what happened, why don't you find lots of female remains with signs of some sort of trauma? Women had to die from childbirth all the time."

"All the time. But the circumstances wouldn't always have been the same—and we do find female skeletons that show various signs of trauma. I don't know. I'm not trying to talk you into anything. It just seems like a possibility to me. Whatever analgesics they had would have been pretty ineffective when it came to serious pain, and experience would have told the midwives that a given situation was going very poorly."

I'm still skeptical. "Only that single square was open, but don't you think I'd have found an infant's skeleton beside her if a baby had died as well?"

"Maybe. But then maybe the child survived."

"Who could look at the pelvis for us?"

Tom John grows suddenly deferential, and in doing so reminds me of the man I've sought to avoid today. "Talk to Harry about this. It's his project. I'm not sure he's going to want to get into a wild-goose chase."

"He will if I demand it," I say, my disgust swelling in me once more. "I think it's fair to say that, at the very least, my darling husband owes me one."

why we endure it

FOR THE LONGEST time, Harry claimed he couldn't tell that I had begun to swell, no doubt in the hope that I wouldn't become convinced that the body I already had real reservations about soon would be something of a lost cause. After a shower at the end of a long day at the clinic, I would prove to him that my belly was growing quickly and that my breasts already were disturbingly big. But he liked to pretend that the dramatic changes still were too subtle to be visible, and that—didn't I know?—babies arrived in bundles held in the beaks of storks.

For my part, I was amazed at how soon my pregnancy had become a physical reality—there was something growing inside me—and with each new sensation I became more directly connected to the women in similar circumstances to whom I previously had given care. So this was what it was like, I noted with revitalized interest—the morning headaches, the nausea, the minor pains and tenderness, my appetite already out of whack and my mood swings surprisingly volatile—and I kidded the guys at the office that if they were ever going to be truly skilled at obstetrics they really had to bear a child or two themselves.

I was nine weeks pregnant and already the issue of whether I ought to be, whether Harry and I were ready to drastically reshape our lives, seemed immaterial, seemed silly, selfish, in fact. We were having a baby—the two of us were—and on my buoyant days that truth seemed so clear, so easy, so fundamentally right that it was hard to remember that only recently I had been uncertain indeed. This is why we endure it, I now realized, the reason we toil awkwardly through adolescence and make stabbing attempts at maturity and finally mate in ways that are always sacrificial. We do it for this, for the sublime creative joy of making new human beings. All we can really do with our lives, it now seemed obvious, is to pass on the opportunity, to offer life in return for life.

the lessons of disease

"YOU LIVED TO tell about it, I see." I can hear Tom John addressing Harry, who is sprawled on the living room sofa.

"Where's the doctor? I feel like I'm going to die."

"That'll teach you to turn forty. She's in the kitchen. You look like you could use some medical attention."

"Maybe we could talk her into putting me to sleep. It'd be the humane thing to do."

"Let me get my bag," I say as I come into the room, my gait more clumsy than usual because, although my head doesn't ache like Harry's does, I am exhausted too. "I'll put you out of your misery if Tom John'll put me out of mine," I say as I slump into an overstuffed chair.

"This is too morbid for me. I'm going home to a highball or two and little Joaõ Gilberto." Tom John leans over to kiss my forehead, then tweaks Harry's toe as if to treat pain with pain.

"If I ever touch alcohol again ... it won't be till tomorrow at least," Harry says plaintively. "Where'd you two go?"

"We ran away. I wrote you a note. But I missed Teddy, so we turned around and came back."

"What were you running away from?" Harry's in such poor condition that it's hard for him to muster interest.

"From the filthy mess this place was in," Tom John interjects.

"I was a good boy. I played softball and then I came home and went to work, but unfortunately I finally sobered up. It's done though. I got everything cleaned up before I started to die."

"I'm out of here," Tom John says as he makes his exit.

I reach for his arm as he sweeps past me. "Thanks," I say, catching his eye. "A lot. Really. It was a nice day."

"Wasn't it?" he says, and he makes a momentary face at me, one that seems to say good luck with whatever follows, before he is out the door.

Now it's only the two of us, and this, in fact, is what I ran away from. I wanted to escape being alone with Harry, to get away from necessarily keeping silent about last night—or the ugly inevitability of shouting it out—and who knew which of the two would be worse? Yet already it is easier to sit near him, to admit him back into my life, than I imagined it would be. As he lies nearby with his eyes closed and as I survey his face, I can't seem to muster my huge anger any longer. He is a bastard—that much is evident—but in the dazed stupor of his hangover he also seems weak, vulnerable even, and although his infirmity is temporary and every bit his own making, for the moment we seem to share something—bodies that have become victims, bodies that are far from invincible.

"Are you hungry?" I ask Harry as I stroke Teddy's forehead, the dog's muzzle pressed between my legs.

"No. Thanks. I think all I need is to crawl into bed. In fact..." Harry hikes himself onto an elbow and swings both legs off the long couch. "Listen," he says, stopping en route to the bedroom, slumping onto the arm of my chair, "despite the fact that I feel truly terrible and want this wretched life to be over, I had a great time last night. Don't you ever do anything like that again, but...I did appreciate it. I really did." He kisses the top of my head, smooths back the hair that has fallen onto my forehead, then walks away to his sickbed.

The television's remote control can't summon anything I want to watch, but I leave the set tuned to the medical drama that people repeatedly tell me I should see. This episode is full of crisis and heartbreak and is accompanied by music that implies some sad futility—and that *is* the bitter reality, I agree, at least for the moment: the only lessons of disease I've ever noted are that nothing lasts forever and that no one escapes alive. I click off the TV but continue to sit in the big chair for a long time, Teddy curled at my feet. I think about what in the world I'm going to do with this relationship, with this marriage that's bound together by true comradeship and caring and time, but which, for one of us at least, is less than the passionate bond he longs for. And as the last of the summer sunlight finally filters out of the sky, it's curious that I also begin to think again about children—about what-might-have-beens, and fears, and regrets I know I never can name.

a kind of feeling amongst us

THE TRIP HAD been a present from Harry's parents, a much delayed honeymoon, a sojourn intended to get us truly away for once, an opportunity to spend some time together and away from clinics and calls, offices and mindless meetings, a last opportunity to escape our regular schedules before the baby arrived. We had flown to Prestwick airport and then rented a car, exploring Strathclyde and the Grampians for a week, spending three nights at an inn on Lockgilphead that served haggis and mash at every meal and that boasted what seemed to be the largest bathtubs in the western world. In Edinburgh the following week, we slipped into the back of a lecture hall at the medical school and listened to a man with a magical accent describe alimentation and the upper gastrointestinal tract. We hiked up to Arthur's Seat to survey the gray and gorgeous city that spread north to the Firth of Forth, and in George Street, Harry discovered a pub called The Dog and Crow that he declared he could never leave.

Outside the town of Innerleithen, where the River Tweed wound through the bare green hills of the Borders so slowly that it seemed to dread its meeting with the cold North Sea, we found the estate where Harry's great-great-grandparents had lived before they emigrated to Michigan late in the nineteenth century. "Why on earth would they leave this place?" Harry wondered, more convinced than ever that his kin were a strange sort of people.

In England during the final two weeks of the trip, we exchanged the car for second-class seats on British Rail, making overnight excursions from London to Oxford and Bath, reveling in the amalgamation of world cultures that nowadays London had become, then taking a train south to the channel-side town of Seaford, where we planned to stay for two nights before we were scheduled to catch a plane at Gatwick that would return us to Colorado.

Since the year before the United States entered the Second World War, my mother had corresponded with Madie Purcell, then a young woman near her own age who worked as a civil defense officer in crowded and chaotic London tube stations during the terrible months of the air-raids, the two of them simply pen-pals at first (their letters initiated by Madie's tiny notice in *Collier's*) but becoming dear, if distant, friends through years of marriages and children, divorces and deaths, their lengthy if irregular letters serving as important ballast for each of them along the way. When Madie's husband Bill died in 1972, she moved to Seaford to retire, and although my mother and Madie had visited each other several times over the years, somehow I never had met this plump, rosy-cheeked woman whom I nonetheless presumed I knew very well, a beloved auntie of sorts who hugged me and Harry inside Seaford's little train station as warmly as if we were children of her own.

A lamb roast was waiting that evening at Madie's little row house, which sat adjacent to the churchyard where, she told us, vicars had been burying townspeople for four hundred years. The three of us ate and drank sherry and talked late into the night about our families, aspirations, and the ways in which England seemed like a very different country from the one in which Madie had grown up, about how Colorado, in comparison, still was a bona fide frontier. It was midnight before Madie sent Harry and me up to bed with hot-water bottles in hand, wishing us the sleep of the innocent, telling us we were welcome to lie in as late as we liked in the morning.

But I was wide awake in the night, counting three chimes of the church-tower clock as I first felt a strange sensation, then what was a sharp and sudden cramp, then steady and buckling cramps when I got out of bed to find that I'd begun to bleed. I tried not to alarm Harry, but I told him I thought I probably ought to get to a hospital, and he threw on pants and a shirt and quickly was knocking on Madie's door, saying, nearly shouting, "Sorry, but it's Sarah. It's the baby. She thinks she ought to get some attention. Is there a hospital nearby?"

Madie's vintage Renault was in a car park around the corner, and by the time Harry returned to Church Lane, Madie and I were standing at the edge of the street, her parka pulled on over my nightgown, a towel clutched between my thighs, plus a scarf tied to cover my ears at Madie's insistence. "Steady, love," she counseled in the back seat once we were under way, her arm around my shoulder, offering Harry directions as we drove. "Left here. Through the roundabout and onto Alfriston Road. Steady, steady. There's a good girl."

But the miscarriage was complete by the time I lay on an examining table and a young doctor began to attend to me. When I told him I was a physician as well, he said, "Then I needn't explain, I suppose. I'm very sorry. I've given you an injection of Demerol, and we'll let you rest through what's left of the night. Tomorrow, if you agree to it, I'll schedule a D&C. I am sorry."

When the doctor let Harry and Madie in to see me, I'm sure I looked pretty awful but I tried to manage a smile. "So much for a good night's sleep," I said.

Madie embraced me first, enveloping me and holding me tight, shedding tears because tears were all she could offer. "You dear, sweet girl," she said. "I'm so sorry this had to happen here. That it happened at all." Then she moved away, momentarily embarrassed as she realized that Harry still stood behind her.

"You okay?" he asked, propped on the edge of the table now, smoothing my hair, trying to find words for whatever else there might be to say.

"I'm fine. Better. But I'm so sorry, Hank," I said, my lip quivering before I bit it to hold it still.

On the afternoon of the second day, I was well enough for a walk already, and the three of us got back into Madie's Renault and drove to the edge of town where the brambled and grassy slopes of Seaford Head swept up to sheer white cliffs that dropped away to the sea. The wind was brisk, and Madie worried whether I was warm enough, but the path beside the cliff-face was wonderful to walk along—big breakers crashing far below us, the downs undulating into the misty distance, Beachy Head and the line of white cliffs called the Seven Sisters stretching away like massive fortresses, keeping the island nation safe.

"Your mum told me this morning not to let you go home until you were strong enough," Madie reminded me. "I'm not at all sure we should put you on that aircraft tomorrow."

"I'll be fine," I said, "and I'll have Harry." I reached for his arm. "This wouldn't have been nearly as easy if we'd been in London. We're so lucky that we happened to be with you."

"Your mum said the same thing, and I told her that as sad as I am for the two of you, I'm happy at least to have been able to offer the odd cup of tea."

"A ton more than that," Harry insisted.

"Back in the war," Madie said, stopping to look at the two of us, "back when your mother and I first began to write letters, we Londoners would spend nights cramped like sardines down on the waiting platforms in the tube stations. We barely got any sleep and none of us could be absolutely certain we'd survive the night, but there was a kind of feeling amongst us, one I'll never forget. I remembered it again last night. It has to do with fear, I suppose, but more than that, it has to do with getting through something together, doesn't it?"

It wasn't until Madie said that that I finally began to cry.

the tall grass that rings the pond

I AM SITTING on a folding chair inside the dilapidated trailer parked in the trees that serve as a makeshift laboratory. The trailer's aluminum doors are propped open to try to dispel the heat; its floor is powdered with dirt. Hand-tools and cardboard boxes, folders and notebooks crowd the counters in what once was somebody's kitchen.

Alice hands me the piece of bone and stands close beside me to point to the stains. "See these dark streaks on the inside of the pubis? They're faint, but they're there. Maybe she did have a kid." She wears a blue bandanna to hold back her hair and the cap sleeves of her T-shirt expose biceps that are tanned and slender. "This is getting kind of interesting. My friend in Albuquerque says she finds these on about eighty percent of the female pelvises she examines, and she's convinced that they're some sort of bruising from giving birth."

"And males never have them?"

"I guess not. Bone does bruise, doesn't it?" she wants to know.

"Well, not exactly, no, but sure, bones often are permanently discolored from trauma, some kind of injury. Does your friend ever find these marks on prepubescent females? If you found them on the skeleton of a girl who was five or six when she died, then you'd think they pretty obviously couldn't have come from childbearing."

"I don't know. She's convinced that that's what causes them, so surely she's compared plenty of bones. Why don't we send these remains to her? She won't charge much. Harry's big-time budget can handle it."

"I'll talk to him."

"Tell him if he wants to get close to *your* pubis anytime soon, he'd better let Steph take a look at this one." She makes a conspiratorial kind of face, then turns toward the counter to put the bone back into its box, and I am dumbfounded for a moment. If Alice is having sex on the sly with my husband, can she be comfortable joking like this with me? It's the kind of thing Alice says dozens of times a day and normally I'd hardly notice, but didn't she seduce Harry—or coyly allow him to have his way with her—only a couple of nights ago? I have known Alice for a very long time by now, and she can be maddeningly matter-of-fact in situations that would make me sputter with embarrassment, but I don't think even Alice could so glibly refer to my sex life with Harry if she and he had begun some sort of thing. In the span of only a second or two, I conclude that they must not have made love in the night on the tall grass that rings the pond, but before Alice reaches the open doorway, her body blocking much of the light it lets into the trailer, I am unsure again.

"What time did things finally break up the other night?" I ask her, and although her face is in shadow, I can see that my sudden shift to that question has unsettled her. She tucks in her shirt as she responds.

"Oh . . . God . . . late-thirty." This time she clearly is having to work at her nonchalance. "There must have been about six of us— with Harry at the helm—who were bent on self-destruction. There was a point there after which I really don't remember much." In the dim light it seems certain that she is searching my face for information, some physical clue as to what has triggered the change of subject and why I've asked the question. And now she seems eager to be on her way. "Well," she says, "I guess I'd better get back to the salt mine."

Alone, I fumble my way out of the chair and stumble down the steps of the trailer, then make my way across the hard-packed ground to the picnic table that sits underneath an arbor built out of juniper branches. My field notebook lies open where I left it, and I try to go back to work on my rudimentary report on the burial I unearthed back in early June, but all I can think about is whether I am ludicrously naive or simply stupid. All I can wonder about is whether I might be less angry at Alice than envious— envious of someone who seems to be able to do whatever she wants precisely when she wants to, unencumbered by incessant circular thinking or by consequences.

to cry every time i came

WE FLEW HOME from England on schedule and I went back to work on the morning I had intended to, seeing kids and expectant mothers among the Monday patients, assuring myself amid the flutter of activity that nothing remotely tragic had happened to me. Miscarriages were commonplace, and I routinely told women who had lost second-trimester fetuses that we had to presume it was for the best—that a healthy infant probably wouldn't have been the product had the pregnancy come to term.

Most of us were standing in the lab eating lunch when I mentioned the events of the days before, describing them as if they were merely of medical interest, as if I were a patient of mine with whom I was hardly acquainted. The men immediately said they were sorry—and they meant it, I know—and John Briem joked that Harry and I would have to get back to work right away, but the female nurses and lab techs suspected that despite my composed veneer, I had to be grieving for a child I already had come to count on. They wanted to hug me, to hold me, each one saying she knew how I had to feel. But I was fine, I tried to convince them, I really was, and then I invented a pressing obligation across the street at Community Hospital so I could leave their company and shed the tears I couldn't contain in private.

Looking back on those days, I know there was an element of deep mourning intertwined with my return to my workaday life, but at the time I did my best to believe that my rather stoic response was precisely what you'd expect from a female physician, from a woman who had glimpsed what it meant to harbor new life inside her, but who knew too that gestation and birth were fragile and manifold miracles. Every woman could not succeed every time, and that was simply that.

Harry did his best to be buoyant during that empty autumn, keeping us busy with camping trips and rock concerts, taking on more than his share of the household chores, as though the miscarriage had left me a kind of invalid, assuring me regularly that there would be a tribe of MacLeishes one day, making love with me so tenderly that I seemed to cry every time I came. But I knew too that he wasn't grieving in the way that I was, and there were many times when I sensed in him real relief that now we weren't about to become parents.

"Why do you think it happened?" he wanted to know as we lounged on the couch—my head resting in his lap—one night a couple of months after we had embraced Madie like the best and oldest of friends and flown home.

"Henry..." I said.

"Something had to have been wrong, didn't it?"

"I think so. If not with the baby, then with me."

"Now that it's happened once, is it more likely to happen again?"

"Statistically, yes. But only a little. It's not like I've become certifiably barren." I smiled up at him, but I could see little but his whisker-stubbled throat and the strong thrust of his chin. I told him I had been sure the fetus was a girl, sure in that way that's wrong as often as it's right, and I decided to say too that I had begun to wonder about naming her Mary Margaret—Oma's name. But somehow in hearing me suggest a name for our child, I think she suddenly became too palpable for him, an absent reality he could not confront.

"There'd be lots of good names," he said flatly, almost absently.

"Yeah," I said. "Sure."

"Do you want to try again?" he asked after a long silence.

I didn't respond, and he asked me a second time, but I don't think I ever answered.

out onto the rocky ground

THEY'RE SITTING IN Harry's pickup as I approach, the truck's doors open wide like wings, Harry's arm stretched across the back of the seat, Alice's boots propped up on the dash. The walk from the trailer to the trailhead where several dusty vehicles are parked is little more than a hundred yards long, but I'm tasked by even that much exertion, by the baking July weather, and by the growing reminders that the coordination and energy I possessed even a month ago now have begun to ebb.

"You've quit already? What's the flimsy excuse?" I ask to catch their attention as I walk to the side of the cab where Harry sits.

"All work, no play, you know. Alice convinced me it was Miller time, despite my better judgment."

"Did she?" I glance across the seat to Alice, who raises her beer in a desultory kind of toast.

"Here. Get in out of the sun," Harry instructs me as he steps out of the truck, taking my cane and arm, boosting me up as I grasp the steering wheel and struggle to pull myself onto the seat. "And in my rush to wrap my lip around a beer can, I realize I forgot to cover the transit, so I've got to go back to the site. You want something from the cooler?"

"Some water. Thanks." I take the bottle Harry offers me, drink from it, then pour water into my palm and splash it onto my face. "This is getting to be too much like work," I say, alone with Alice now.

"While it's hot, you don't need to come out every day, do you?"

"Alice..." I draw out her name to punctuate what I'm about to say. "I guess I don't have to do a goddamn thing, do I?"

Alice doesn't respond. She sips at her beer and stares into a stand of drought-stunted piñon trees. "I talked to Harry about having Stephanie examine that pelvis," she finally says to end the silence.

"You don't have to do my talking for me, you know." This time, my glance at Alice is rancorous. "Talking, for the meantime, is something I'm perfectly capable of doing."

"What brings out the bitch in Sarah this afternoon?" Alice is willing to spar with me now. "I didn't realize I had to check with you before I spoke with the human race."

"I told you I'd talk to Harry about having your friend look at it. You didn't have to intercede for me. You didn't have to help me out."

"What's the matter with you?" There is a kind of conciliation in Alice's question.

I turn my face to the breeze that wafts into the cab of the pickup, and my voice is weary when I speak. "I'm getting so tired of people tiptoeing around me all the time. 'Let's do this for the poor little thing.' 'We can't trouble her with that triviality.' 'No, she mustn't hear about that in her invalid state.' You know, contrary to the way I must appear, I'm not helpless. I'm really not."

"Do I act like you're helpless?"

"You act like I'm somebody you used to know."

Instead of being wounded by my remark, Alice is only icy. "I don't know what you mean."

"Then never mind."

Alice drinks the last of her beer, then with more than a measure of melodrama, she throws the can out onto the rocky ground. "I'd ask you again what's the matter, but I guess I really don't give a shit," she announces. She steps out of the cab of the truck, collects the can with an indignant sweep of her arm, then gets into her car and drives away in a hail of contentious dust.

My head is tipped back against the seat and my eyes are closed when Harry returns. "Alice take off?" he asks.

"Yes."

"You okay?"

"No."

"Tell me," he says, and something in his tone assures me that he does want to hear.

I turn to the west, toward the high hump of Ute Mountain, the landmark to which Harry long ago laid a kind of personal claim, a big and beautiful breast of a mountain that rises at the rough center of Harry's adopted world. "I've been pretending that this was going to be nothing worse than a nuisance," I say tearfully, "when the truth is that it's already the focal fact of my life. This disease doesn't just haywire your central nervous system, it also quite cleverly ruins everything else."

Harry purses his lips and blows out a long and anguished breath.

like stories you told your children

THERE HAD BEEN a time in his undergraduate years at Stanford during which Harry planned to major in Latin American history and to go on to graduate work in Santiago or Mexico City. But for some reason—and he knew the summer he'd dug in the dirt with Tom John Brown had played a principal part in it—the hemisphere's prehistory began to more readily draw his attention. The epoch that had begun with Columbus, Cortés, and Coronado, and which continued today, it seemed to him, was more thickly woven with human tragedy and triumph than an historian could comb in a lifetime of work. Yet the cultures that had flourished and failed before the arrival of Europeans had seemed to embody a kind of clarity in comparison, a kind of stature supported by what they achieved despite their detachment from the rest of the world, and Harry had become a student of anthropology in the end as a means of getting at what might be essentially American, at what, if anything, was peculiar to human lives that were lived on the two "new" continents that separated the planet's imposing oceans.

By the time he had narrowed his focus to the archaeology of the southwestern United States at the University of Colorado (an institution he had been raised to regard as a bit beneath his family's station), Harry had come to believe in an odd sort of way that there was an ancestral aspect to his occupation. Despite the tartans and coats-of-arms his parents possessed, supposed proof of his proud Scottish heritage, Harry liked to think that his personal roots, like those of the peoples he studied, reached only into western American soil. And when he first had encountered me, I know he had been delighted to consider that my grandfather had raised oats and alfalfa on the same ground where the Anasazi once had nurtured short stands of maize. That was the real ancestry, wasn't it?—generations attached to the same enduring place, the same peaks that rose in the eastern distance, the creeks that flowed where they had since before history commenced, cultures connected not so much by blood as by a shared possession of landscape.

The Ancient Puebloan people, Harry could convince you—if the evening was long and the liquor was in steady supply—had inhabited the misshapen circle of the Four Corners country for reasons that ultimately had something to do with liking the place. The summers here were too dry, the growing season too short. Because of the high elevation, land that literally baked in July and August often lay under a foot of snow from the winter solstice until the equinox that at long last presaged the spring. The region contained good soil, but only in wind-deposited pockets at long removes from rivers and springs. There was timber for fuel, but it was too stunted, too twisted to be of perfect use in construction. There was game in abundance, but killing a deer, or even a rabbit, had to have been an event laced with luck as much as with skill. Yet despite the hardships, in spite of burdens that would have been easier to flee from than confront, the Puebloan people somehow were at home here. Harry liked to think that they would have been no better than he was at explaining the strange and sustaining lure of a place that seldom made life easy. He liked to imagine that it was the trickling creeks, the high peaks, and the jutting cliff-lines of the mesas that had kept them in place—landforms like stories you told your children, terrain like food you ate every day.

the substantial stuff

WE WERE AT a Broncos game in Denver and I had just made the innocent observation that the entire population of Montezuma County wouldn't have filled the stadium's isolated south stands. "I tend to forget what a hayseed I really am," I had told him. "I'm not sure I actually like being in this close proximity to this many maniacal people."

"We could move down there, you know. There's a big, long-term project that's getting started next spring. A woman from the BLM called me on Friday to talk about it. I think I might be able to get a job. We could get you back to the hayseed life," he said with a grin on his face, and I asked him whether he was out of his bleeding mind.

But the fact became inescapable in the following days that Harry was serious about this outlandish possibility. He was growing excited by the prospect of heading up a substantive, many-season excavation—one that would offer him his own equivalent of Tom John's career-consuming work at Cow Canyon—and the idea of settling somewhere into the environs of greater metro Cortez seemed to him like perfect bliss. "Come on. Give it some fair thought," he would plead on the evenings when we tried to talk out this fearsome new possibility. "I'd get out of the university treadmill, and we'd both get away from the Front Range."

"But I *like* Boulder."

"But you don't like the likelihood that Rocky Flats is going to make us all glow in the dark, and you don't like the way Denver's oozing in this direction, and you don't, my dear, like the fact that we haven't been able to afford a single one of the country houses we've looked at and liked."

"Harry." I would try, at this point, to slow him down to a sub-sonic pace. "Think about it from my perspective for a minute. It would be like you moving back to Cherry Hills, for heaven's sake. I'd like to be nearer Barbara and Oma; that aspect sounds great. And yes, it's a wonderful part of the world in its own bizarre way, and yes, I know it would be a terrific opportunity for you. But the thought of me actually living in Cortez again makes me want to run shrieking into the night."

"Why?" His voice at these moments would lend a measure of pain to his incomprehension.

"Because...because I grew up there and was this precious little girl who didn't turn out quite so preciously, and because I was an adolescent there who pulled any number of teenage stunts, and because I left town feeling like I'd escaped from prison, and—"

"You were a kid. Of course, you hated it. That's part of grow-ing up. But that was fifteen years ago. It's going to feel very different now."

"What's this 'it's going to' business? Your bags are already packed?"

"They offered me the job."

This statement wasn't normally part of the conversation, and I was flabbergasted. "When?"

"Today. I got a letter." He was setting me up—not playing fair for a second—yet his face wore the beaming visage of a boy who'd just made the baseball team.

"You bastard," I said, trying to sound lighthearted, my slight smile an effort to stall for time. "This is going to be a done deal and I'm still going to be in the freaking-out stage."

"I'm going to go down and look things over and hear them out. I want you to come with me—you and your open mind. If we don't both agree it's great, the right thing for both of us, then it's history. I promise."

"Have you considered the fact that I've got a very real commitment to my partners to think about?" It seemed as though it was time for me to get serious. "Have you wondered about whether a new doctor could make any money in Cortez? Do you want our kids to go to podunk schools?"

"We don't have any kids, Sarah." He seemed to think he needed to remind me.

"If and when we have kids, do you—"

"You want them to grow up here and become coke-heads by the time they're thirteen?"

"Is this really about kids and cocaine?"

Harry hoisted himself out of his chair and went to the window that looked out on Sixth Street, and he had begun to feign oppression again. "I love it down there, you know that. And I'd love to work in the field for a few years. The field's the only thing I truly enjoy in this ridiculous line of work. But I'm not going without you. And if we both go, we've both got to feel good about it."

"So either I give in and make your life perfect, or we stay here and I'm the wicked witch forever and ever. Thanks, Hank." I'd gotten snide, but my alternatives seemed to be vanishing, my options limited now to making a selfish scene or lying by saying his news had made me the happiest girl in the world.

"I'm the bad guy," he said. "I know this is hitting you hard, but I know you too. And I really think there's a chance we'd love it down there."

Harry moved to the chair where I was sitting and began to massage my shoulders—a blatant bribe aimed at my acquiescence. But I didn't succumb, didn't offer him any hope. I just sat compliantly, trying to figure out how to explain to him that, for me, going back to Cortez would feel very much like a defeat. I had spent much of my life trying to convince the people I encountered—and myself most of all—that, despite my paltry beginnings and the haggard place I hailed from, I was a person of substance, that I could thrive in the world at large.

Yes, I cared about Montezuma County; I loved the feel and the smell of forests of piñon and juniper trees; I loved the cliff-line of the mesa gone red at sunset and the certain paradise of summer mornings; and I know I liked it when people remembered my name on the occasions when I returned to visit, stopping me on Main Street or in the produce section at the market to say, *my land!*, how I had grown up, and hadn't they heard that I was a doctor somewhere? But I hated my hometown as well, hated the foot-shuffling, self-denigrating, we're-just-dipshits attitudes, the perverse pride so many people seemed to take in not having a thought on any subject, hated the specter of poverty that was characterized by so many runny-nosed kids sitting in the open doorways of so many trailers with old tires in rows on their roofs, hated a certain style of affluence as well—diamond rings stuck on pinky fingers and toothpicks stuck in blue lips that seldom parted to issue words.

Cortez and the whole splendid geography of its region were places I knew I never would come to terms with; I belonged to them in ways that alternately made me swell with pride or feel as though I had to rush to take a shower to try to wash something off before it stuck. Unlike Harry, for whom Cortez was truly exotic, intriguing in its ratty and rustic simplicity, flavored by the aromatic scent of the backwater West, for me it was a place I knew too well and was too much connected to, a place about which I couldn't possibly be objective, a home I couldn't appreciate, a home I couldn't come home to.

worry turned to inattention

SOUTHWESTERN COLORADO LAY under snow in early December, when Harry and I arrived to make our reconnaissance. From the pastures at Oma's place, where we had set a ski-track in the crust and drifts, Mesa Verde, capped in white, commanded the southern horizon, and in the northeast, the towering alpine peaks of the San Juans seemed to have crept closer with the coming of snow.

Inside her house, with the furnace working furiously and the temperature cresting eighty degrees, Oma nonetheless was worried about keeping warm. Her propane tank had been filled only recently and the furnace never had failed her, but in her advancing years, and compounded by her increasingly sedentary days, winter had become a season with which she did battle—fretting about the sudden attacks of storms, watching like a wary spy as the gray sky descended and the world outside her window froze, then seemed to stand still.

Harry had gone to a meeting with the Bureau of Land Management's area manager on the second morning of our visit, and I had stayed at home with Oma, to be with her by myself—not so much because there were subjects that were better discussed in Harry's absence, but because both silence and the shared pleasure of saying next to nothing, being together in ways that didn't need many words, were easier without him. Yet we did talk about my miscarriage for a few moments, long enough for Oma to assure herself that I was doing okay and for her to assure me that miscarried babies get to grow up in heaven.

"That's a nice thought," I said.

"It's what my grandmother used to say. Back in those days, people lost lots of children, both before they were born and after. But it seemed too like new brothers and sisters got on their way sooner than they do now." She smiled instead of saying outright that it was time I was pregnant again.

"We're trying, Oma," I told her. "We know what causes it now, and we're trying."

"Bless your hearts," she said, her face flushing a bit.

But then the strangest thing happened. I had gone to the kitchen to make us tea, and as I was carrying Oma's wonderful old ironstone teapot from its cabinet to the counter across the way, it fell from my hand and shattered on the linoleum floor. I was horrified, and the noise was enough for Oma to get out of her chair to see what in the world had happened, but it wasn't until I was on my knees trying to pick up the pieces that I realized I couldn't make my right hand move. My fingers didn't seem numb, and it wasn't as though my arm had gone to sleep, but even with concentration, I couldn't make my fingers flex, couldn't fold my thumb into my palm.

"Honey, what happened?" Oma was worried about me and seemed unconcerned about the teapot.

"I don't know. I just let it go. My hand's... sort of strange."

"Did you cut yourself?"

"No. But..." Had I pinched a nerve? What was it? "This is crazy." I massaged my elbow, assuming the culprit must be my ulnar nerve. "I guess my hand went to sleep. I've got skin sensation, but I can't make my fingers work. But look what I did to your teapot. I'm so sorry."

"Oh, don't even think about that," she said. "I broke the handle once. It was glued back on. I bet it just fell off again."

"It wasn't the handle," I said, trying to sound less perplexed than I was, trying as best I could to collect the pieces while Oma poured boiling water from the kettle into cups instead of the pot.

My hand slowly improved as we sat in the living room sipping our tea, but my end of the conversation surely lagged, my thoughts occupied by whatever it was I was experiencing and whether I could isolate some sort of cause. Yet I couldn't come up with anything, and by the time Harry returned in a surge of enthusiasm, his spirits high and his body a whirl of nervous excitement as he sat in a chair that was much too small for him, I had begun to think about other things—Harry's job prospect in particular—and, with my hand virtually normal now, my worry turned to inattention.

Harry had met the woman from the BLM at the site, a huge horseshoe-shaped ruin wrapped around the head of Tse Canyon west of Cortez, a place where the valley swept upward as if bent on reaching great heights until a succession of canyons cut off its steady climb. Unexcavated until now, and surprisingly free of the vandalism that had left many sites cratered if not completely destroyed, Harry explained to Oma and me that this ruin was as large as any he was aware of in the region. It was a site that once had been a very large village, and even amid the rubble, the tangle of trees and brush, and the snow, it was easy to spot a perimeter wall that once had enclosed it and kept it safe.

"It's a gorgeous spot. Ute Mountain looks enormous from there. You girls will have to come see it," Harry enthused.

"Is it near the old Goodman Point schoolhouse?" Oma asked.

"West of there a couple of miles."

"I haven't been over that way in donkeys' years," she said. "Time was, that would have been a long day's trip from here."

"I'll take you!" It seemed like a perfect plan to Harry. "The three of us'll have a little outing."

"Oh, gracious," Oma countered, "I can't go traipse around in this snow."

"Would you like to just go for the drive?" Harry was undeterred.

"Darlin', what I'd like to do is sit here in this chair of mine." She meant what she said. Like Kitty, her cat, Oma always had been content to stay at home, and it was precisely the same nesting desire that made me long to remain in Boulder.

But I was willing to see the ruin, at least, and Oma encouraged us on our way. As we zigzagged south and west on the county roads, Harry pointed out several farmsteads where signs
marked them for sale. "What about this one?" he would ask, slowing the car as we passed, variously pointing out orchards or outbuildings or ponds, but I wouldn't play along.

"You're getting way ahead of yourself, mister," I told him
finally, and then I explained the strange thing that had happened
in Oma's kitchen.

"Weird," he said, but then an idea flashed in his head. "I bet
you dropped it because you were just so damned excited about
moving back here." He gave me his smile and I shook my head in
disgust, but before I had a chance to respond, to tell him he was
as full of shit down here as he was at home in Boulder, he has-
tened to explain what more he had learned about the scope and
the timetable of the Tse Canyon project, his words a whirl of per-
suasive information, his eyes turning to me for emphasis and in
the hope of seeing my acquiescence, his face animated by antici-
pation, the road ahead of us plowed and packed hard, the snow
spreading in smooth folds across pastures and fields, the valley
reaching up toward both the mesa and Harry's mountain.

propped against a life preserver

I HAVEN'T BEEN able to hike for a year now, and scrambling up peaks the way Harry and I did in our early years together is plainly an impossibility, but I still can ride a horse: Harry can saddle the sedate old gelding we call Mr. Ed and, holding the horn, I can keep my balance as Ed dutifully and rather depressively follows Harry's horse on the trail that winds toward the canyon rim from our farm. Canoeing, too, remains a successful way for the two of us, or the three, to get away for a day. I sit in the bow of the boat and manage my paddle as best I can; Teddy rides between the thwarts and does my balance a steady disservice as he lunges to look at rising fish or plops himself down on the hull in a kind of exhausted ennui; and Harry works from the stern to actually get the canoe where it's going, ruddering, J-stroking, complaining, and paddling hard to keep us in the quick current and pointed principally downstream—down the cold and clear and often trickling Dolores, its water released by a giant gate valve beside a dam, its canyon cutting deeply and angling north into an ochre desert; down the storied San Juan, so thick with silt it sometimes seems like liquid earth, brown and broad and lazy, its bed braided into several channels where it enters Utah, the river languishing between the sandstone cliffs that flank it and the tamarisks that try to suck it dry.

On a warm morning in mid-July—the afternoon's heat still at bay and the air moist and sweet by the river's bank—Harry hauls the canoe down from the pickup's rack and eases it into the water. The big, boxy cooler, the already-dripping-wet dog, and I are soon on board and Harry pushes the boat away from the sandy shore, pushes it out until the brown water rises above his bare knees. Then he too steps into the canoe and we are river-borne, floating down the San Juan from the Navajo settlement of Montezuma Creek, past abandoned cars and a derelict pumping plant, past metal-sided shacks and assorted oil-boom relics, past the tattered drive-in movie screen that has been blank since the middle 1950s, and finally into empty territory, the current carrying us beneath the clustered, cliff-side nests of canyon wrens now, the presence of our canoe disturbing a downstream heron enough that he lumbers into the air to elude us.

At lunch time, we find a place to pull ashore where three enormous old cottonwood trees crowd together beside the bank—a spot where we always stop on this almost-annual excursion down this stretch of the river, a place where the shade spreads wide and a deep eddy is fine for swimming, and before we eat the meatloaf sandwiches I've packed, we take off our clothes and wade into the chocolate water, holding hands to keep me steady, Harry letting me go when the water is deep enough, then swimming quickly to the top of the eddy where he can catch me before I'm carried too near the downstream current. It is something I still can do—I still can swim, at least after a fashion, and I revel in the water for half an hour, circling the long eddy, Teddy trailing Harry and me from the shore, our eyes irritated by grit and our bodies tanned with a layer of silt by the time our feet find the riverbed and we lurch our way back to the shore.

"I love it that you're as big a klutz as I am when you try to get out of the water," I say, laughing, as I watch Harry stumble and splash his way toward me.

"I'm pleased that you enjoy yourself at my expense," he says.

"I should just live in the water, shouldn't I? No one would ever know there was anything wrong with me."

"You'd get terminally wrinkled fingers and toes."

"I suppose I would," I say, patting the sand beside me as a signal to Harry to sit. "But it would be worth it. You can't imagine
how nice it would be to look normal, even if the awful truth was
that you weren't. People not knowing—that would be winning half
the battle. If I just had to deal with my wacky neurons and the
bizarre responses my body makes, but other people weren't aware
that anything was out of the ordinary, I don't think I would feel as
fucked up as I do. If this were like diabetes—which is grim and no
fun whatsoever, but most of the rest of the world doesn't necessarily have to know you have it—it would be a whole lot easier."

"Do you really think people are treating you differently now?"
Harry is listening to me but he's also building a mound of sand
with his hands.

"You're kidding."

"What?"

"I can't believe you're asking that question."

"Is there—?"

"You're not aware of it?"

"I'm not sure what *it* is."

"God," I say, "former patients I run into in the store, people my
parents' age, the gang out at Tse Canyon, you, Alice, Tom John at
times—everybody acts like I'm entirely different. It's like you all
lower your voices when you're around me, and you'd think I was
twelve years old, the things people say."

"I treat you like you're twelve?"

"You treat me like I'm your dependent. Yes, you do."

"Well, tell me to cool it when I do." Harry is trying to avoid
one of our pitched conversational battles, the kind that can quickly become a sortie of words and phrases, its subject all but forgotten amid the stinging remarks. But I—at least not yet—do not
want to let it go.

"Cool it! There. Has that done the trick? Now can you think of
me as the same woman you hooked up with forever ago?"

"But you aren't the same person. And neither am I, thank God.
I'm not sure that—"

"But see? I do feel the same. I am the same, except for the fact
that the package has been run over by a truck. Jesus, can I finally

empathize with people in their seventies who hate being treated like doddering fools."

Harry's mound of sand has risen between his knees now, and his eyes keep close attention to his task as he continues to talk. "I may be dense, Sarah, no, I *know* I'm dense, but honestly, thinking back about the night of the party, for instance, I don't see how everyone was so weird around you."

"I don't think we really want to talk about the party, do we?" I pull my knees up to my chin and wrap my arms around them. I stare out into the river and watch a driftwood stick bob, then disappear, then surface again as it passes.

"Because...?"

"No, Harry."

"What?"

He has to wait for my answer. He turns to look at me and has to wait until I feel tears well in my eyes. "Like I told you, someday I'm just going to disappear."

"What are—?"

"I'm just going to go away."

"And I can't come?" He puts his hand on the nape of my neck.

"No." This time I turn to look at him. "Of course you can't."

Even in the shade, it is hot by the time we finish eating, Teddy paying entranced attention to our meal, giving up hope only when it's clear that none of our food is meant for him and when Harry throws a stick into the water for him instead. My straw hat helps shield me a bit from the sun when we are afloat on the broad brown back of the river again, but I'm weak when we reach Sand Island and pull ashore late in the afternoon, and I fall fast asleep in the cab of the pickup, my head propped against a life preserver, on the ride home to Colorado.

the curve on mancos hill

BACK IN BOULDER, I acquiesced. Faced with Harry's conviction that the Tse Canyon project was the kind of professional opportunity he might never have again, and with his boyish, over-the-top exuberance about living in the back of beyond, I told him I willingly would return to Montezuma County, at least for a year, maybe two. Four years before, I had vowed in front of Father Abraham that I would stick by Henry MacLeish for better or worse, and although I still felt that following Harry to Cortez was decidedly worse, I did realize that my sacrifice was not a saintly one, all things considered. There would be work for me in my hometown, it turned out; two family practitioners whom I met and liked during that short December visit were running themselves ragged—their waiting room overflowing from ten until six every day—and they assured me on our first meeting that they would welcome my helping hand. Staff privileges at Cortez's small hospital could be acquired as a matter of course, and my call schedule, shared with my partners and two other docs, would be surprisingly merciful—one night a week and only one weekend in five.

My colleagues at the clinic in Boulder professed sorrow to see me go—they did their best to induce great guilt, in fact, when I first announced the impending move—but before long they were warmly supportive and the several of us promised each other we would stay in touch. At a going-away party on the weekend before Harry climbed into the cab of a Ryder truck with the self-assurance of someone who'd been highballing the nation's highways since he was seventeen, a slightly drunken and very married John Briem told me that I was a fine physician and then finally confessed to the crush he said he'd maintained since I had joined the practice. I blushed, I know, and told him he was crazy, then also tried my best to let him know that I was flattered by his bad judgment.

Harry towed our car behind the rental truck as we pulled out of Boulder, the rig barely crawling up to Eisenhower Tunnel and over Fremont and Poncha and Wolf Creek passes, and I patiently followed in the pickup Harry already had purchased as a means of making his cow-country image complete. When we rounded the curve on Mancos Hill on a warm and welcoming evening in early May—snow still capping the peaks of the La Platas and the cottonwoods leafing beside the little river a mile off to the west—I was shocked to discover that I was excited somehow. The profoundly familiar valley tilted up in the northern and western distances and the Abajos and San Juans seemed to float far beyond; Ute Mountain heaved up out of the earth as it always had, and the mesa still sealed off the south, but something discernible had changed. Something in the rich aroma of springtime—or perhaps in the soft light that languished till dusk—was arresting and appealing and unlike everything that I was sure I knew and understood about the place.

I noticed that my left hip was numb from the long hours I had been stuck on the pickup seat, and I tried to stretch to relieve it, but I didn't pay it much mind in the midst of that strange and swelling sense that there might be things in this place that bore discovery, after all, that deserved some investigation, that could recapture my interest despite my lifelong familiarity and the fact that I once had run kicking and screaming away. On the straight stretch of highway that cut west toward the lights of Cortez, I gave myself up completely to the notion of coming home. In Harry's whining pickup, with the radio blaring and the disheveled sweep of the valley surrounding me now, I finally surrendered whatever it was that had kept me so leery so long. And by the time the two of us lay in a bed in the Best Western motel on the east side of town—the patch of numbness still unabated and seeming to extend down my leg now—I was nonetheless relaxed and at ease in a way I hadn't been for half a year, all our possessions packed in the truck that stood outside the door, our plans for the coming days still only vaguely decided.

fertility of every kind

LIONEL, MY MOTHER'S boyfriend, is crouched on the packed earth of an open kiva, excavated only this summer, the floor of the cylindrical pit nine feet below the surface of the surrounding ground. Etched in the sandstone slab that makes up much of the kiva's floor is a stick-figure depiction of a bent-backed man with a formidably erect penis who seems to be playing some sort of flute: Kokopelli, an ancient character, surely symbolic, that's still common among contemporary Pueblo people.

"I've seen these on jewelry and in artwork," Lionel says, turning up toward Harry, who stands high above him at the lip of the kiva's wall, and me, sitting at its edge, my legs dangling into space, "but I had no idea they were as old as this."

"Yep. This character—whoever he is—has been around for a long time," Harry tells him.

"Do you normally find them in places like this?"

"No. This is unusual. It isn't earth-shattering or anything, but engraved kiva floors are pretty rare."

"And they mean...?" I anticipate Lionel's next question, and I know Harry's answer before he gives it.

Harry's laugh is practiced, as is his response. "People think archaeologists ought to be able to explain things. I'm not sure I can, in this case, but we've assumed for a long time that Kokopelli probably has something to do with fertility, that cock of his being pretty imposing, after all. You find him painted on pottery, on plastered walls; occasionally you find a ceramic figurine. People argue about whether he's a hunchback or if he's carrying a pack. And the flute? Well, maybe he's a kind of Pied Piper calling forth fertility of every kind—babies, game, rain, good crops. Or there's always the possibility that he's simply an erotic figure—pornography of a sort. Whatever, I've kind of always liked the fact that he seems to prove that these folks weren't religious fundamentalists who would've been aghast at drawings of big-time hard-ons."

Lionel chuckles as he stands up, grinning as he glances at me, and surveys the circular chamber. "And these kivas were ceremonial, weren't they?"

"Well, presumably. As you can tell, I'm a little reluctant to get categorical."

"Yes. I've noticed." Lionel begins to climb the aluminum ladder that leans against the kiva's block and mortar wall. "Why?"

"Oh, I'm more than willing to make pronouncements about things we can observe, the physical stuff. I can cite you chapter and verse about unit-pueblo room blocks or types of projectile points or the range of a particular type of polychrome ceramics. Whatever the scientific process allows us to conclude, I'm happy to conclude, but all we've got to work with are those pieces of physical evidence." Harry extends his hand and Lionel takes it as he steps up and off the ladder. "We find the knife stuck in the body, say, and there are enough pots and pans around that we're pretty sure we're in the kitchen, but that isn't enough information to prove that the cook's the killer."

"Hercule Poirot gone prehistoric," I suggest.

"Precisely, *mes amis.*"

"And now no more tedious questions. I promise." Lionel puts his hand on Harry's shoulder and I see that Harry notes the touch. Despite what seems to both of us to be an eccentricity or two, Harry has liked my mother's boyfriend from the beginning, and thus far I think I do as well.

Harry wants to show Lionel a nearby site anchored to the absolute lip of the canyon, and because of the rough ground, I decline to make the short walk with them, yet the slab of rock that cups the place where they stop throws their voices loudly back to me where I remain at the kiva's edge. I can hear that Lionel is stunned by the panorama I picture in my mind: the canyon cutting away from them in a series of sudden turns, its sides sheer-walled in places, the buff sandstone smooth and rounded by weather, the green-timbered summit of Ute Mountain looming high in the near distance, the air at the canyon rim rich with the smell of piñon pitch and sage.

"Well, they did know how to pick a spot. I'll give them that." Lionel's voice carries easily to me as he surveys this southwestern-most piece of Colorado. "I'd live here, given the opportunity."

"In a second," Harry agrees.

Then I catch a conversation they surely suspect I can't. "Are you two happy, happy here?" Lionel asks, and now I want to be sure I hear every word.

"I am, sure. This is a great job, it's important, and look where I get to work every day. This place isn't Paris, but it suits me. I don't know if that compliments me or slurs Cortez."

"What about Sarah?"

"Oh, gosh," I hear Harry say, and I can tell he needs a moment to craft a response. "She didn't want to move back here. The idea scared the shit out of her at first, but I was gung-ho and she was supportive enough that she ultimately agreed to it. Then before long, she was pleasantly surprised to discover this wasn't precisely the same place she'd grown up in. And she's enough of a nester, somebody who loves the security of a true home, that now she's the one who'd have a hard time moving again. The MS, of course, is a huge thing to deal with, and she told me last week that sometimes she likes the idea of just going away, someplace where nobody knows her, but I suspect that what actually would be her preference would be for me and a few of the rest of us to go away instead and leave her comfortably at home." It's a bit of an effort to catch each of Harry's words, but I want to hear them—and do— and although I want to shout that what I say is exactly what I mean, instead I have to silently acknowledge that Harry does know parts of me pretty well.

"I asked Sarah if I could go away with her when she told me that. She said no, I couldn't, and it was strange. For the first time in all of this, I found myself wondering whether we might belong apart, whether that would be best for her."

"Would it be best for you?" Lionel, bless him, asks exactly the question I want to ask from the place where I sit thirty yards away.

"I don't know," Harry says, his voice soft but still discernible. "I believe in the death-do-us-part stuff. But I also believe that people change, that they *should* change. What I don't want is for either of us not to have the fullest life we can just because we're afraid of what comes at us."

"I suspect that what's come at Sarah is something of a freight train," Lionel tells the husband who—it seems certain from where I sit—is trying to find the simplest way out of a marriage that doesn't make sense for him anymore.

"Yes," I hear Harry say, "...and why her? Of all people, why should Sarah have to suffer?"

contentment seems like surrender

IN THE AFTERNOON, Harry and Lionel have driven to Mesa Verde to look at still more ruins and for Harry to take the skull of the Puebloan girl whom I unearthed some weeks ago to the park service's lab for more investigation. Declining to join them frees my mother and me for a few hours from the subtle but nonetheless consuming attention to men that so often occupies our separate days—Lionel living in her house since early July, me attached to Harry for twenty summers by now, both of us the sorts of women for whom playing a nurturing role to the men in our lives always has been something we've only awkwardly accomplished.

When they arrived on Thursday, at first my mother and Lionel had insisted that they would stay in a motel in town, but I finally convinced them that they would be more comfortable out in the country with us. And after two nights spent under the same roof, after two dinners accentuated by unwelcome attention to my health and Harry's booze-fueled ramblings about all the places in the world he and I ought to inhabit, the four of us still are getting on remarkably well—Harry and Lionel very at ease with each other in part because no blood or expectations connect them, me enjoying my mother the way I wish I could all the time, admiring her, thinking *I want to be that secure and self-satisfied when I'm sixty.*

129

Tonight, Mother and Lionel are scheduled to have dinner at Barbara's house, and already she is bracing herself for an encounter with the son-in-law whose name she seldom mentions, whose virtual inattention to husbanding and parenthood has vexed her for fifteen years. But this afternoon is going to be a pleasant one; she and her two daughters are going to do nothing at all. Perhaps we'll make rum drinks and take them outside to the shade, or we might sit at the kitchen table with photo albums spread out before us to trigger our musings, but nothing more taxing than that—just the three of us together for a few hours, a mother and her daughters entering a stage akin to friendship now.

Yet when Barbara arrives at one o'clock, wearing a scoop-neck T-shirt that shows too much cleavage for my mother's taste, she makes clear, Barbara has a different idea about how to fill the afternoon. "Let's go visit Oma," she suggests. "She'd love to see you, Mom."

Mother isn't sure how to respond, how to say, *No, dear, let's not*, without actually saying so. But when she does say, "Well, I guess we could drive out," it is clear to both Barbara and me that our mother is more than a little hesitant.

"Let's do." Barbara still tries to encourage her.

"Honey, you know I love Oma, I really do. We send each other notes a couple of times a year and she's the sweetest woman in the world, but...well, you can understand that our relationship changed rather dramatically quite a few years ago."

"So?" Barbara inquires.

"Will you explain this to your sister?" she turns to me, seeking some help.

"You two decide," I say, unwilling to press my sister's point, but neither am I ready to nix the idea. "I'd be happy to go, but it's up to you, Mom."

"I called her and said we were coming out. She was tickled to death."

"Barbara! You called her before you—"

"I'll call and cancel then. Forget it."

"I think we'd better go." Now I'm trying to referee. "Just for a little while."

"Well, we should in that case," Mother agrees, but her aggravation hasn't subsided. "But I am amazed, Barbara, that you don't think these things through sometimes. I wish you'd try to understand the awkward position it puts me in."

"It'll only be awkward if you let it be," Barbara counters. "She's a darling old lady who thinks very fondly of you, and I think it's as simple as that."

"We're going," I say in an effort to settle their conversation.

"Well, give me a minute," my mother says, leaving the room with her irritation still hanging in the air, me offering Barbara a something of a confederate smile but also shaking my head at her tactics.

In the car on the short drive northwest to Lewis, the highway flanked by fields where hay bales wait to be gathered and stacked, Barbara attempts to make amends. "I'm sorry, Mom. I thought it'd be fun for all of us."

"It will be," Mother assures her. "I just—well, I'm sure it will be," she says, and the tiff is officially finished. "How has she been?"

"Great, I think. Hasn't she, Sarah?"

"She's a rock. I check her vitals occasionally, and I'm always amazed. She's probably in better shape than Barbara is."

"Says who?"

"You of double-cheeseburger fame. You of the fried cholesterol breakfast."

"I don't even want to think about what your family eats," my mother says with a kind of wince.

"We eat like a normal American family, thank you very much. And excuse me for living today." Barbara has begun to feel put upon.

"Only kidding, dear sister." I turn toward Barbara and offer her a smile I hope shows that I really am. At least so far this afternoon—and despite the fact that Harry's words from this morning, those he spoke about all the change he's eager to initiate—still swirl in my mind, I'm having a surprisingly pleasant time.

"I would much rather talk about Mom's new man." Barbara seems willing to forego another row. "And what I want to know, Sarah, is whether he's way cute."

"He's cute."

"Hunkier than Harry?"

"Harry who?"

Mother is sitting in the back seat. "You two," she scolds and we laugh. "You can judge for yourself this evening, Barbara. And I won't need to tell you either that he's also a wonderful man." Mother is trying to play along, but it doesn't come easily for her.

"Well, we want him to be a wonderful man. That's the kind we like, Mom. But didn't it crowd you a little to have him move in?"

"It's taken some give and take, to be honest. I lived alone for quite a few years, and I got to where I kind of liked it that way."

"Sounds like paradise," Barbara muses from behind the steering wheel. "A dependable vibrator and nobody else in the house."

This time our mother is abashed. "I can't believe the things you say. Did I really raise you?"

"I seem to remember waking up in your house every day."

"I seem to remember being pestered till I wanted to choke you to death," I add.

"Yeah, that was me, Mom. I guess you did raise me."

"We did have fun sometimes, didn't we?" She sounds surprisingly wistful.

"It was agony, to tell the truth." It's hard for Barbara to respond any other way. "No, I actually guess it was okay. Sarah was always a pain in the ass, but you didn't cause me too much grief, and Dad hit the road. Plus, I had the advantage of watching her blow it on a regular basis. The only good thing about being younger is that you get to go to school on the older one's idiotic mistakes."

"Some of them were pretty awesome, weren't they?"

"You grew up in a confusing time," my mother says, as if to offer me a kind of excuse.

"I think I grew up in a great time. If things had been more complacent back then, I probably would have become one of the Nixon youth."

Barbara says, "I think you secretly wanted to be the homecoming queen, but when you realized you didn't have the hot bod for it, you decided to go the revolutionary route instead."

I laugh. "I see. That's the explanation, is it? And speak for your-self about the wish for a hot bod."

"In my case, there wasn't any need to wish," Barbara says, toy-ing with me. "Still isn't. I don't wear my ring to work and I get asked out all the time."

In the back seat our mother is smiling, relishing the repartee, knowing that her daughters' sparring often isn't done in such fun. But then she sees Oma's whitewashed, lap-sided house at the top of the rise, a place she hasn't seen for longer than she wants to remember, and her smile fades as memories and long-worn mis-givings flood back into her mind.

Barbara turns the car into the lane, and I try to anticipate my mother's reaction. "I bet seeing this brings back stuff from a mil-lion years ago," I say, twisting in my seat to speak.

"It does. It makes me realize that I've lived two or three very different lives."

"Good for you." Barbara's door is open but she hasn't begun to get out.

"Why was it so hard for you to be happy here?" I want to know now.

"I'm not sure," my mother answers, sounding as if it's a ques-tion for which she'd love to secure an answer herself. "I think I was always taken aback by how placid people seemed to be. Contentment was something I was always skeptical of; it seemed fine for cows but not for people. Contentment seems like surren-der to me."

half a lifetime yet

I HAD EXPECTED moving home to be emotionally chaotic somehow; I had assumed that at the same time Harry was acting like a little boy at a rodeo, I would be caught in a tumult of rank recollections of an earlier time, as well as stony contempt for what the present-day place had become. But moving back to Montezuma County was remarkably easy, in fact, and it seems to me now that when people tell say you can't go home again, what they're correct about is only that you can't reconstruct a time—you can't set the same chain of circumstances in random motion again.

Cortez late in the 1980s turned out to be a surprisingly different place from what it had been in the middle 1960s. The suspicious and paralyzing fear of a world in which change was becoming the only constant seemed almost to have vanished by the time I returned. Satellite dishes now appeared to be planted atop every farmhouse, and working-class men looked like the hippies who had seemed so terribly subversive two decades before. Although attitudes toward Utes and Navajos still seemed mired in stereotype too often, I actually sensed a nascent appreciation for the fact that this was a place in which faces were several-hued—reds and browns and sun-scarred whites in an increasingly comfortable mix. I was one of only two female physicians on staff at Cortez's hospital, it was true, but a woman was

Cortez's city manager these days and a woman was also the district judge—evidence that people in this outback region had decided there was room in their world for the future.

Yet despite the fact that the denizens of the Four Corners country seemed to have resigned themselves to the turning of the twenty-first century, Cortez and its environs still sometimes reminded me of my early days. "Toto, something tells me we're not in Boulder anymore," Harry liked to joke, and I would laugh sarcastically at the understatement. Three decades after the oil boom of the early 1950s, parts of Montezuma County still looked as though a Korean War battle or two had been fought on American soil, and any sort of land-use planning was still plainly and simply a Communist plot; the mannequins in the windows of The Toggery still looked like they belonged to an era epitomized by Desi's exasperation with Lucy, and poverty still seemed to leave too many lives forlorn.

Unlike my patients in Boulder, who often wanted an hour-long explanation of even the simplest disease's pathology, and who too often wanted to debate whether the drug I'd just prescribed was the next worst thing to thalidomide, patients in Cortez tended not to question my diagnoses or plans for therapy. "Well, you're the doctor," they'd say, as if the M.D. were proof that I could work any number of miracles, and I soon learned that a patient sent away without some sort of prescription was a patient who'd be certain I'd stolen his money. Yet I liked most of the people in my hometown who came to me for care. I liked the wry old geezer farmers who swore they'd never been sick a day in their lives, unless you counted that time when a combine took two of their fingers; I liked the prim and matronly ladies, some petite and fragile, others substantial and portly, who would wear their best dresses just to sit in our waiting room, and who seemed nothing short of astonished that a sweet girl like me had managed the mysteries of medical school; I liked the teenagers who proudly announced that they were getting out of this shit-town, and that before they stopped anywhere along the way, they were going to see the ocean.

Most of all, I think, I was attracted to the young mothers, a couple of whom once sat across the aisle from me in high school, a few of whom had high-schoolers of their own already, women who knew before their fortieth birthdays that life wasn't going to keep the promises they once were sure it had made. Too often they were women for whom child-rearing had seemed all-consuming at one time, everything they could ask for, but who now sensed—some of them still with toddlers in tow—that their kids would force their way free in seemingly no time at all, leaving them with half a lifetime yet to live and little enthusiasm for what those years would hold. They were women with husbands who would get drunk and want to make love with them on Saturday nights, but who would spend the rest of the week in a strange and private isolation that refused to be broken down, the wives wishing in the end that someday the men just wouldn't come home.

As I treated these contemporaries of mine for migraines or irritable bowel syndrome, for insomnia or duodenal ulcers or any one of a dozen other disorders whose primary cause likely was chronic stress, I sometimes wanted to say, *Hey, go away: Go home and pack a bag and leave a note on the kitchen table saying you don't know if you'll ever be back.* I wanted to tell them to start new lives surrounded by different scenery, but somehow I never did, in part because I knew I'd be afraid to start again myself.

Barbara was one of those women—although both of us realized right from the start that I was in every way the wrong person to be her doctor—and as I began to get to know my sister again, to truly encounter her as an adult for the first time, I couldn't help but hold myself up in comparison. Yet was I so different from Barbara and the other women who worked at the local banks, who were school secretaries or auto-parts clerks or Jazzercise instructors in addition to raising a couple of kids and trying to come to some sort of truce with their husbands? I had grown up in precisely the same place and in much the same way they had. Did the fact that I didn't have any children (and was beginning to wonder whether I ever would) and that I had gone away for a decade and become a "professional" in the process really set my circumstances apart from theirs? Did Harry and I share something vital and invigorating that their marriages sadly lacked? Was I a free and fulfilled resident of a place in which they plainly were trapped?

I wanted to think that the answer in every case was yes, but the longer I lived in Montezuma County this second time around, the harder it was for me to convince myself that I was in any way different. There were days when it came as a real comfort to me to feel that I lived in a place where I belonged, but there were days too when I was sure that Harry and I and this place might as well be strangers, none of us truly connected in the ways we wished we were.

a wider swath of the world

MY MOTHER'S APPRAISAL of the town where she raised her daughters hasn't changed at the end of her visit, but both she and Lionel admit on Sunday that they have enjoyed their short sojourn north out of New Mexico, even if it has taken them only a few miles beyond the border, even if she still hasn't been able to persuade me or Barbara or our spouses that perhaps it is time to move on, to discover a wider swath of the world.

On Sunday afternoon, we all gather at our farm for a barbecue—Lionel serving as chef, the work and the rave reviews for his ribs further helping forge for him a fledgling connection to this clan, Barbara's boys and I ensconced in a very low-stakes game of poker before Lionel serves the meal, Harry and Rudy playing horseshoes and knocking back several beers, Rudy surprisingly at ease on this occasion, going so far as to tell Mother she looks great as we sit down to eat, telling Barbara that her family seems to specialize in handsome women, Barbara winking at me in the ensuing seconds as if to say, well, I guess he can't be an asshole all the time.

Barbara's clan leaves for home as dusk descends on the summer weekend, and before the four of us who remain call it an early night, we agree on a reunion in Santa Fe in September—Harry mentioning the conference he has to attend in Albuquerque and

me saying sure, I'll agree to see my mother's herbal therapist—
this woman who purportedly can cure any disease suffered by
humankind—but only as a matter of curiosity. "If she prescribes
something truly disgusting, I'm not guaranteeing I'm going to
swallow it," I say, and then I laugh at myself. "God, I sound like
one of my patients."

Harry is up at six on Monday morning, and Lionel and
Mother hope to get an early start as well, but as I try to get out
of bed to go make breakfast, my legs collapse, crumpling
beneath my weight, sprawling me on the bedroom rug, stranding
me there much like the night I was stuck out in the sagebrush,
except that this time I haven't tripped. This time, both legs have
simply surrendered.

When Harry gets out of the shower, he tries to get me onto my
feet, to hold me until I regain my balance, but although I try
repeatedly, I can't place one foot in front of the other. Collecting
all my concentration, I can't lift either instep, and I start to cry.
"Goddamn it," I wail, "*goddamn* it. I don't need this right now."

"Is this another exacerbation?" Harry asks.

"I can't walk and my eye is all blurry and that's fucking exactly what it is. Jesus."

Harry lifts me back into bed. He props pillows behind my back
and straightens my robe and smooths the comforter he spreads
across my legs. "Do you have any prednisone?"

"No," I respond, sobbing lightly, wiping my eyes.

"You want to prescribe yourself some? I'll run and get it."

"No. There's no rush. We'll wait until Mom and Lionel leave."

"I'll take care of their breakfast," Harry says and I nod my
assent, but when Harry encounters the two of them in kitchen
and explains what has happened, Mother rushes into my room,
the two men trailing behind her. She sits on the edge of the bed
and studies my face as she strokes my cheek, her own expression
etched with anguish, her eyes moist and hollow with pain. "What
happened to you?" She is attending to her child once more, and
her voice bespeaks her concern.

"I'm okay. It's just snuck up on me again. This hasn't happened
in quite a while."

"What do you mean 'this'?"

"It called an exacerbation; surely I've explained it before. The symptoms periodically get bad, but they don't usually last too long. A few days, a couple of weeks. I'll be up and around again soon." I'm trying to sound lighthearted, but my face betrays my worry.

Mother turns to Lionel. "Can we stay today? Can you cancel your appointments for tomorrow?"

"Sure. Of course I can," Lionel says, laying his hand on her shoulder.

"No. You go on. Really. There's not a thing you can do for me."

"Well, I can feed you and take you to the toilet and I can keep you company, at the very least."

"I can stay home with her." Harry can tell that despite my mother's concern, I'm determined not to fall back into the role of a sixth-grader stuck at home with the flu, and he tries his best to dissuade her. "Alice and I can take turns being here for the next few days. Your daughter isn't the world's most cooperative patient, you probably know."

"I want all of you to take off," I insist. "Harry, you can bring me a piece of toast and a thermos of tea...and maybe the bedpan, but then you're all out of here. This has happened before."

"You haven't ever been completely unable to walk," Harry counters.

I glare at him for a moment. I can't believe he thinks anyone else needs to know this. Mother turns to him for an explanation, then back to me as she realizes her query will go unanswered. "Out," I say. "I'll kiss each of you and then you're on your way."

Harry is the first one to acquiesce. He bends over to kiss my forehead and tells me he'll bring back my breakfast.

"I'll call in a prescription later and you can pick it up on your way home."

"You sure? I can go get it now."

"I'm sure."

"Sweetheart, I just can't leave you here like this." Mother wants to cooperate, to do as her daughter desires, but she believes I'm helpless here in this bed, and after all, she remains my mother.

"We'll just stay today. You'll be better tomorrow and we'll leave first thing in the morning."

"Mom." I'm teary again. "Don't make me get mean. This god-damn stuff is just part of my life now. Mine, not yours. And I can take care of myself."

a kind of corporeal siege

MY HAND HAD betrayed me that winter day at Oma's—gone numb and dumb and as awkward as a club—and the skin on my butt and thigh had lost sensation for several days at the time Harry and I moved back to Cortez in May. But another year and a half passed before more symptoms arrived unannounced and unwanted. It was October 1989 when my vision blurred for the first time. My right eye was fine, I was able to determine, but when I closed it and relied solely on the left eye, images were out of focus, colors were as flat as those in a photograph left out in the sun, and in my peripheral field of vision, a large swatch of the world simply had vanished.

Rather than grow alarmed however, rather than rush to an ophthalmologist seeking an explanation, I remember I chose instead to ignore the fact that my left eye couldn't, *wouldn't* offer a clear report. The symptoms were a nuisance and they lasted for nearly two weeks, but I ignored them, and I know I did so because by now I was sure what was the matter. I had diagnosed this disease often in my career—I should say that I had strongly suspected MS on several occasions and sent patients on to neurologists for confirmation—and if a woman my age had presented in an exam room with precisely my history and current complaints, surely I'd have done so again.

But I was the patient this time; this time I was under a kind of corporeal siege, and instead of freezing with fright at something unknown, I was strangely acquiescent at first. During the string of days in which my vision was compromised and my energy utterly seemed to vanish, I explained to myself the unfortunate facts: at thirty-two, I remained well within the age group most likely to contract the disease; I was a middle-class Caucasian woman who had been raised in a temperate climate, and those several factors further made me MS's potential target. But more particularly, I think, I recognized with an absent composure that if humans somehow had to contract this disease that made a mess of the brain's otherwise splendid circuitry, it could as readily choose to haunt me as anyone else. Physicians sometimes tried to pretend that their profession insulated them from personal susceptibility to sickness and suffering, but I knew that notion was nothing more than make-believe, and I made my way through the demands of those days feeling a chaotic range of emotions, feeling alternately worried or wistful, sad or sarcastic or even strangely sanguine about what would become of my life.

Only late at night, lying awake beside the man to whom I couldn't yet mention this, did I understand how truly terrified I was.

absolutely everything

MOTHER AND LIONEL finally leave at noon, arguing even as they say good-bye that they ought to stay to see me through the day, still trying to convince me that it isn't safe for me to be in the house alone. But I remain uncooperative, steadfastly assuring them that I will be fine by myself, adamant as I explain that I want to be left alone with my stupid predicament.

But then Alice arrives in mid-afternoon. It's clear from the way she's dressed that she hasn't come from Tse Canyon, and I'm puzzled by why she isn't at work and how she's heard already that I'm at home in bed.

"Harry stopped by this morning and told me," she says in response to the querulous look on my face.

"He drove into town before he went to work?"

"He...had some errands or something."

"Well, what made him think you'd still be at home?"

"He probably assumed I hadn't left yet. Which I hadn't. I was feeling lousy—cramps that were killing me. I wasn't going to work today anyway. So, once I began to feel like living this afternoon, I decided I'd drive out to see if you needed anything."

"I don't need anything," I reply too bluntly. "I'm sorry about your cramps."

"I'm okay. I'm—" She is about to say she is sorry about my exacerbation, about the fact that I woke up unable to walk, but

144

she realizes how the comparison will sound and stops herself. "How are you?"

"I've been better."

"How long will this last?"

"Who knows? I might be ready to run tomorrow, or I might not walk again for...a while. We'll see." I'm cold and aloof and I just can't bring myself to play the brave soldier with Alice. I can't assure her with a game, sick-lady smile that soon I'll be much better.

Alice is obviously uncomfortable. She doesn't know what to say now, and she isn't the type who starts tidying up the room as a means of making herself seem useful. She walks to the bureau and picks up a framed photograph of Harry and me, the two of us all dressed up and holding drinks in our hands, looking unlike ourselves.

"Where was this taken?" she asks.

"Harry's parents' house. Christmas Eve a year or two ago."

"You look lovely." She means it, it seems, and I suspect too that she is trying to cut through the tension that so plainly puts us at odds. "Harry looks like he wishes he was someplace else."

"He's getting better about being there. He can spend three or four whole nights with his parents these days without having to get roaring drunk before every dinner."

"Harry..." she says, shaking her head.

"Are you sleeping with him?" I inquire. I might as well be asking if those are new shoes she is wearing. When the question simply issues out of my mouth, it appears to bear no malice and neither does it seem to demand a detailed response.

"What?"

"I'm not really sure that I want to know, but...by all appearances you are, and I guess I don't want to be the last person on earth who knows about it."

Alice walks to the window now and keeps her back to the bed. She doesn't speak. She's still looking out at the orchard when she finally asks, "Isn't that a question you should put to Harry?"

"It's not a question I want to ask either of you," I say, "but...but I've asked it, haven't I? I guess it was easier to ask on a day like today."

Alice turns, moves toward me. She sits down on the far side of the bed. In all the years I've known her, I've never seen her cry, and she isn't crying now, but each eye is glazed with a tear that she wipes away with a finger. "I've never had better friends than you guys," she begins. "Never. And I've hated the way things have been so weird lately. I know you think I've been a horrible bitch, and I probably have been, but I haven't meant to be. Not that that's an excuse."

"Is this the answer to my question?" My voice sounds almost empathetic and that's how I feel for a moment before a cold kind of anger rises again.

"It's different from what you think it is." She smooths the bedspread with the palm of her hand.

"Everything's different, isn't it?" I say to her after a long silence, after I've tried but failed to tell her to get out of my house and out of my life forever. "Everything's as different as it can be."

the bearer of very bad news

THE SNOW HAD not yet begun to fall that winter, and Harry had
stayed at home to begin surveying small sites outlying Tse Canyon
Pueblo—working with Alice Adelman, the tall, trim, and vastly
overqualified assistant he recently had hired—and I had made the
trip back to Boulder alone, telling my husband I needed to discuss
taxes with my former partners as well as try to convince the people in the accounting department at Community Hospital that I
was still owed some money. What I hadn't explained to Harry was
that I also had scheduled an appointment with Stephen Worster,
a neurologist to whom I had referred patients while I practiced in
Boulder, a fellow whom I liked and respected and from whom I
was sure I would receive a professional opinion that concurred
with my own. Dr. Worster's diagnosis, I knew, would be relapsing-
remitting multiple sclerosis.

I sat across a broad teak desk from Steve Worster on a bright,
sun-splashed day in mid-December and this time I waited for
him to speak. Forty-five minutes earlier, he had greeted me
warmly and we had shared collegial gossip for a bit before I began
to outline the history of my complaint, describing each of the
unusual episodes in detail, explaining that color still seemed flat
in my left eye, confessing that nowadays I was chronically and
debilitatingly tired. In a small room across from his office, Steve

147

had examined me at length, comparing my eyes and the reflexes in each limb, testing skin sensation and balance, asking a battery of questions as he performed a long and linked series of simple tests, telling me that when I was dressed again he would meet me back in his office.

"Well," he said as he leaned back in his leather chair—and that single word seemed to carry the weight and force of all the words that followed—"you'd make a good neurologist. I'm sorry to say that I'm sure you made the right call. I could order evoked potentials and/or a lumbar puncture, if you'd like to do everything we can in the way of confirmation, but I don't really think they're necessary. Your history, the current symptoms, the exam just now— I'm sure that MS is what we're dealing with."

"Okay..." I looked out the window, and I was surprised that I could see in the distance the building where occasionally I too had been the bearer of very bad news. "Okay."

"There are a couple of things I want to tell you, though." He leaned forward now, his elbows on the desk's dark and shiny surface. "The first is to remind you that you didn't have your first demyelinating episode until you were thirty years old—to remind you that that's very much in your favor. The other is just a piece of advice: don't try to manage your own care. Come back and see me regularly—which would be my pleasure—or find somebody down there you're happy with, but don't try to treat yourself."

"Sure," I said in agreement. "It's probably not much fun to order your own wheelchair."

"I'm not at all sure it'll come to that, Sarah."

"You'll guarantee me?"

Steve exhaled a long breath. "You know I would if I could."

where i think i'm going

BEFORE ALICE DRIVES away from the farm on Monday afternoon, she accedes to my curious request: she helps pack a suitcase, collecting shirts and shoes, underwear and trousers and a toiletries bag at my bidding, the two of us arranging them in an old Samsonite case that lies open on Harry's half of the bed.

"Listen," I tell her, "I want you to help me with this. Will you? I don't want to talk about Harry or you or hear any explanations—or have you beg me not to go. I just . . . I just can't lie here in this bed. That's all."

Alice wants to know where I think I'm going and how in the hell I'm going to get there. I think she surprises herself by sounding rather like herself in the midst of this stunning and singular visit—Alice as incapacitated till now by my quiet and all-too-passive confrontation as I suddenly am by disease—but I turn her query away.

"It doesn't matter. I'm just going to get out of here for a while. You should take off too, and tell Harry that I'm perfectly fine and that I'll call him when I get wherever I get to. Okay?" My voice begin to break. "Will you go? Please?"

"Okay," Alice says, standing up, still holding onto the bedspread as if leaving is something she desperately does not want to do. "You're crazy. You are definitely crazy, but okay. Can I give you a hug?"

"Just go!" I implore and Alice turns and walks out the door.

his barks meant to persuade us

I WILL CALL Tom John first, I decide, and if I can't reach him, Barbara will be at work and can get away if she feigns a family emergency. But Tom John picks up the phone as I start to leave a message, telling me he's just walked in the door, saying, "Sweet thing, how nice to hear your voice."

"Not so fast," I caution him. "I'm calling to ask for a favor I can't believe I'm going to ask. I need some help, Tom John."

"Whatever I can do," he assures me, sensing now that he's taking something of a risk in saying so.

"Wait. Wait till you hear. You'd better not be so sure."

What I want Tom John to do is to gather some clothes and close up his house and drive into Cortez, where he can pick up a prescription at the pharmacy. And a wheelchair will be waiting for him at the medical supply company as well. "I'm afraid I'm going to need some wheels for a while, and what I'm asking is for you to get me out of here."

"Where are we going?" he wants to know.

"Far enough away that nothing looks like this place. You pick. Are you sure you can?"

"Well, no. No, I can't, if you put it that way. I've got a million things I have to do and I ought to stay put and attend to them, but . . . You sound like you need a chauffeur."

"I love you," I say. "God, I really do love you." Tom John can tell I'm close to crying now, so he tells me he has to get off the phone and get moving if he's going to make it to town before the store closes.

"I trust I'm going to get some sort of an explanation once we've warmed up the tires," he adds.

By the time Tom John arrives, the wheelchair folded and stowed in the bed of his pickup, I've spoken with Oma, telling her I won't be out to visit for a few days, saying I have to attend a meeting in Denver, saying I'll call. Then I ask my grandmother to *promise* me she is all right.

"Well, I'm just fine, honey," Oma says, "I'm still old, but I'm fine."

"You're wonderful," I say, my tone brightened by my grandmother's response, brightened but breaking with chaotic emotion.

Tom John takes the suitcase out to the truck and opens the passenger door before he comes back inside for me. When he carries me out of the house a few moments later—clothed now and cradled in his arms—Teddy is sitting on the vinyl seat, certain that this impending excursion will include him as well, his eyes pressed forward in the presumed direction of travel and away from any possibility of being directed out of the truck.

"Teddy," I sigh, and I start to cry as Tom John eases me onto the seat. "We can't take you with us." The dog crouches down at the tone of my voice as if to try to make himself disappear. "Can we?" I glance at Tom John.

"You're the tour director. It's fine with me."

"Oh, but you'd be miserable—wouldn't you?—and that fucking Harry wouldn't know what to do without you. I don't . . ."

"Are we leaving a note this time?"

"We are just driving out the driveway. And . . . I guess we'd better leave this guy behind." I hold Teddy close to me for a long time, burying my face in the thick fur at his neck, telling him what a fine fellow he is, before Tom John lifts him off the seat and lowers him to the ground.

I turn to watch Teddy as Tom John's truck crosses the cattle guard and pulls onto the county road, and I can see him racing along the fence line behind us now, his swift pursuit a frantic attempt to join us, his barks meant to persuade us to come back home.

three

the spires and buttes and hoodoo rocks

UTE MOUNTAIN IS nothing more than a nipple on the southern horizon and the high cliff-line of Mesa Verde has sunk from sight by the time Tom John addresses my latest predicament. What he wants to know is whether I'll ever walk again, but all he is courageous enough to ask at the moment is if I'm going to have to get good at driving a wheelchair.

"I hope not," I tell him. "It's not like my arms are a whole lot more cooperative than my legs are. If this is like the other exacerbations I've had, I'll be back on my feet in a week or two, but...I guess I've got to face the fact that this is going to be a permanent fucking situation someday."

"Whew." Tom John doesn't know what else to say.

"Yeah." Neither do I, but silence always has been something Tom John and I comfortably can share, and we quietly cross the Utah line as thunderheads rumble above the Abajos and a thin rain starts to spit at the windshield.

Earlier, once we neared the highway and dear Teddy had surrendered the chase, Tom John said the one thing he really did need to know was where in the world we were going. "This truck's going to have to turn one of two directions right up here, so think fast." But I still didn't know where I wanted to go because it hardly seemed to matter, and we sat at the stop sign for a while, watching the trucks roar past and imagining ideal destinations.

"We could go see Cynthia in Tucson," he finally suggested, certain he'd struck on the perfect plan, "drag her with us down to Puerto Peñasco for a day or two. We'll sit on the sand and eat shrimp all day and watch the waves splash till we get wise." Cynthia is yet another comrade archaeologist, a mutual friend who recently returned to the University of Arizona determined to finish the Ph.D. she's repeatedly abandoned, and although it did sound wonderful to see her and do a little lounging beside the Sea of Cortez, I said no, reminding Tom John how heat makes all my symptoms worse and readily saps whatever strength I otherwise can muster.

"Right. Bad idea," he said as he pulled onto the lane of the highway that pointed us northwest. "We'll aim for the North Pole. We can't tarry too long in Utah or they'll try to get us into the Mormon underwear, but then we'll either go to Montana to court some cowboys or I'll take you to the Oregon coast and show you the prettiest sights you ever saw."

"You're on," I said, doubtful that we'd really get very far afield, but pleased to pretend that we would, and as we wind down now into the Lisbon Valley, the spires and buttes and hoodoo rocks of the canyonlands stand red in the early evening light, and I tell Tom John that I'm sure we've taken the proper road.

We dine tonight at the Taco Bell in Moab so I won't have to be maneuvered in and out of the truck, and we stop as well for gasoline and the quart of beer Tom John makes his dessert, then we drive on into the dusk, the sky as dark red as the rock now, the storm behind us and kicking its heels up in Colorado, the highway empty and hot from the heat of the day, my mood oddly buoyant until Tom John finally demands to know some details.

I'm reluctant to play it all out again, to try to describe a situation that, so far, I've only run from, but I owe him that much, owe him more than I'll ever be able to repay, so I begin by explaining the way the day began—my legs on sudden hiatus, my mother and Lionel determined to be of some help, Harry sweet and understanding and out the door at his regular hour, Alice arriving in the afternoon, kind and solicitous until I asked her the question.

"But you didn't really talk about it?"

"What was there to talk about?"

"Well, I don't know, the sordid details. Whether it's love or only something a little more carnal."

"Oh, I think I understand. There hasn't been any calculated attempt to ruin my life, nor do I suppose they've spent much time crying about being star-crossed lovers. I guess they just...well, it's really pretty simple, isn't it?"

"Sarah, can I say something?"

"You can."

Tom John pauses before he begins, and it's clear as he gathers his thoughts that he hopes I'll really hear him. "I think by now I've got a pretty clear idea of how men's minds and penile appendages operate, and we are not the noblest of creatures, which you probably already understand too. It is possible that as ugly as all this is, it doesn't truly mean too much. *Mean* in that big-picture way, in a way that has to change everyone's lives."

"There's a part of me that thinks this is all very understandable," I tell him, "but me ending up with MS and then Harry fucking our best friend is bizarrely symbolic of something that's fundamental, that's at the core of my relationship with him. It isn't just that I'm a cripple now. Forever, always, I've never been *enough* for him. He loves me—goddamnit, he does love me, but there's always been this look of disappointment that spreads onto his face that just kills me. He wants me, but you can see it in his eyes, this longing for more than me. And I suspect that sex with me, even in the best of times, has left him desperate for more, better, *other*. It's pretty hard on your self-esteem after years and years, and you end up just wanting to walk away."

"We're walking, we're walking," Tom John assures me. "Rolling at any rate. And I don't know what to say, other than to tell you I love you. The mysteries of how two people connect, or only partially connect, or never truly connect at all—I feel damn stupid about all of that. I do know Harry, think I do, and I also think I know what it's like for a man to want everything under the sun.

It's accepting the fact that you just plain can't have everything that makes some men crazy. I do suspect that Harry is sick to death at this minute, and he's hearing nothing but my answering machine, and he's put two and two together and he thinks I'm a son of a bitch."

"If Harry can have Alice, then why can't I have you?"

"Wouldn't that have been something?" His voice is wistful, and in it I hear that he is aware, like I am, that the two of us just *might* have connected completely. Tom John finds my hand in the darkness and I squeeze his hand inside both of mine. Night nuzzles close to the land in Utah and I can't imagine tomorrow morning or any of my mornings to come.

a story i'd never tell

FLYING ACROSS THE alpine spine of the Rockies, I could see that the early snow had been swept from the mountains' ridge-lines but it already was mounded smoothly in the bowls and cirques below them, and I felt as though as I was headed home to die. As a child, I had hated being stuck at home on school days suffering from a cold or a case of chicken pox, and in a similar way that I couldn't explain but still overwhelmingly sensed, I hated to think that it was Cortez where I would wither away.

Although I had imagined for a month that MS had singled me out, it wasn't until Steve Worster had given me his concurring opinion that I really began to think of myself as sick. I was a patient, for God's sake, someone who now would have to be cared for, protected, and tended to as if she were less than complete, and I was repulsed by that realization. I could already imagine peoples' voices growing quiet in my midst and their conversations becoming oddly condescending, their laughter, their cordial kidding disappearing, seeming inappropriate under the new circumstances, and I knew for now, at least, that I couldn't deal with those demeaning reactions.

But no one really would have to know, not for a while. I would tell Harry when he met me at the airport—I'd break down when I did and tell him I was so sorry I'd screwed up his life—but this strange malady otherwise would be our secret. My family, our friends, my colleagues and patients, and the people I passed on the street wouldn't know that my brain had begun to demyelinate, that my sight sometimes was suspect and my coordination occasionally was out of control. Harry and I would keep my corporeal troubles in confidence; I'd mask my shortcomings with a kind of easy élan, and if I had to grow chronically ill in my hometown, at least I'd do so with some measure of privacy, my disease a story I'd never tell.

Near the end of the short flight, the small plane angled down from the summits of the San Juans toward the broad plate of the valley, toward the mesas that spread away to the south and west and the canyons that cut them into long and sinewy strips. I tried, as I always did, to find our farm among the gridwork of roads and winding canals in the lowlands, and I did catch a glimpse of it—the ice on our little pond shimmering in the sunlight—before the plane banked into a turn and all that remained to see was sky. Racing over rooftops in Cortez a few seconds later, dropping down so suddenly that I always sensed a moment or two of the impending end of time, I now could see the hospital and the clinic where I plied my trade, and I wondered how safe my secret really would be. As the plane settled down on the runway south of town, among the ugly detritus of an old oil boom gone bust, I saw Harry standing outside the door of the little terminal, and I knew when I saw him that I'd never been so scared.

Would my news be the thing that at last would send Harry away from me? Would the quiet and secure and love-surrounded life I'd always wanted become instead a kind of enforced confinement in which love was supplanted by pity? What did my future hold, and why did it now seem so utterly out of my own control?

a string of ridiculous accidents

IT IS ALMOST midnight before Tom John pulls off the interstate in Provo, Utah, to find a room for the night. But all the motels are full, we find—packed with Mormon graduates of Brigham Young University in town for a rousing and faith-promoting homecoming weekend. I'm about to resign to driving on to Salt Lake City when Tom John returns to the truck with news that he's made a call and secured us the honeymoon suite in a nearby bed and breakfast—a penthouse room in a remodeled Victorian mansion boasting a king-sized bed with satin sheets and a huge, red two-person tub as a kind of centerpiece. Tom John struggles to carry me up two flights of stairs, and we laugh as we cross the threshold into the room—me in his arms again, my hands clasped around his sun-leathered neck—and survey our accommodation, resplendent with silk floral arrangements and gold-glittered mirrors and bath towels as red as the tub. "Our boudoir, my darling," Tom John announces as he lays me down on the bed.

"Be gentle with me," I purr and Tom John bellows before he asks if he ought to bring in the wheelchair. "Oh, sorry, but I guess you probably should. Unless you want to carry me in to pee in the middle of the night."

"I'd have to help you into and out of the chair, wouldn't I?"

"I guess you probably would."

"Then the hell with it. I'll draw a bath instead." He turns on the tub's faucets and tests the temperature of the water for a bit before he begins to take off his clothes. "You'll join me, won't you? This is exactly what I need after six hours of highway."

"I think I'll stay here and just enjoy you in all your naked splendor," I say as I look at a man who is, in fact, quite easy to look at, whose tanned and still-toned body might well belong to someone twenty years his junior.

"True, that'll be fun for you," Tom John jokes as he steps into the tub. Settled, submerged except for his head, he lets out a long and contented sigh. "What a crazy life this is. Here we are in a honeymoon suite in Mormon heaven. But I don't date girls and you're not at your best at the moment. We should have received a substantial discount."

"It's my treat, whatever it cost. But God, I wish I had a camera."

"Blackmail? Forget it. I don't suppose there's a single soul who's interested."

"Surely there's somebody who'd get a little crazy seeing pictures, isn't there?"

"I wish that there was. But I'm afraid I'm so celibate at the moment that a careful description of the whole situation would come close to breaking your heart." He pats the water's surface with his palms. "The problem with getting old is that although the rest of the world thinks you're inconsequential, you still feel like you're as young and dashing as you ever were. You don't feel old on the inside."

"You don't look old on the outside either. I think you're still a very attractive man."

Tom John blushes. "If you call me 'well-preserved,' I'll throw this washcloth at you." He lifts it out of the water in a threatening gesture, but I'm silent and so he doesn't attack. He submerges his head for a moment, then begins to shampoo his hair as I pose a question.

"Do you suppose there's ever been a relationship that one way or another didn't end up screwed up?"

"Well, Ronnie and Nancy set us a shining example."

"Seriously."

"Don't make me be serious. I'll end up saying no, because I kind of doubt it. Although if the subject is you at the moment,

I . . . I keep wanting to say that I'm still not sure what the current circumstances mean."

Tom John is serious in spite of himself, and I try to consider what I want to say in return. "What I don't want to do is be boringly predictable. I don't want to cause scenes or make ultimatums or any of that kind of crap. For far too long I've let Harry take our collective lead, but this time I can't stand the idea of being stuck with his decisions. And the last thing I want is a marriage that's simply delivered like doses of medicine, brought to my bedside a couple of times a day."

His hair lathered into a kind of cap, Tom John rests his head against the rim of the tub and looks up at the textured ceiling. "Marriage," he says slowly, drawing the word out as if to discern whether he's ever heard it before, "is so far from my own frame of reference I can't even imagine it. It sounds lovely sometimes, it does sound lovely, but I can't think what it would be like to live my life in concert with someone."

"It ain't for the faint of heart, I'm afraid." My mood lightens a bit. "You know, there was a time—I was doing my residency—when I absolutely knew I'd never be married. I would have bet very big money. Then along came Harry and the rest is a tragic record."

"No," he counters, still relaxed in the soothing water, "the rest is just what happened. Sometimes it all seems like the grandest kind of plan, and other times it's just a string of ridiculous accidents."

"It's all accidents, Mr. Brown, I can assure you—meeting a man or catching a cold or . . . catching something more complicated. If I learned anything from the practice of medicine, it was that nobody deserves what comes their way, but neither is anybody offered prizes."

Tom John sits up in the tub, shampoo everywhere now as well as on his head, and I laugh at the silly sight of him. "Even our night in the honeymoon haven? You don't think we've been moving inexorably toward this moment since the very tip-off of time?" With the lather stiffening his long hair, he twists and stretches it into antennae, into horns, two erect pigtails on top of his lovely head.

I shake my head—no, I don't believe so—and I laugh so hard that Tom John decides I deserve the washcloth he launches at me like a missile.

if only the cottonwoods would leaf

ON THE DRIVE home from the airport, I told Harry I was fine. But he insisted that I looked tired—or was I troubled?—and so I simply confessed that yes, I did have some unusual news.

"Is he sure?" he wanted to know a moment later, shocked by what I had told him, unsure of what else to say.

"Steve Worster's sure. I'm sure. Yes, it looks very certain."

Harry turned off the tape player to listen, not so much to my words as to the absence of words, the questions that couldn't be answered that filled the interior of the car with fear. Even the name of this disease was frightening—it sounded like a body turning to stone, to crust, certainly to decay. He didn't ask, but he must have wondered immediately whether multiple sclerosis meant that I was about to die.

In the calmest tone I could muster, adopting my doctor's voice with its steady detachment, I reminded Harry of the time I'd dropped the teapot out at Oma's, my hand mysteriously useless, of that other time my butt and thigh had gone numb because of what we'd assumed were too many hours on his pickup's uncomfortable seat. I admitted what I hadn't before—that my eye had blurred and gone partially blank in October—and Harry nodded in agreement when I added that lately I hadn't seemed to have my normal energy.

These, I said, had been the initial episodes, my first fleeting encounters with a disease so unpredictable that physicians could do little more than counsel patients to expect the unexpected. I explained to Harry that this was a disease in which a patient's own immune system bizarrely and very selectively destroys the insulating white-matter sheath called myelin that surrounds nerve fibers in the brain and central nervous system, slowing, interrupting impulses aimed at muscles, interrupting as well the return of sensory information. Sometimes the myelin is only briefly and incidentally damaged and functions return to normal; other times, or in other patients, sclerotic tissues form at sites where the myelin sheath has been compromised, causing permanent damage and loss of use of whole muscle groups, of legs or arms or eyes. "It's impossible to predict," I told him, his face visibly blanched by all he heard. "With some people, these episodes—the things that so far have happened to me—occur once, twice, three times, then never again till they die in their sleep at a robust ninety-three; other patients end up unable to walk, to feed themselves, to talk by the time they're thirty."

"And as far as you're—"

"With me it's just wait and see," I interrupted, but an honest answer that day would have been that I assumed I was in for a struggle.

Harry, on the other hand, decided that I would be one of the fortunate few when nothing new had befallen me by the beginning of his field-season the following spring. Snow still sat deep and crusted in the high country, but the valleys were bare and brown. The floors of the juniper forests were dry, and I felt perfectly fine. I was free of symptoms, energetic, and we seldom spoke about the disease neither of us liked to name. It seemed that if only the cottonwoods would leaf and the grass would begin to grow, our lives—and even our marriage—would offer few kinds of complaint.

But as we were hurrying to leave the house one morning— Harry buoyant about being back at work outside, me quietly considering how to proceed with two new patients I'd acquired in a long night on call—I noticed that my right leg was dragging; it was slow to respond, and it was a real effort to lift it far off the floor. Skin sensation in my leg seemed to be fine, but as I tried purposefully to place one foot heel-to-toe in front of the other to test the problem, I crashed into the kitchen counter.

"You okay?" Harry asked as he walked into the room, ready to leave.

"I just stumbled. Something snuck out and bit me." I was upright again and was sure I appeared okay, but Harry's troubled look betrayed his abrupt suspicion.

"What was it? Are you ... ?"

"I don't know. Just a klutz, I guess. I'm fine, but I've got to go." I blew a kiss at him and got in the car, and I worried all the way into town.

Walking into the hospital on the way to do my morning rounds, there was no ignoring my recalcitrant leg. I had to clutch the handrail to climb the rear stairs, and I told a nurse who inquired about my awkward gait that I had sprained my ankle. By noon, numbness extended from my pelvis down to my knee, and the whole leg now seemed disconnected from the rest of my body. Somehow I made it distractedly through the rest of the day at the office, then drove home with my left foot on the accelerator, my right leg splayed out into the passenger's space, mocking proof that I suffered from a disease of sudden surprises.

I was using a ski pole as a cane when Harry came home at seven, and despite myself, I started to cry when he saw me bumbling my way across the living room. He kept his hands in his pockets and waited for me to reach him, and he watched me with eyes so sad I hated to see what I was doing to him. But then he hugged me tightly, holding me without any words, and he wiped my cheeks as I pulled back a bit because I needed to gauge his expression again.

I don't know how he did it, but in the next seconds he offered me his splendid and self-defining smile, the smile that had seduced me into a life's alliance with him in the first place. But he couldn't sustain it for long and he had to hold me close again to hide the pain that quickly replaced it. It one of the very few instances in all our years together when Harry had seemed utterly focused on me for a moment—a version of me he wasn't hoping to bend into a better shape—but the cruel truth was that now we both had physical proof that I was less than the person we wanted me to be. As I began to cry again, he whispered that everything was okay. Except, of course, that it wasn't.

her shoes

I HAVE BEEN to Boise before; I've been here twice with Harry in the years my father has lived here, his return to Cortez to live having been rather brief, he and Fran, my stepmother, taking administrative and teaching jobs in her hometown just two years after I left for college.

I'm traveling with Tom John Brown on my third excursion to Idaho; I'm confined to a wheelchair—or to the strong and enveloping arms of my friend—and Fran is one of those women who feel intruded upon if you haven't called ahead at least a week before you plan to stop by. Under these circumstances, I'm not at all sure whether I should call.

"But your daddy is just across town," Tom John persuades me, "and I think I've proven I'm an able driver. Besides, take good advice from me. You always should see your people when you've got the chance to."

"Don't shame me into this," I say, lifting the phone's receiver.

"It's up to you," Tom John responds, deferring to me entirely now, but still perplexed about why I seem so hesitant.

Although my father is the link between Oma and me, and although it's from him that I inherited the family that's given me so much of my sense of myself and has rooted me in a particular place on earth, my father and I somehow always have been wary of each other, unsure which words are the right ones, our love often labored and almost impossible to express. When Dad began a new life with a new mate, I felt betrayed by him; I couldn't understand what I or Barbara or my mother had done to deserve his departure, and although he tried—often awkwardly—to maintain an emotional link to his daughters, I know I built something of a barrier over the years to prevent him from hurting me again. We dutifully sent each other cards on birthdays and at Christmastime; we shared a meal or two each March when he and Fran made their annual spring-break journey south to find some sun and to visit Oma. We had little left to argue about, and nothing provoked confrontation, yet it was apparent to both of us that we didn't really know each other now that I was nearing fifty and he lately had retired.

I'd slept late in the honeymoon suite in Provo. Tom John wanted to let me get as much rest as I could. He left me a note, ate breakfast, drove up the canyon to Robert Redford's Sundance resort, and was back by the time I stirred and awoke and needed some assistance in the bathroom.

"I'm sorry about this, Tom John," I said when he lifted me off the toilet.

"Not a word," he said to silence me. "I used to do this back home when Grannie Lester came to live with us. You do all kinds of things for the people you love, don't you?"

"But it's not exactly how you'd like your friends to see you."

"But better this than not."

As the truck skirted the barren, white-crusted shore of the Great Salt Lake at midday, Tom John raised the issue of destination again, and he reminded me as well that Harry was bound to be worried.

"I'll call. Before long. But what do you say we go on out to the coast? You'll miss Montana, but wet and green and the utter absence of southwestern sleaze sound like a cure to me at the moment."

"You're the doctor," Tom John easily acquiesced and we'd made it all the way to Boise before it was obvious that I was weary again and we needed to stop.

But now we're traveling again, if only across town, and I can imagine how Fran must have winced when my father invited us over for dinner. And as Tom John takes the wheelchair out of the bed of the pickup in front of the lap-sided house on the edge of Camelback Park, I know I probably should have mentioned on the phone something about my condition. Instead, my father already is out on the curb and leaning into my open door before he notices the chair and makes a startling realization.

"Hi, Dad. It's not really as bad as it looks. I had a relapse a couple of days ago and I haven't bounced back quite yet."

"You...need a wheelchair, sweetheart?" My father—stocky, ruddy-faced, and balding now, looking more like a rancher than a rancher's son—doesn't know whether he ought to ask any questions; he doesn't know what to think.

"Only when I have to get around." I try to joke as I hold out my arms to embrace him. After he hugs me, he steps back, still a bit baffled. He shakes hands with Tom John and tells him he's pleased to meet him, and he watches as Tom John clutches me beneath my armpits, then lifts me out of the truck and into the waiting chair.

"We'll, uh...the steps here," Dad says, attempting to take a host's control of a situation he hasn't expected, pointing toward the entry, unsure how to proceed.

"If one of us is on either side of her, I think we can just lift the chair up," Tom John suggests.

"I'll play Cleopatra," I say, and this time my father smiles—awkwardly, terribly ill at ease, his daughter evidently an invalid now.

Inside the house, Fran is equally ill at ease, yet her concerns seem centered on whether the chair's wheels will damage the carpet and if it can be maneuvered between a banquette and the dining room table. Despite Fran's well-intentioned attempts to ingratiate herself with her stepdaughters over the years, I still can't help but think of her as "the ostrich," as Barbara and I privately referred to her—a woman rather long of neck and leg who always fretted about whether Barbara and I would track dirt onto her pristine carpets, to say nothing now, I'm sure, about the certainty that a wheelchair, its occupant, and my rather strange and exotic friend will throw her house into utter disarray.

As soon as my father serves drinks—drinks are going to be very important this evening, we all readily would agree—I do try to explain my physical circumstances, to describe the exacerbations I've suffered previously as well as the events of the days before, assuring them, assuring myself that I'll be walking again not too far down the line. But as for why I'm passing through in the midst of this recent assault, or why Harry remains unmentioned as yet, or just who this picturesque Southerner in present company is, I see no immediate need to explain at all.

"Have you lived in Montezuma County quite a while?" Finally, Dad has to make some inquiries.

"Summers since the early sixties," Tom John brightly replies; by all appearances, he isn't feeling awkward. "Year-round for ten or twelve years. Long enough that I've thrown my suitcase away."

"You're happy there?" Although she hasn't meant it to, Fran's question implies incredulity.

"Not so much happy as just at home. A lot like you are here in Boise, I suppose."

"It's Boy-see," Fran corrects him. "There isn't the zee sound."

"Oh, sorry," Tom John says, chastened and saying nothing else for the moment.

"Tom John's an archaeologist," I explain. "Harry worked for him years ago. Nowadays they spend their time taking professional potshots at each other." My grin and my mention of Harry open a door that Dad's been anxious to peer into for some minutes.

"And Harry. How is he? He couldn't make this trip?"

"We didn't invite him," I say cryptically.

"Oh?" He won't surrender quite yet.

"He and Teddy are at home. Tom John and I just got a terrible case of cabin fever and decided to take a drive." I motion with both hands toward my legs. "In the midst of this, going someplace helps you feel like you aren't quite so stuck." I try to grin again.

"Sure." Dad doesn't know what else to say.

Fran says, "Well, we should eat, shouldn't we?" and as we move into the dining room, she apologizes for what she's about to serve, saying she'd have offered a better meal if she'd had a little more warning.

"I'm sorry about that," I say. "We weren't even sure we were driving through here until about noon today."

"This is sort of a seat-of-the-pants adventure," Tom John adds by way of explanation.

"And you're headed...?"

"West. Northwest. Who knows?" I say with some animation. "Tom John's the driver, but I make all the decisions."

"You should go to Cannon Beach in Oregon," says Fran, almost as if we should go this very moment. "It's the loveliest place in the world."

"I was there years ago, and I agree with you completely," says Tom John, "assuming there aren't condos all over the rocks by now."

"There aren't," Fran assures him.

"Well?" He turns to me as if to secure my consent.

"We'll see," I say, hoping to sound buoyant still, if rather unwilling to let Fran participate in our travel plans. "I make no commitments until the last possible moment. It's far better that way."

"Sure," my father says a second time. His smile offers proof that he indeed is my father. Unlike me, he didn't inherit his father's red hair, but Win Lewis is reflected in his mouth, his jaws, his big and wide-set eyes. I note too that as my father grows older—he is sixty-six now—the visage of my grandfather that I remember so vividly seems in several ways to be returning to life. The way my father walks, the way he literally cocks his head as he listens, and the way he lets the words at the ends of his sentences trail away (the way I too often do myself, to my dismay) are Winton Lewis's legacy—Dad, me, the eldest of Barbara's boys, it's already obvious, all of us keeping his mannerisms immortal, sustaining his placid face.

As the subject shifts to Oma, to Barbara and her boys, to inquiries about their health and stories about their escapades, I no longer feel as if I have secrets to keep, and as I relax, I can sense my dinner partners relaxing as well. My father, leaning back in his chair and angling his head toward a shoulder, wants to hear what I know about Jason's skateboarding passion. He grimaces when he hears that his grandson now looks just a touch more outlandish than he did in the Christmas photo, but Dad is reassured by the news that, so far at least, Ryan seems to have no interest in emulating his older brother. I try to put a bright face on everything I say about Barbara, about Rudy and the domestic complexities of their lives, and my father in turn seems to interpret everything he hears optimistically—as if from a far distance all he comfortably can consume is good news. Yet when Oma is at the center of the conversation, his confidence turns to a kind of guilty anxiety. She is all by herself in that drafty and tumble-down house, and what will happen to her if she falls one day and is stranded? Wouldn't she be happier living near other elderly people, women with whom she could share the long and quiet days? Shouldn't she be nearer a hospital? It would take an ambulance thirty minutes just to reach her.

"Dad," I begin to lecture when he's completed his catalog of concerns, "nobody, not you or Aunt Ruth or anybody, is shirking their responsibility by letting Oma stay in her house. And as sharp as she remains, it seems like it ought to be totally her decision. She doesn't want to hang out with a bunch of old gals she doesn't know, most of whom probably couldn't offer much in the way of a conversation anyway."

"But like it or not, she's getting fragile, and—"

"What's the matter with fragile? I'm fragile myself at the moment. That's probably why this seems so clear to me. Just because you're compromised doesn't mean you have to give up your life and go decay somewhere."

"Your situation and your grandmother's aren't the same, sweetheart." Dad can voice his concerns about his mother, but directly addressing my condition is still something he can't do.

"Well, yes, they are. They're different in the sense that the last thing I want is to be stuck at home like a poor little cripple. I won't do that. But for Oma, that house, her place is everything. It's been her whole life and she deserves to stay there till the end of her life, if she possibly can, because that where she wants to be."

"Even if the risks of an accident or a very bad situation of some kind get greater every day?"

"Even if." I speak the two words resolutely. "We check on her all the time. Between Barbara and me, we talk to her every day, at least, and we see her twice a week. But I'll tell you, Dad. If someday she doesn't answer her phone and we drive out and find her in her bed or on the living room floor or someplace and she's gone, well, I'm going to feel like she was very lucky till the end."

"Well," Fran says before my father can respond, "let me get these plates cleared." She gets up and quickly gathers the dishes, her whirl of activity making it apparent that the subject of death isn't a common one at her table. "Your grandmother is awfully strong willed," she says as she disappears into the kitchen.

"I hadn't met her until recently," adds Tom John, seeing no reason why he shouldn't pitch in as well. "I thought she was wonderful."

"Well, thank you." It's a compliment Dad feels free to accept. "She is something, isn't she Sarah?" He is surrendering his position, giving it up for Fran's sake, and for mine in the midst of an evening that is awkward enough already. I let Tom John and my father chat instead about the bountiful attractions of Boise until, as Fran is serving us coffee, I issue another statement: "You know, all Oma really needs is to know that you trust her decisions, and that you respect them."

Dad looks blank for a moment before he says, "Okay. All right then. If you seem to understand the situation so completely and think..." His voice trails away as it often does, but this time it bears his hurt.

"I just..." I realize I've said too much. "Sorry. It's just that I feel like I'm in her shoes these days."

"But you've got your whole life ahead of you," Fran offers. Despite the fact that I haven't given her much notice and have brought a strange man and this wheeled contraption into her house, and that it all has been most unusual, she now wants to be supportive, hopeful, maternal if somehow she can be.

"Well, yes and no," I say in response.

far better days

FOR SIX YEARS, I managed my disease much like a parent trying to keep furtive track of a delinquent child. The nagging knowledge of it, the dread, and the fanciful wish that it would all get better were always with me. During the months the disease remained in remission—my health perfect by all appearances—I nonetheless knew that one day it would be back. I got out of bed each morning mindful that it might, in fact, have visited in the night, and my first acts always were to query muscle groups, to study my coordination as I made my way to the bathroom, to stand at the window and examine each eye, to determine whether the barn still was bright red and whether the mesa was distinct in the south. During those occasional periods when multiple sclerosis was very much with me again—times when I stumbled down stairs or couldn't hold a pen in my hand or seemed so fatigued that bed was my only solace—I tried to steel myself to the truth: this would be the exacerbation following which I wouldn't return to normal; this time, my deficits would not disappear.

Yet what actually transpired during that long succession of seasons was something akin, I think, to the process of growing old. After each relapse, I did suffer some permanent loss, but at first so subtly that I was unaware of it. Later, I simply forgot that I once could climb up a scree field much more successfully than I could now; somehow I didn't realize that I was far from the rider I once had been. And then in a sort of third stage, I was shocked one warm and otherwise wonderful summer—in the midst of my attempts to see that the vegetable garden flourished and that the house was re-stained and that the horses weren't going to ruin, all in chaotic addition to keeping abreast of my practice—when I realized that I was in sorry shape. I walked no better than Oma did anymore; I had to consider how hot it was and whether I was likely to exhaust myself before I began the simplest task; and I was forced to acknowledge now too that I had become disabled, bit by gruesome bit.

In the ocher and yellow autumn of 1998, when I finally admitted that I couldn't depend on my fingers to palpate an enlarged spleen anymore, when I began to dread the way I displayed my clumsiness each time I walked into an examining room, when morning rounds at the hospital became certain to leave me spent for the rest of the day, I decided to call it quits. I tearfully confessed to a few chronically ill patients whom I had come to cherish that—here was an irony for them—I had joined their ranks and was closing my practice, going home to become a housewife until even that occupation grew problematic. I gave in to a disease I'd sworn I wouldn't give in to, and I imagined that Oma and I were contemporaries now—two old gals who once were game for anything, but who now had to practice patience and acquiesce to inability, stuck inside bodies that had seen far better days.

to be proud of that place

BAKER, NORTH POWDER, La Grande, Perry, Pendleton—the towns tick by on Interstate 84 and I complain to Tom John that the idea was to leave these burnt and brown landscapes behind. This slice of the state of Oregon looks to me like wind-seared Wyoming, like the low *llano* of eastern New Mexico, too much like the crumpled country in Colorado I wanted to shed like a skin.

"Well, if you'll be patient for about half a second here," Tom John scolds, "we're about to meet the mighty Columbia River, and the most amazing thing's going to happen. Driving downstream beside it, the desert disappears all of a sudden and the river's as wide as the world and you're in the lush Northwest hardly before you know it."

"So keep driving," I say. "The trouble with you is that you'd rather describe these exotic locales than actually encounter them."

"Just whose truck is it that's moving down the road at seventy miles an hour? I'd be careful if I were you not to take your driver to task."

"When were you up here before?" The teasing tone is gone from my voice now. I adjust myself on the seat and turn toward him to listen.

He scratches at his gray hair, tied back with a black scrunchy, as if to help recall a time some years ago. "Would have been the

summer of 1968, I think. It definitely was, because it was that awful
year when everything that could happen did happen—all the
assassinations. You were just a baby then so you wouldn't remember, but it seemed like the only thing that made any sense in the
midst of the world going completely crazy was to be blissfully in
love with somebody. Or maybe with everybody."

"I was just a baby then." I wink at him and he returns the hint
of a grin.

"At the end of that summer field season, I was so in love I actually ached. We came up this very same route, just going to be
going somewhere, sleeping out on the ground, laughing, telling
our sad stories, holding onto each other in the low campfire light.
We got to the Oregon coast near Lincoln City and climbed a thing
called Cascade Head above a little saltwater estuary, and the way
the ocean met America there—all misty and majestic and huge
rocks everywhere like they had floated up out of the middle of the
earth—well, it was one of those things that'll never leave me."

"Was this with someone I know?"

"I don't suppose it was. Turned out in the end that I didn't
know him all that well myself, but the feeling for a while ... my
God, the feeling."

I watch Tom John watch the highway as it banks into a broad
left turn. "Do you want to go back there—that place on the coast?"

"You don't mind if we don't go right there, do you?" He turns
to look at me. "I promise I'll show you better."

"I don't mind a bit," I say, reaching across to touch his shoulder. "Just get me out of the Great American Desert and into any
place that looks like I didn't grow up there."

We hadn't stayed late at my father's the night before. Fran
served us dessert and the subject shifted from Oma to education—to my father's career and fledgling retirement and Fran's
current job at a junior college—before I admitted I was tired and
a kind of visible relief framed their faces. Dad said he wished we
could stay longer; Fran said she was sorry we had to go, and what
both of them meant was that it had been good to see me and to be
back in touch, but that rendezvous like these were best kept brief.
I assured my father I soon would be well as Tom John wheeled me

to the front door, and I kissed his cheek once the two men had lowered me down the steps and lifted me into the truck again. "When I see Oma, I'll give her a hug for both of you," I said through the open window, noting as I spoke that neither of them as yet had made that request, my father and Fran already waving from where they stood on the nearby sidewalk, the night air sweet in Boise.

And this afternoon, just as Tom John predicted it would, the interstate bears down on the broad Columbia, and instead of fording the river, it now makes its way at its flank. Round hills on either side of the river are tawny and bare and treeless, and the river itself seems sedate, stately as it slows and tumbles over low dams and rolls on. Just as Tom John described, stunted evergreens at last begin to cling to the grassy skin of the hills—taller, sturdier trees finding footing, finding water in the lees and gullies between them. As the river, a half-mile wide and unimpeded again, begins to cut into a shallow gorge, fir trees lay tentative claim to the rocky side-slopes and forests stand thick and dark and substantial on the benchlands above. The gorge grows deeper; occasional cliffs jut out from the blanketing cover of trees; rivulets, waterfalls, creeks spill down from hills that nearly are mountains now, and at occasional moments, Tom John and I can see the splendidly white and shocking summit of Mount Hood away in the southwest, its slender volcanic cone rising impossibly high above a world grown wet and green.

At a turnout below the town of Hood River, I insist that it's time for a stop, and with my door open to the tepid summer wind—a wind ferrying moisture instead of dust, I notice to my satisfaction—I watch the windsurfers who are negotiating the dark chop of the river's surface, their sails, many dozens of them, brightly colored and alive in the insistent breeze, darting, spinning, racing between the distant shores.

"Isn't that terrific?" I ask Tom John, who is out of the truck now, leaning against the cab near my open door.

"How do they keep from killing themselves?"

"I'd love to be able to do that. It looks so..."

"Dangerous."

"Nah. You just fall in the water when you fall. What's so scary about that?"

"The water. The cold water. The dark, cold, moving water with suspicious things swimming in it and no, thank you very much."

"What a dud you are, Tom John."

"Listen," he explains, "I grew up in a place where the water was full of slugs and snakes and all manner of aggravation, and now I've lived for ages in a place where there's hardly any water at all, and I'm not about to try to turn into a fish at this age."

"I'd try," I tell him. "Imagine a place like this where, if anything, there's too much water instead of too little. The river, the rain, everything wet. I think I might even like the winter drizzle, and I know this disease of mine would be easier to contend with. Wouldn't it be kind of cozy? It probably gets a little intense after four or five months, but—"

"What I've heard, everybody's in the process of committing suicide when the sun finally comes out at last."

"Shall we see if we can make it? I'm sure the fall's very nice, it must be, then we'll try to survive till spring. You can spend the winter making some sense of your checkered professional life—write up what you've been digging into for a hundred summers. I'll...watch it rain, I guess. A climate like this is great for your skin. We'd both grow old so gracefully."

"If I agreed to stay, would you call your husband and tell him where we were?"

"You think he'd need to know?"

"I think it's long past time you called. You know that's what I think."

"I'm going to call. I will." I'm still watching the bright sails abroad on the river. "But let me decide when the time's right, will you?"

"I don't want to be your mother hen."

"Then don't worry."

"If I left everything up to you, you'd have me out on one of those surfboards scared out of my skin this afternoon while you were off looking at high-priced property."

I look at him now to try to explain a new sensation: "Every place we've been on this trip—Provo included, for God's sake—

seems like it would be a better place for me than Cortez. I think maybe I'm suited to running away."

"I don't think your home situation would break too many hearts, sweet thing."

"No, it's not that. It's just . . . I don't know." My voice trails away as my father's often does.

Driving downstream again, past the vast concrete impoundment of Bonneville Dam and the high, wind-whipped plume of Multnomah Falls, its thin cascade seeming to tumble out of the sky, I pose a question out of the cool and pleasant silence.

"Do you regret that you haven't seen more of the world, lived in more places?" I ask Tom John after a while.

"Not daily I don't."

If I hoped for a well-considered, justifying sort of answer, I realize now that I'm not going to get one. "Don't you have these occasional terrifying feelings that you've got to get on with it? Go where you can, do what you can, discover a thing or two before it's too late?"

"In my case, my dear, too late may well be upon us."

"Bullshit."

"No, I've always been something of a nester, actually—too lazy or too limited in other ways, I guess, for adventuring to seem like the thing at the top of the list. I may still build a house someday, something to suit just me, but I have a suspicion I'll build it there in the Four Corners somewhere. Shoot, girl, after thirty years you finally think you're getting the feel of a place."

"If I had an unequivocal kind of love for Cortez," I tell him, "I don't think this would be an issue with me. If I could be truly at ease there—secure and safe and anchored—I don't suppose I'd ever want to move on."

"Do you suppose it's unconditional love that has kept your grandma so secure down there for so long?"

"What do you mean?" He mentions Oma just as she crosses my mind as well.

"She never once went away, did she? You suppose that's because she's always been tickled to pieces?"

"Her life and mine, Tom John, have been as different as you can imagine."

"All I'm saying is that I'm not sure a good, full life has to be spent in motion."

"No," I agree, "but I'd love to know how Harry and I might have been, what we might have made together, in another place. Maybe somewhere where we didn't have such history."

Tom John smiles, and the smile seems to linger as he considers the thought. "Oh, I'd have been somebody else if I'd stayed in Arkansas, all right. Good God, that's a thought that unnerves me. But, I ended up in your home place instead. It's funny. Montezuma County has always seemed so different from my hometown that it might as well have been heaven. I think I did find a place where I fit. That's why I'm there. It's a lot more than the gnats and the digging in the dirt that's kept me near Cortez."

"I've think I've always wanted to be really proud of that place . . . wanted everyone else who lives there to be proud too, to look around every morning and say to themselves, *sweet Jesus*."

"And your dear grandma would tell you that pride's a sin, wouldn't she?"

"No, Oma would understand," I tell him, aware as I am that the tree-shrouded outskirts of Portland, Oregon, are a very long way away from Oma's open back door.

into similar disrepair

WHAT I DID, I know, was to take out my frustration, my rage at the body that had betrayed me, on everyone who had the misfortune to draw near me. Stuck in the house all day, with no work to define who I was or to give me the vaguest sense of purpose, the valley I successfully had gone home to and had been happy in for longer than I once could have imagined, now seemed shriveled, shut off by its isolation, crippled by poverty and a kind of ennui that were passed on like heirlooms.

I still drove, although I probably shouldn't have, and as I interrupted my days with trips to Oma's house or excursions into town to the market, I scrutinized the hardscrabble place that my family had been connected to for four generations—five now with Barbara's boys—with an increasingly jaundiced eye. Out in the broad bowl of the valley, too many farms had been split into sterile, treeless little ranchettes as Californians had begun to aim their westering quests back toward the Rockies in droves. Nowadays, far too many houses stood uncomfortably shoulder to shoulder alongside county roads; too many trailers were propped on blocks in the middle of fields, appearing as though their occupants someday might need to haul them away in a hurry. Everywhere, junked cars sat like ruins of a highway war; ancient farm machinery rusted in pastures and in derelict sales lots; and high chain-link fences surrounded oil-field equipment that had lain idle for half a lifetime already. It was a place that broke my heart on a daily basis in those days, a haggard setting into which I'd returned only to fall into similar disrepair. It seemed to me that we were both, this place and me, far past our primes—if, in fact, we ever had had them, and the depression that descended on me was one even I became aware of after a while. Alice was wonderful in the way she tried to keep me light-hearted, steering my swelling disgust, as best she could, toward her own brand of benign and comical cynicism. Tom John still shared with me his delightfully bohemian outlook on the local human condition. And one night Harry told me he loved me, not for my awkward arms or legs, but plainly and simply for me, and I knew as he said it that he deeply wished it were true.

I never did get entirely desperate. I know Oma kept a close watch on me; so did Barbara and the several friends with whom we had seemed to circle the wagons against calamities of several kinds. Our scrappy little farmstead too was something I couldn't surrender, couldn't imagine anyone else being as good to, as appreciative as I was of its subtle and nurturing gifts, and so I stuck it out for the short term—a native inhabitant at crescendo-ing odds with her homeland, a physician who couldn't give care or comfort, a woman who had almost everything she could hope for except, perhaps, the salve of hope itself.

like such a liberation

THE PREDNISONE SEEMS to be helping this time. My strength hasn't completely ebbed, my vision hasn't blurred, and the kind of quiet euphoria the medicine induces is always something I welcome. During the long hours in the truck, I try to command my legs to move as I command them, and although they still refuse to function, my skin sensation seems normal, and a few minutes ago—I shouted at Tom John with such glee that I'm sure I scared him—I actually succeeded in rubbing my feet together. I haven't been incapacitated to this degree before, of course, and it does not bode well for what I'll face in the future, yet somehow—maybe it's the optimism induced by the road, the promise of aimless travel—I'm sure I'll walk again, at least for a while. I'll spend another year or two on my feet before I have to sit down and stay.

But for now, the pickup truck and the wheelchair remain my means of locomotion, and Tom John and I still are wandering into the wet Northwest, a region I'm fascinated by already, a place on the dramatic cusp between the continent and the Pacific, a landscape that is subordinate to the sea, I have to assume, lush with the stink of decay and the sweet aroma of regeneration. Yet what an outsider I am, we are, Tom John and I both agreeing that there is a kind of claustrophobia in such thick and dripping forests as these, and we share the continuing sense that we need to chop down a million trees, or at least climb into their uppermost branches. We need to see, to get a gauge on the country, to stare into the comfort of distance, and we soon discover that it is only at the water's edge—beside the swollen Columbia, or Puget Sound, or the glistening Strait of Georgia—where we feel unencumbered and at ease, the horizon a reassuring reach away.

After a night in a downtown hotel, we re-appraise our plans in Portland, crossing into Washington on the high bridge that arcs over the ocean-bound Columbia, leaving Tom John's emotional memories of the Oregon coast alone and undisturbed, deciding—what the hell?—we're traveling so we ought to really travel, north by northwest again, ridding ourselves of the interstate in Olympia and seeing open water at last as we near the spry little spray-battered town of Port Townsend, the smell and the feel of the place entirely watery now, soft gray clouds scudding across the sky, the calm, soup-green sound surrounding the town on three sides.

Our options this afternoon are these: we can stay in Port Townsend and drink Rainier beer with the tourists in the dockside bars; we can drive to Port Angeles and board a ferry for Victoria, shedding even the United States as we flee from home; or the ferry from Port Townsend will deliver us to Whidbey Island, where, Tom John has it on the word of a friend of a friend, life is serene and simple. Although Tom John does confess an interest in a bit of beer drinking, moving on still seems like the best thing to do, and en route to Whidbey Island, he marvels at where in the world we are.

"My truck's been all over hell and gone," he tells me, "but it has not been to sea before." We are out on the ferry's open-air upper deck; the pickup that's still caked with Colorado dirt is parked three decks below. The cool wind whips our hair and dampens our reddened faces, and Tom John strains at the railing to see all that he can see—fishing boats bobbing on the swells, slow freighters bound for Seattle's piers, the mist-shrouded shore of the island stretching away to the north and south.

As Tom John surveys the scene like a boy in lucky command of this ship, I set the wheelchair's brake and flip the footrests out of my way. I reach for the railing and get a good hold and with all the strength I can muster, I pull myself up and onto my feet. My legs want to buckle and I have to lean into the railing to keep from falling, but at last I'm standing beside him, my rubbery legs sustaining my weight, my hands holding on for dear life, my face, I'm sure, evidencing the fact that I've accomplished a wonderful feat.

"Girl! Girl!" Tom John shouts into the loud roar of the ferry's motor and the steady of rush of the wind as I stand next to him now. "Look at you! Look at you this minute!" And as he embraces me, I lose my tenuous control of the situation, tipping toward him, falling into his arms, his arms enveloping me and keeping me upright until I have hold of the railing again and my legs are steady and my balance, such as it is, is back. "If you aren't a pretty sight!" he continues, his hand under my elbow. "If you aren't something to see."

"Can you believe it?" I shout back at him, my smile, my joy impossible to contain.

"You're right here in front of my eyes and you're tickling me to death!"

"Let me see if I can stand here for a bit."

"I'm right here," he assures me, and I cling tightly to the railing. Just to stand, to be on my feet and out of the chair seems like such a liberation; it is splendid to be upright, to have achieved merely that much, and I want to cry and shout and hug him tightly all in that instant, but instead I try my best to concentrate, to sustain this act, my grip on the railing as determined as I can make it, a grateful euphoria rising from the soles of my feet to the taut and tingling skin of my scalp. I am standing again! And I don't sit down once more until the ferry is about to dock and people are making their way to their cars.

"What got into you?" Tom John asks as he wheels me toward the elevator.

"I just thought I'd give it a try. You looked so fine standing there with your face into the wind, staring out at the water. I thought I'd join you."

He is still giddy with my success. "Good Lord, we'll have you hiking here in a minute."

"Whoa, mister," I caution. "It really wasn't all that impressive."

"The hell it wasn't. It calls for a celebration at the very least. Some sort of triumphant merrymaking. A bottle of champagne? A couple of quarts of quality beer? What do you think?"

"I want to try again."

"Of course."

"Maybe I could use the wheelchair like a walker and try to take a few steps."

Tom John has never seemed so enthusiastic. "Let's go buy you a walker. Do you suppose Whidbey Island's got those shops for old people on it?"

I laugh. "Hold your horses, big guy. Let's make sure first that I'm up to a repeat performance." I reach over my shoulder to grasp his hand and I squeeze it instead of trying to tell him, my God, how very much he means to me. "We could look for a phone, too," I tell him. "It's an hour later back there, and that Harry might be at home."

some sort of hobby

ON AN EVENING at home some months after I'd quit my practice, Harry said, "Why don't you come out to the canyon? I could use your help. Honestly. You might enjoy it if you don't overdo."

"You don't care who you hire, do you?" I was slouched in an armchair, Teddy asleep at my feet.

"I demand high moral standards, good personal hygiene, a hat, heavy socks."

"Socks I've got. But the Indiana Jones image, I don't know. I really don't know a thing about your business, dear."

"You're a smart girl. You'll catch on. I'm serious. There's no fancy footwork required, and we'll assign the heavy lifting to somebody else. It does get hot out there, but..."

"You'd let me dig?"

"Sure. After the briefest bit of training, I would. I have a hunch that it's a little like doing an autopsy. You go at it real slowly; you make sure you don't miss anything or screw anything up as you work, and you find what you find."

"If it's very much like an autopsy, I think I'd probably say no."

Harry got up and came to my chair; he sat on its overstuffed arm and peered into my eyes, his expression at once serious and full of mischief. "If you'll come out to the canyon," he said, "just one or two days a week, I'll...I'll do something for you in return."

189

"Like?"

"I don't know. Never drink another drop?"

"Have I ever asked you to stop drinking?"

"You've asked me to be a little more moderate about a million times."

"I don't want you to surrender to me," I told him, the subject suddenly shifted. "I hate it that you see me as the one who keeps you in check, who always holds you back, who won't let you have any fun."

"Then why do you end up in that role so often? Am I that incorrigibly rotten?"

"No, you—"

"Let's see, I drink way too much; I ogle every woman I meet; you think I'm a pervert and am on some sort of sexual overdrive, and you're afraid that I'm seconds away from ditching this marriage for a life of orgies and booze and crazy abandon."

"I'm afraid," I said, struggling to understand precisely what it is I'm afraid of, "that we're discovering that we want different kinds of things out of life. I'm afraid it's taken us this long to figure out that we've wasted our time together. I'm afraid this disgusting disease makes those differences all the more plain. I'm—"

"Listen, be who you are, okay? I'm not trying to turn you into some wild-ass version of me. And you certainly don't have to come work in the field," he said, evidencing his hurt. "I just thought maybe you'd—"

"I know what you thought," I told him.

interstate flight

WITH TOM JOHN'S pickup on the firm footing of Whidbey Island now, we set about our several errands, finding champagne at a store in Coupeville to help us celebrate my standing up, finding odds and ends for our supper at the supermarket in Oak Harbor, its electronic doors wide open for the after-work rush, a bank of telephones beside them.

With a finger stuck in one ear and the phone's receiver pressed firmly against the other, I wait to see if Harry will answer. At last he does just as I'm about to hang up.

"Hi. It's me," I say, sounding cautious, tentative, uncertain about how he'll sound in response.

"Sarah! God, I almost didn't make it to the phone. I just got home." I can hear his hard breaths and imagine him having darted in from the lawn where, I can imagine, he's been rewarding Teddy's day-long sentry duty with a game of fetch.

"I thought it might be a little early yet."

"No, no, I'm here. I'm here. Where are you?" I can hear his sense of relief as well as a very uncharacteristic hesitation in Harry's voice.

"You'll be surprised."

"I'm sure I will."

"Tom John's with me."

"Yes, I assumed he was." He sounds wary now.

"Do you know where Whidbey Island is? North of Seattle?"

"You're in Seattle?"

I laugh, and I'm aware how nervous I am. "No. We're on Whidbey Island, in Puget Sound, north of Seattle."

"Where are you going?" Harry doesn't return the laughter, nor does he share my enthusiasm at how far-flung we find ourselves.

"We're just going. Seeing the sights. I'd never been up this way before, and Tom John hadn't for a hundred years, he said, so...How's Teddy?"

"He's fine. He misses you." There is a pause before Harry asks me how I am.

"I'm better. Better. I stood up this afternoon, on my own, which isn't bad for..."

"That's great. It is. Wonderful," he says, and I can feel him begin to soften. "Are you holding up okay?" he now wants to know.

"I'm okay. I sleep a lot in the truck, and Tom John puts me to bed by nine."

"Tell him to take good care of you," Harry says instead of addressing the subject he isn't sure how to bring up.

"I will. I'll tell him. Harry, I can't hear you all that well, but listen, I just wanted to let you know that I'm okay. We're fine and we're having fun and one of these days we'll turn around and come home." Neither can I say anything substantial yet—certainly nothing about him and Alice and his marriage to me, nothing about broken vows or years of misconnection.

"I hated for you to leave like that," he offers.

"It...I just...Harry, I can't talk till I see you. Okay? We'll talk but...but not on the phone."

"Come home," he says. He doesn't plead, but I can hear emotion rise in his voice. "There's lots to talk about."

"Will you hug Ted for me?"

"Sure. And remind Tom John about laws against interstate flight with your best friend's wife?"

"You're sure you want to bring up friends and wives?" I ask, surprising myself, but then I let it go. "Tom John's been wonderful."

"I'm sure. But come home, okay?"

"I...I've got to go," I say. "Bye. Okay?"

the simplest sort of meaning

I HAD VISITED the ruins of Tse Canyon Pueblo often in the years during which Harry had managed their excavation, and I knew what a splendid site the builders of that Puebloan town had selected back at the beginning of the thirteenth century. From the place where a wide plaza once formed the community's busy nexus, the canyon cut away with a certain resolve. Between its buff and red-rock walls an intermittent creek wound toward broader McElmo Canyon with its wider and steadier stream, the water courses and the canyons making their way toward the dark and dramatic shoulder of Ute Mountain in the south, its high summit holding a kind of haughty local command. From atop the mortared-rock wall that protected the town on three sides, or perhaps from the vantage of a high, rough-plastered roof, the view would have been—and still was—equally grand in the other directions, all of Montezuma Valley sweeping down and away in a succession of juniper forests and fields before it angled upward again, climbing steadily toward a line of snow-crusted alpine peaks that must have seemed proof to early people that the earth encompassed many mysterious worlds.

The site at the lip of Tse Canyon offered available water from springs; fertile ground lay at its flanks and perhaps its high vistas even afforded protection. Yet as I began to spend long and always exhausting days there, seeing the ancient village in the soft light and sweet aroma of the morning, the harsh and hot and colorless glare of midday, as well as on settled evenings as the sky turned wondrously red, I began to think that this place had been claimed and settled at least in part because it was beautiful. And what a pleasure it was—the true tonic of landscape—to lay my own kind of claim to Tse Canyon, just as Harry and Alice and the others had done before me, custodians, all of us, in our diverse and unspoken ways of a pristine place that somehow still stirred with the lives that were lived there a very long time ago.

I liked digging in the dry and rocky dirt, as it turned out; the pace suited my capabilities and the pursuits seemed to spur my curiosity, and I remember thinking that I ought to attempt to understand as best I could something of the scope of what once had animated that environ. I wanted to truly imagine, in some way to reconstruct, the winter fires that once had smoldered in rooms without chimneys or ventilation, the butchering of squawking turkeys in the warm and welcome spring sun, the awful stink and noise and communal chaos of the plaza from first light until well past dusk every day, couples stealing away in the placid evenings to copulate in rooms where they could claim some privacy, children playing out among the branch-stripped trees. But strangely, before long I found myself wanting little more than to try to come to terms with what lay underneath my trowel, to attach only the simplest sort of meaning to a grinding-stone split into two pieces, a slender dog's jaw, a painted cup whose handle was darkened by human touch.

It was the focused investigation, the microcosm of a meter-square hole in the earth, that ultimately captured my attention, and a world reduced to that size was one I could manage somehow. Coming to grips with the totality of what once had stood at the edge of Tse Canyon seemed clearly out of the question as my first season in the field came to a close and the leaves fell from the cottonwoods that stood beside the seep-springs. Impossible to answer too were the broader questions about how the Ancient Puebloans had lived so well for so long there, or why we seemed to be living in the same place so poorly in many ways.

In time, too, I began to pay perceptibly less attention to the physical deficits brought on by my disease or to compiling lists of how they'd shattered my life. My depression seemed to ebb undeniably as I dug there on the high edge of a world I was beginning to be at home in again, looking only for objects that might have survived centuries and the slow blanketing of the brown earth, artifacts that offered only their own eloquent explanations: a rough cooking pot still black with soot, a child's tiny ceramic rattle, a beaded bracelet carved from a deer bone.

replacing the soil

IT WAS LATE October and a killing frost long since had defeated my garden. The harvest moon was full and fat and golden, and in the chilly sunrise, the yellow leaves of the cottonwood trees rustled with the portent of winter and fell to the frozen ground. We were out of bed early that morning and quickly off to the canyon, working against the deadline that the first snow soon would impose, backfilling test-squares and the several whole rooms and kivas that the crew painstakingly had unearthed during the preceding seven months. There was a peculiar aspect to the task, it was true, dumping the finely sifted soil back into the holes it had come from—working with shovels and wheelbarrows and the battered old Bobcat that Harry managed to keep running— and when I had observed this final job of the field season for the first time the previous fall, it had seemed to me like a melancholy one as well.

Yet as far as Harry was concerned, this was the one job he performed without qualm or question, without any of his ongoing concerns about the ethics of disturbing human remains, or the possibility of inadvertently destroying information, or whether a given site simply ought to be left alone until some future time. Once the digging was done, once maps and drawings were made, photographs and assorted samples were taken, artifacts collected, and stacks of records completed, replacing the soil became for him a benevolent and fiercely protective act, sealing the site against vandals and the coming winter's weather and the prospect of further destruction, leaving it peaceably alone again into succeeding centuries.

Alice shared Harry's perspectives, but instead of rhapsodizing about how important this work was, she tended to focus on how it strained her back and put blisters on her hands. Alice tended to issue complaints about most of life's little aggravations and petty travails, and I'd always enjoyed her particular style of lighthearted whining. Now that manual labor had become problematic for me—sometimes a bona fide struggle—I was glad to hear her giving bitchy voice to what I often felt as well. And our present task that morning, amid Alice's groaning complaints, was to finish backfilling two tiny rooms that had been excavated on a side-slope near the head of the canyon, work that at least provided some warmth.

By ten o'clock, we both were sweaty and almost hot, and already half the job was finished. We sat on a slab of rock with our faces aimed at the sun and drank hot chocolate from a battered thermos. As we shoveled, Alice had been describing some of the peculiarities of her childhood in Berwyn, Pennsylvania, and during the break from work she continued to make me laugh with stories about a mother who was obsessed with keeping the bathrooms clean but who seemed allergic to her kitchen, about a father who called each of his daughters "Bunny," she was sure, because he couldn't remember their names.

"I swear it," she said. "We had macaroni and cheese five nights a week. We went to my grandmother's on Saturdays and to Warbury's Cafeteria in Wayne on Sundays. The reason I can't cook is that I always thought food just came already hot."

"You could have made somebody a lovely little Main Line wife, Alice, cooking expertise or no. How'd you go so wrong?"

"Good question." She tossed her head back as if the answer might be scribbled across the sky. "Better question: how on earth did I end up shoveling dirt for a living out in the Wild West? I mean, how did this happen to me? My mother hoped for so much more."

"I think when I got my diagnosis, my mom—in addition to being shocked, then very sad—thought well, at least they'll have to leave Cortez now."

"Nah."

"I'm sure she did."

"Where did she grow up?"

"Denver."

"Oh, really cosmopolitan, huh?"

I laughed. "Part of it was the divorce, and how I'm sure she was aware that she never would have lived here if it weren't for my dad. Plus—and this I can relate to now that I live here in my middle age—she never understood why so many people here seemed to live so slovenly."

Alice nodded her head. "The problem with places like this is that there's too much space. The scale is grand enough that people don't develop that kind of gardening, caretaking mentality that people like you wish they had. They have five or six ancient pickups on blocks, rusting away in the front yard. And then you get quite cranky about it."

"I do get cranky," I said.

"But the Puebloans weren't much different, I don't think. They certainly appear to have wreaked their share of havoc around here as well."

"But they didn't squander things in the same way; they couldn't have. And the thing I've never understood is more general than that, anyway."

Alice turned to me with a hint of exasperation on her face. "This is still the stupid frontier, Sarah. We're all still recent arrivals. Think about it. How long have Anglos lived here? A hundred years? A hundred and twenty? Your own great-grandparents were among the people who tried to start something here, and in the big scheme of things, a hundred years ago was yesterday. By the time they built this particular village, Puebloan people had lived here twelve hundred years, and they'd long since cut down all the nearby timber for building and for fuel. Let's see what this place looks like a thousand years from now."

I was slowly getting to my feet. "I'll meet you here and we'll check it out," I said.

"No, some future dipshit will find our bones and think, well, they weren't much at making the most of the place, but God, they must have been comely and intelligent creatures." Alice's grin was infectious and I felt it spreading to my face as well.

"From our bones, they'll deduce this?"

"I've got great bones," Alice said as we went back to work, burying once more a part of a house that hadn't been lived in for a very long time.

a hell of a tingling time

THE FOUR OF us were dining at Nero's that night. Harry and Alice and I were weary from a raw autumn day spent backfilling the Tse Canyon excavation, and Tom John had been invited along to add some animation to our otherwise exhausted group. In a week, once all the exposed holes at the Tse Canyon site were safely blanketed with soil, Alice was migrating south to Mérida to meet a Mexican friend and visit familiar haunts in the Yucatán. Harry and I were heading south of the border as well, returning to Guatemala for a many-times-postponed archaeological sojourn there, in addition to spending a week at the medical mission in Mariscos prior to a week's rendezvous with Alice in Mexico City. Tom John was staying home and was making it clear during dinner that although he wouldn't have joined us anyway, an invitation might have been proffered at least.

"Don't you worry about me," he assured us, pretending to be rising above the insult. "I'm getting used to being the old guy who gets forgotten. I'll just stay here, maybe drive out to the empty Rez for a fun time, or go line-dance with the oilfield jocks in Farmington if I'm feeling sporty. I'll be fine."

"Why don't you come stay at our house?" I encouraged him. "Teddy wouldn't have to go to the kennel that way, and he'd be thrilled, and you could watch some TV for a scintillating change. The pantry and the fridge would be yours for the marauding."

"Oh, so you need a housesitter? That's why I wasn't invited to travel to foreign lands."

"You're invited, you're invited," Harry said. "Pack a bag and let's go, for God's sake."

"I do have some self-esteem," Tom John declared in stoic response. "Besides, the older I get, the less interested I am in gallivanting all over the place. The Navajos say you shouldn't travel so far from home that you can't get back by dark, and that's my creed too. Oh, there are places I'd like to see, see again. I'd like to see the Nile for some crazy reason; Australia, Ayers Rock; and I'd go back to the Oregon coast. I was up there once a long time ago and, oh my, talk about your drama."

"Well, let's go sometime," said Alice.

But Tom John didn't seize her offer. "It's not something that's going to make an awful lot of difference one way or the other, I don't suppose."

"You're starting to sound like one of these locals who went to Albuquerque once but couldn't stand it because sometimes there were three whole lanes of traffic going in the same direction." Harry kidded him, but still Tom John stood his ground.

"Y'all are too young to know this feeling, aren't you? You get to a point where it feels perfectly fine to be on your home ground."

"You sound like my grandmother," I said.

"If you come from someplace like this, sure, you've got go see what the air at the ocean smells like, and you should see how the stupid people in the cities live, and it's probably a hell of a good idea to go someplace once in a while that isn't the U.S. of A. All that's true enough. But the idea that you're an asshole if you don't keep moving all your life, that's a different story."

Harry was exasperated. "Jesus, Tom John, we're just taking your basic winter vacation here. It's not like we're about to join the Bedouins."

"Hey, I'd do it," Alice interjected.

Tom John grinned across the table at the friend he took such pains to trouble. "I know," he said, surrendering. "I know. You're heading off to do what you ought to be doing, and I'm just tickled to death that I'm not going with you."

"I am ready for a break from that slave labor out there," I interjected, "and I'd also put this disease on a long hiatus if I could."

No one knew quite what to say for a moment because it was a subject I seldom raised, one I guarded as means of protecting myself from a certain truth, and I tried to close it as quickly as I'd raised it by adding that Harry too was someone from whom I deserved a substantial respite.

"Separate vacations, starting next spring. No doubt about it." He seemed glad to continue the light-hearted sparring.

"Then can I go with him?" Alice asked, "Show him a hell of a tingling time?"

"You can if you can bear him," I said.

"Girls, girls," said Harry, pretending that surely there was enough of him to go around.

all about alaska

A NARROW HIGHWAY winds through tall and tangled coastal firs; ferns and deadfall mat the moist earth beneath them; the bridge at Deception Pass links Whidbey Island with Fidalgo Island, but in order to cross the placid water this time, the pick-up truck doesn't need to board a boat. But another ferry ride is in the offing: from the fishing port of Anacortes, Tom John and I plan to take a ferry to Lopez Island, where a friend of a friend of Tom John's raises Shropshire sheep and is reputed to welcome strangers, then perhaps we'll go on to Orcas or San Juan Island as well, where we'll wander with no one to see, unimpeded by schedules until it's time to head home—or at least to consider starting the long drive south.

But as we eat breakfast at a bakery near the harbor in Anacortes—me still in my chair and adapting all-too-easily to its special logistics—I'm struck by a new possibility, by an idea that's a little outlandish, yes, but one too that seems to seize the place and the opportunity, and I hope it will be the perfect climax to a journey that already has brought us many miles and a much-appreciated emotional distance from the complexities of home.

"This is Friday, isn't it?" I ask, closing the newspaper I've been perusing. "You know where we could go instead of the San Juans?"

"The San Juans are said to be wonderful," Tom John responds with suspicion, a bit reluctant even to hear what I suddenly have in mind.

"But think about this," I urge, my voice animated by my excitement. "And don't freak out, okay? Just think about it for a minute. We could drive to Bellingham today—it's not far—and this evening we can take a ferry to Alaska! I'm serious. We can go up the Inside Passage all the way to Juneau. It'd be incredible. It's supposedly just incredible."

Tom John fills his fork with scrambled egg, then takes a bite, which gains him valuable time. "For a second there," he tells me, "I thought you were suggesting we go to Alaska."

"Come on! We could be back here in a week. We wouldn't need to take the truck, so it wouldn't be that expensive, and it's my treat anyway, and—"

"A week? You know, I do have an obligation or two left in this life, and you ... How do you know whether we could get on at the last minute?"

"We'll call and find out. Without the truck, I bet we can."

Tom John's expression evidences real pain now. "And would we sleep in deck-chairs for that long duration? What sort of accommodations does this sailing ship have?"

"I don't know. Maybe berths like a train or something. Maybe deck chairs, I don't know. But think about what a wonderful trip it would be—all the islands and glaciers and eagles and whales and no roads, just this crystalline water the entire way. Let's call and find out."

"I think this sinking feeling in my substantial stomach means you're serious about this." Tom John leans back from the table as if to distance himself from my proposal as well as his unfinished eggs.

"I am. I think it's a great idea."

Now he has to try to explain. "You are a sweet thing, I hope I've told you twice a day, and I have truly enjoyed this jaunt of ours. I have. But I know I'd spend the week on that boat worrying about how neglectful I was of a million other obligations, and I'd turn into a sourpuss and say ugly things, and then where would we be?"

"Has this been an obligation?"

"No, I don't mean that for a minute, but—"

"Well, if it hasn't—and if you're being honest—then why don't we do something absolutely crazy and wonderful? We could have long talks with people who're traveling home and hear all about Alaska. And you could beat me at pinochle as often as you wanted to, and just imagine where we'd be, what we'd see!"

Tom John exhales a troubled breath. "Sarah girl, I—"

"Listen," I say, still undeterred, the idea of a trip through the Inside Passage one I'm passionate about already, "I know I've taken terrible advantage of you since I called you that afternoon, and you've been wonderful to me. But let me try to explain something, if I can." I adjust myself in my chair, then fold my hands on the table. "I'm running away. I know that's what I'm doing and I feel perfectly fine about it because it's so unlike me. It feels so good to do something that isn't absolutely predictable, and about the only other alternative I can think of is closing myself up in the garage with the motor running. I'm running away from Harry, and from a clear answer to the question of where our marriage is headed. And for a while longer, at least, I just want to keep running. This time, for once in my life, I don't want to be a good girl. I don't want to do the safe thing." I search Tom John's lovely, sun-worn face to see if perhaps he understands. "The other thing is that I'm going to be totally and completely stuck one of these days, and it really is terrifying." I don't mean to cry, and I don't, but my voice falters as I speak. "Sitting on a ship that's going exotic places, that's something I can still do, do you see? And I can't be hesitant about things like this anymore."

The smile Tom John returns to me is warm with friendship and the most straightforward kind of love, and it's unmistakable proof that yes, he does understand, but the sadness that spreads across in his face in the next instant also implies the truth that my circumstances are unfortunately mine alone. "Girl, I'll go to Alaska with you if you want to," he tells me, his voice quivering now with something that must be contagious, his hands enveloping mine, pressing in the point. "I will, and a week's time doesn't mean a thing to me, if you want to know the truth. But before we end up in China, you've got to promise me that, after this, you're going to let me take you home. There's stuff, sweetheart, that's waiting for you back there, I need not remind you. And there are people there, damn it, who need to see your shining face."

I squeeze his hands as tightly as this disease will allow me to, and my teary eyes look at him with a gratitude I can't otherwise convey. "If we can get on that ferry, and if I can get clear to Juneau, Alaska, even though I couldn't walk to that counter over there if my life depended on it, well, God, then let's go. Let's *do* it!"

Tom John nods, saying nothing more because it's clear that he's my ally in this now, my friend and fellow traveler, and the questions that follow confirm his willingness to join me on a journey of a thousand miles more. "Even if, when it's over, I have to take you back to Colorado and heaven knows godly what? Even if Harry MacLeish decides to strangle me for the wicked part I've played in all of this? Even if you don't win one game of pinochle all up or down that cold Pacific coast?"

the small bones of the feet

THE DRY JUNE air and the baking, relentless sun long since had sucked the winter's moisture out of the soil. The swelling heat of the coming summer similarly had sapped my strength, but although I often wobbled unsteadily as I walked, and worked so slowly my progress was hard to measure, I still went to the canyon with Harry five days a week, still dug in that complex dirt, looking for remnants of a time before my time, looking for answers, I suppose, to questions I couldn't shape and wasn't sure of, keeping my hands active as a hedge against the day when they might no longer move.

I was working alone that day, excavating a test square Harry had surveyed in the spring, slowly removing layers of soil, rubble, and ash from a midden below a room-block that appeared to have been built late in the village's occupation. Potsherds were scattered everywhere—surely they were pieces of vessels that had been broken and thrown away—and I found dozens of tiny bones I presumed were the remains of many turkey dinners before I bumped my trowel against something large and rigid.

Using a whittled bamboo stick as I proceeded, I scraped enough soil away from the object that I could see it was dome-shaped and darkly mottled, perhaps an overturned bowl, perhaps part of a water jar. I was intrigued now, excited in much the same way that Harry said he still could be, and although I needed to be careful, I wanted to work quickly to see what lay beneath my hands. After only a little more work, I was sure I'd found an unpainted cooking pot, cracked but still holding its shape. Then in a few more moments, my certainty turned to shock. I encountered a round hole, packed hard with sediment, in the object's convex surface, then another hole beside it, holes that were circular and smooth and that hadn't been chipped into place, and I know I pulled away in fright as well as amazement when I realized that this was bone.

My next impulse was to go find Harry, to tell him, *my God*, he had to come see this and explain to me what to do. But I already knew what to do, and now I knew too what was buried beneath me, and I could imagine how it lay underneath that thin cover of soil: the whole of the skull, fissured and stained and gray, turned on its side; nearby it the strong humerus and radius bones of the arms; ribs clustered like kindling; the thick vertebrae still in a row; there too the pubis and fan-shaped ilium that comprised the pelvis; the big leg bones bent at the knees; the small bones of the feet hard to distinguish from those that belonged to turkeys.

I felt uncomfortable, callous somehow, kneeling there above the area where I presumed the skeleton lay in its burial position, but the space in the hole afforded me no alternative. Still stunned, uneasy about every move I made, I went back to work, chipping sediment away from this human skull, careful not to jar it out of position, holding my breath with something that must have been awe, uncovering enough of it before I briefly left in search of Harry that the eye sockets were plain to see. The dome of the cranium seemed to bulge up out of the soil, and the mandible—a row of twisted teeth still firmly attached to it—seemed to gape open in anguish, as if I were causing pain, as if the bright light and the dry air and the twentieth century were simply too much.

going home

STILL OUTBOUND, HEADING northwestward still into a world of water and wilderness, Tom John and I purchase round-trip tickets on the Alaska Marine Highway ferry in the middle of the afternoon. We are scheduled to board the ship in Bellingham at seven o'clock that evening, then to sail at eight, and we spend the intervening hours in the village of Fairhaven near the ferry terminal, Tom John pushing me up the hilly sidewalks, the two of us wandering into tourist shops and browsing at length in a bookstore. Tom John buys two books by Michael Ondaatje and a collection of stories by Alice Munro because the impending cruise seems likely to offer more scenery than he will properly appreciate. I buy maps—folded maps of Washington and British Columbia and the straits and sounds off their western shores, a rolled map of the state of Alaska, and a navigational chart of the Inside Passage I admit I doubt we'll need, before I try to reach Harry again to tell him about our astonishing itinerary and to say that we'll probably be home in a week and a half or so.

Tom John helps wheel me to a telephone in the bookstore's basement, then waits for me in the adjoining café as I make the call. But when I find him a few moments later, our seafaring plans are scuttled and it seems likely that my maps will be as much of the passage as I'll see.

"It's Oma," I say as I roll myself to his table, and I suspect the look of concern on my face I see Tom John react to is, for the moment at least, more the sort that physicians wear than a grand-daughter's sudden visage of fear. "She's in the hospital. Her gall bladder, I guess. Her white count's off the chart, and they think there may be some other GI problems as well."

"When?"

"Harry said they admitted her yesterday. He was very relieved that I'd called since he didn't have a way to reach us. He came home early, he said, just in case I called. Barbara got hold of my dad and my aunt. They're both standing by, but evidently neither of them has left for Cortez yet."

"What do you want to do?" Tom John's question makes it clear, of course, that he will agree with whatever seems best to her.

"Oh, I've got to go back," I say. I can hear a kind of calm resolve in my voice, and I offer him a small smile. "I'm sorry. But you're probably not too terribly disappointed, are you? And we will do this another time, won't we?"

"Would you like to try to get a plane out of Seattle?"

"Let's just drive," I say. "Let's have a sandwich or something here, and then we'll just head south."

The decision is so easy to make because, for each of us, there really is nothing to weigh or carefully consider; my grandmother is ill and I need to be by her side. "We'll drive till I get too drowsy," Tom John tells her, "and then I'll crash for an hour or two, and then another big push. But it'll be tomorrow afternoon or there-abouts before I can get you there. All right?"

I nod and pat my palms on the armrests of my chair. "I guess we're going home, Mr. Brown," I say, aware that Alaska is already far from my mind.

four

the clear and simple buoyancy

I'LL SAIL THE Inside Passage someday. Perhaps I'll travel with Tom John, perhaps with Harry MacLeish. I'll walk as I go onboard the huge steel ship, and I'll stroll its observation decks for hours every day. My suspect legs will serve me, and with my hands I'll scribble postcards describing wondrous sights. But that will happen someday, and in the meantime, it's certain that I need to be on dry land—in a place so dry this summer that the reservoirs are nearly drained and crops haven't grown high enough to harvest.

My few days on the islands and shores of Puget Sound have been days I'll remember, despite—or perhaps because of—the special circumstances and my often-reeling state of mind. I've been fascinated by a place so shaped by water, a place where land seems subservient to bays and straits and the spreading sea, where lush foliage successfully shrouds so much of society's wreckage, and where the gray and scudding sky seems to hover just out of reach, covering both land and water like a lid. I would have loved to stay longer, but Oma is ill and in the hospital and I know I belong at her bedside—explaining for her what I can explain about gall bladders and guts and systems gone awry, making certain that my former colleagues know she indeed is a VIP and that she receives the best possible kind of care, simply being there for her the way she always has been for me.

The sun has settled into the Pacific and the sky is black by the time we drive through elongated and water-bound Seattle, the highway skirting close to the downtown towers that are lit up as though the workday is far from finished, and Tom John suggests that the next time we're up this way, we ought to investigate the urban Northwest as well.

"I'm going to remember that and hold you to it," I tell him in reply. But although I do want to return, it would be impossible tonight for me to feel resentment at having to leave. Heading south instead of north now, driving toward a specific destination this time, I feel the clear and simple buoyancy of doing what has to be done, and I can already sense that I owe Oma for this, for helping me come home to some sort of purpose.

It must be midnight by the time we drive out of Yakima Valley and cross the Columbia again, and in the preceding miles, I've imagined mature and lovely apple orchards—their fruit beginning to grow red—reaching away from the road forever. I'm still wide-awake and strangely energetic in these hours, and I describe for Tom John how the country looks outside our windows. Then at last I tell him too what Harry told me by telephone—that Alice was at our house when I called.

"Jesus," Tom John says disdainfully, "I can't believe he thought you needed that news."

"He said she'd arrived just as he had, that he hadn't seen her since the day you and I left. He said he thought she'd left town as well."

"Surely he didn't think she was with us."

"No. I guess they'd talked and she had told him about my conversation with her—what I asked her, what she said or didn't say."

I can't see Tom John's face in the darkness, but I can tell from the strain in his voice that his confederation with me for these days has left him feeling negatively toward Alice, and then I repeat for him what else Harry said after he'd explained that Oma was ill—that Alice had told him she was looking at potential jobs in a number of other places, that she felt sure she couldn't stay in Cortez, not now. "He told me too that she'd had a call from her friend in Albuquerque who'd spent time examining the pelvic and leg bones of the girl I excavated. I guess the UNM woman is sure she *is* female, sure too that she didn't have any children before she died. She thinks the girl was about eleven or twelve and that her leg was congenitally deformed."

I haven't thought much about the girl in the days we've been away. For a time, my speculations about her life were with me constantly, but getting away from the place where both of us had been born also had put some space between us. Yet I'm glad now to know that she didn't die giving birth, if a bit melancholy to know as well that her life had ended while she was still a child.

"Oh, life does not turn out easily for everyone, does it?" Tom John says as he stares into the wedge of light the truck's head-lights send ahead of us. "Some seem charmed forever, and some—"

"Charmed like Harry's always been. I'm not sure what's ever been hard for him."

"I suspect he does not feel charmed, Sarah, on this night of his life," Tom John says in challenge to me. But then he immediately lets it go. "I'm surprised he wanted to be so chatty."

"I'd assured him we'd be there as soon as we could. I could hear his relief at that. And I could tell he didn't know quite what to say, maybe because Alice was there, but it seemed like he thought a bit of conversation would help lure me home." I can see Tom John nod at what I say, and can hear him blow out a long stream of breath between his lips. "I'm not scared about Oma," I tell him, "but I'm scared to get back, I guess I realize, now that we're head-ing that way."

the first time i can remember

OMA'S ARM IS strapped to the bed to prevent her from dislodging the IV line that's been inserted into a vein in her forearm. A catheter tube curls across the mattress, attached to a urine bag that is pinned to the bottom sheet. Her face is jaundiced and her thin hair is unkempt in a way I've never seen it before; her eyes are closed and her mouth gapes open a bit and I'm sure she's sleeping. I maneuver my chair beside the bed's railing, then reach to comb Oma's hair back with my fingers, but as I do so, my grandmother opens her eyes and, after a moment, sees who I am. She offers me a weak and sedated smile.

"Hi, there," I say. "How are you?"

"I'm in the hospital." Oma's voice is merely a whisper.

"I know you are." I say with a smile. "How did that happen?"

"I guess I just finally got too old."

"Maybe so. But we'll get you out of here soon enough. Are they treating you okay?"

"They're nice as can be." Oma can't keep her eyes open, and she keeps them closed as she speaks. "I'm glad you're back, though. They said something about an operation, and I said not till you were here."

"Good for you," I say as I squeeze her hand. "I just got back, and I haven't talked to any of the doctors yet, but I will, and we'll get this all figured out. Are you comfortable? Are you in any pain?"

Her eyes still are closed. "I'm okay," she whispers, but for the first time I can remember, I know my grandmother isn't telling me the truth.

Tom John pulled off the interstate for a while the night before and he and I slept in the cab of the truck for an hour or so somewhere in eastern Oregon. Then we were driving again by three o'clock and stopped for breakfast before we were out of Idaho, the day dawning clear and calm and confident in Utah, me napping periodically, my curious chattiness finally abating, Tom John chewing gum and challenging the truck's engine with a kind of trucker's hypnotic resolve. It was four in the afternoon by the time we crossed into Colorado again, the tall grain elevator at Dove Creek a concrete beacon signaling that we were back, and thirty minutes later, Tom John helped wheel me into an elevator inside Cortez's small hospital, then down the familiar corridor that led to my grandmother's room before it seemed to him he'd accompanied me far enough, and he told me he'd see me again in a while.

And I choose not to stay long. I don't want Oma to tax herself with conversation, and if she can sleep, she should. Seeing her for only a moment is enough for me for now; it's enough just to see her frail but undaunted smile, to hear her declaration that she is glad to have me back. And I need to get a handle on Oma's condition, to discover what her doctors have encountered and how they've treated her so far. I need to go find one of them—Pete Theobold, the internist, if he's nearby—and hear how Oma seems to him.

At the nurse's station, I inquire whether Dr. Theobold is in the hospital and am told by an RN whose name I can't remember and whose tag I can't quite read that he doesn't usually make rounds until about six, so I ask instead to see Oma's chart. But the nurse hesitates, aware, of course, that I'm not on the hospital's staff anymore and uncertain about how to respond to my request.

"Dr. MacLeish, I . . . the patients' records are—"

"She's my grandmother," I say, my irritation immediately evident, "and I've been out of town, and please, just hand me her chart."

Now the nurse acquiesces, handing me the aluminum folder, pursing her lips and shrugging as if to say *whatever*, then walking away down the corridor to distance herself from what she's agreed to do. But just as I open the folder and begin to try to make sense of what's transpired in the past two days, Tom John comes round the corner, this time with Harry in tow.

"Look who I found in the cafeteria," Tom John says brightly, aware that this won't be the simplest of reunions, but nonetheless speaking brightly.

Harry doesn't move toward me, but something in his expression successfully spans the short distance between us. "I'm glad you're back," he says. "Did you see her?"

"Just for a minute. She seemed pretty weak. But she seemed okay." I try to smile at him. "Have you been here the whole time?"

"Barbara and I've been taking turns," he tells me, speaking tentatively. "Barbara's been great."

"Thanks, Hank," I say from my chair.

Harry nods but doesn't say anything else, and Tom John now wants to make himself absent. "So..." he says. "So, I guess this is the end of the line."

"Yeah," I say, "We're back, aren't we?"

"I think I can make it home," says Tom John, his eyes at last exhibiting his exhaustion, his shoulders slumped, his hands stuffed into the pockets of his pants, "and then I won't move another mile until I've slept for about a week."

I reach for Tom John's hand, then turn to Harry. "Did I ever tell you what an amazing guy this is?"

the rocky road

IN SEVERAL WAYS, Oma was going to be the hardest person to tell. During her long life, she had had to suffer much bad news and, it seemed to me, more than one person's share of sorrowful losses—her mother when she was still a girl, two toddlers and a stillborn child, a son in France in 1944, and her husband two decades later. Yet although each death had scarred her and surely broken her heart, instead of becoming callous or embittered, she simply responded each time by all-the-more lovingly embracing those kin and friends who remained alive.

I always had been acutely aware, on the other hand, of the way she received the news of another person's hardship, a friend or family member's pain or sudden loss. She could bear the intimate suffering that came her way, but hearing what had befallen someone else seemed to be nearly more than she could stand. I knew well by now how a deep sadness would spread across her face as she heard someone else's difficult news—ironically, those were the only times she ever seemed to evidence physical pain—and I couldn't imagine what it would do to her when I finally told her that I now bore a brutal disease.

Harry knew just a day after the neurologist confirmed my diagnosis that December; Alice and Tom John knew soon thereafter, as did Barbara and my mother, but months passed before I finally could bring myself to tell Oma what had happened. Harry had gone skiing, so it was winter still, but it must have been March because I remember Oma telling me that wet and blustery weather like this still reminded her of heating milk for dogie calves, pouring it into pop bottles topped with rubber nipples, then traipsing out to the shed where the poor little things bawled at her as though she was their salvation—which she was, I reminded her.

"They were bums, most of them," she said. "A few finally caught up and got their full size, but for some reason, if they weren't taking the milk right from their mother's teats, most of them seemed to fall so far behind. It's funny how things like that matter as much as they do."

But then Oma wanted to know, and it was awkward for her to ask, whether Harry and I were going to end up raising children. She had queried me once before, and that time I had told her we were trying. The same answer would have sufficed still, but this time I wanted to tell her more.

"It's been more than ten years since I was pregnant," I began, "and it's beginning to look like babies aren't in somebody's big picture. Which, as it turns out, may be just as well." I told her again how Harry and I had wanted to be parents, how once we'd imagined a felicitous nest of little MacLeishes, and how now I actually was relieved that I didn't have young ones who depended directly on me. Then I tried to tell her why.

Her face was blanched and disbelieving at first, and she seemed to need to hear a bit of detail about this bizarre malady before she could begin to connect it to me. "It's in your brain, but it affects the rest of your body?" she asked.

I told her that was exactly right. I reminded her of the time I'd dropped her teapot, then continued to describe as best I could the mysterious pathology of multiple sclerosis, its symptoms and its myriad long-term consequences; I told her the disease could be treated in only cursory ways, and I said it was impossible to know precisely what it had in store for me.

She was silent when I finished and I watched for her reaction, bracing myself, expecting to see her face portray her hurt, knowing that her visage—more than anything else so far—would prove to me that I'd come up against some trouble. But she remained wonderfully inscrutable this time, astounding me with what I assumed was strength but what must have instead been an old and precious woman's wisdom, saying nothing still, her face finally consumed by an expression of care for me that was overwhelming as I went to her and took her hand, her love this time supplanting her pain.

"I wish I could be here to live this out with you," she said, as if someday she would let me down by dying. "I wish I could tell you that at least I'd always be sitting here in this chair."

"You will be for a long time," I told her. "We're peasant stock, the two of us. We'll stick it out a long time."

"Okay, I'll remember that," she said trying to smile now. "You do too. We'll keep our chins up, the both of us, down the rocky road."

the dim and sheltering light

WITH WHAT BARBARA and Harry separately have explained and what I later glean from my conversation with Dr. Theobold, I'm able to piece together what happened during the final days of my escape. On the same evening Harry called Barbara to tell her that I'd finally phoned from somewhere near Seattle, Barbara called Oma to chat and to check on her. And worryingly for Barbara, Oma confessed that she was in some pain. Something she ate must have disagreed with her, she said; her stomach was terribly bloated, her lower back ached as well, and she felt almost as if she were catching the flu. When she was worse the following morning—the pain in her abdomen severe and unrelenting now—Barbara insisted on taking her to the doctor. On examination in Pete Theobold's office, the area surrounding Oma's liver and gall bladder was extremely tender, and the doctor asked Barbara if she thought her skin looked slightly jaundiced. Oma had a fever and her white count was very high.

Dr. Theobold admitted Oma to the hospital directly from his clinic, despite her protestations that first she had to attend to a thing or two at home, despite her faltering claims that soon she would be fine. A battery of tests at the hospital that afternoon confirmed that her gall bladder was greatly swollen and infected and was in real danger of rupturing. Antibiotics might have been able to control the infection, although they would have to be administered in massive doses. But additionally, the doctor cautioned Barbara, surgery also would be required to remove the perilous gall bladder before it burst.

Wasn't it kind of crazy to operate on someone in their nineties?, Barbara asked him as he hurried down a corridor on the second day of Oma's hospitalization, and he had agreed that it was—unless there clearly was no other choice. In her grandmother's case, he said, there was a reasonable chance she would survive the surgery and regain her health; without it, she likely would live only for a few days, days that would be punctuated by terrible pain. He would want to consult with a surgeon, he said; he would, of course, discuss the procedure and the several conceivable outcomes with Oma and the rest of the family, but for now, he saw no other option.

I've referred patients to Pete Theobold in the past, and I believe he's a good physician. He's never too quick to call for the knife, and this time, too, I agree with his assessment of Oma's situation. Sitting in a physician's lounge with him and Barbara and Harry a few hours after my return—Tom John gone home to sleep, me still animated by anxious energy and the insistent guilt that I should have been here when she got ill—I ask only a few questions and nod my head at my colleague's answers. I scribble notes onto a prescription pad, then turn to Barbara.

"When was the last time you talked to Dad and Aunt Ruth?"

"This morning. They know they're probably going to operate. Ruth is going to drive down, and Dad was looking at what his airline options were."

"They should know that there's a possibility she won't survive the surgery," Dr. Theobold says. "They might want to be sure they're here before."

"Well, if she's not going to make it, why can't we just let her go on her own then?" Barbara asks. "Why do we have to put her through that?"

"It'll be your grandmother's decision," the doctor says, glancing at me. "We won't operate unless she agrees that it's the best thing to do."

I reach for Barbara's forearm. "If she was sixty, there wouldn't be any question. The surgery needs to be done. The only real issue is her age. If she really didn't have a chance, we'd just have them give her morphine and make her comfortable... But on the other hand, she may make it through the surgery. And if she does, she'll probably get well."

"She'll probably outlive all of us," says Harry. The rest of us smile wearily but don't offer him second opinions.

Once Pete Theobold leaves—after I've told him I'll be happy to discuss the surgery with him and Oma in the morning—I want to see my grandmother again. Harry pushes my chair down the hall to Oma's room, Barbara joining us for only a moment because her boys are alone at home, kissing Oma's forehead but trying not to disturb her as she says good-bye. "I'll see you tomorrow morning," Barbara whispers, hugging Harry, squeezing my shoulders with her hands.

I move close beside the bed; Harry sits in a corner chair and watches me watch Oma in the dim and sheltering light. The room is silent except for the soft guttural sounds she makes as she sleeps, and after a time, Harry slips out the door.

I know that I've been sleeping too when Oma speaks to me, calling me "honey" in a fragile voice, asking if it is late at night.

"Not very," I say, attempting to lighten my sleepy voice. "I think it's only about eight. How are you?"

"Okay," she says with an interrupted breath, as close as she will come to admitting to the pain.

"You sure?"

Oma turns her head to the side to look at me very directly and purposefully, saying without saying so that, well, now she has some trouble too.

"This operation you've been hearing about?" I ask, and Oma nods her head. "I talked to Dr. Theobold a little while ago, and he and I are going to come in together in the morning and talk about it with you in more detail, let you know what they would try to do, and also what the risks would be."

"If you decide it's the best thing, then that's what we should do," she says.

"I'll tell you what I think, Oma, but you'll have to be the one who makes the decision." I reach for my grandmother's arm; the skin at Oma's biceps is pale and yellowed and crosshatched with hundreds of delicate wrinkles. She closes her eyes before she speaks again.

"I don't know if this is my time yet. It might be, but I don't know. I want to leave it in the Lord's hands, let Him choose the time. You and the other doctors should just do what you think is best." She opens her eyes again. They are clear and calm and unconcerned. "I'm not scared," she says.

"I'm glad you're not," I say, and my exhausted eyes are weeping now.

"But there's something..." She has to stop and gather breath before she can continue. "Remember our pact? The one we made when you got sick? Well, honey, I'm still going to keep my end of the bargain. But I don't want some machine to keep me going. I don't want to live beyond when I was meant to. Do you understand me?"

"Yes," I whisper.

"Then you tell them that," Oma says with the last of her strength, her wide eyes shut once more, her breathing labored now, me falling asleep beside her before Harry walks back into the room and I realize that now it's time for us to talk.

years and years

I INFORMED MY husband in a voice laced with disdain that if life offered worse experiences than moving, I simply couldn't imagine them. We'd been carping at each other constantly since early morning as we filled cardboard boxes and dutifully carried them out to the rental truck, and now that we were nearly finished, I was mollified a bit, but my mood hadn't really had time yet to improve.

Harry's particular dilemma that day was that this move southwest to Cortez had been his scheme from the beginning, and he knew that if he complained too loudly, I might just announce that, in that case, we should stay where we were and scuttle this trauma right now. "If you will cut me some slack, and let me get this finished without discussing every dish and saucepan," he told me as he sat for a moment on the ramp that angled down from the rear of the truck, "I will take you to Señor Miguel's for dinner, and we'll drink margaritas until this task is nothing more than an unpleasant memory. Deal?"

"I think you'll take me regardless," I replied. "I think that's pretty well required."

"Well, then, will you kindly trust me for about another hour that I'm not going to break everything we own?"

"But if I don't keep an eye on you, you will. Who was it who was so sure that all those wine glasses would need was a little newspaper?"

"Sarah!"

"Okay, okay. I'll be inside, surveying how far we are from empty."

We weren't far, as it turned out, and my outlook on life had improved decidedly by six o'clock.

"To us. Off we go," Harry said at the restaurant as he held up his margarita glass to toast our departure.

"Whatever have I done?" I asked incredulously, my smile as generous as I could make it.

"What do you suppose is in store for us down there?" Harry mused after he'd taken a big first sip.

"You're only just now beginning to think about such things?" I said, feigning another snit.

"Just in general. Wouldn't it be interesting if you could compare ten years from now, if we stayed here, with what things'll be like ten years after we move—how different everything would be?"

"Are we going to be in Cortez in ten years?" I'm sure I sounded suspicious.

"But even if we're not—"

"Thank God we can't really know and compare," I interrupted. "If we could, people would regret their lives even more than they do."

"We're not going to regret this," Harry said with confidence.

"Guarantee?"

"Guarantee."

"You jerk," I said, smiling at him again, reaching for his hand and holding it. "You've known from the start of this that I'd go with you wherever in the world you wanted to go. There wasn't ever any doubt for you, was there? Even to darkest Cortez. I want you, and I want a wonderful life with you, but I'm still not at all sure that I want to move back to my hometown. What would you have done if I had said no?"

"You didn't. We talked about it. You agreed it was a great opportunity. It—"

"What if you had to choose between that job in that place or me? What would you choose?" I asked, hoping to hear something declarative in his answer, hoping for reassurance that I would be his choice

"It'll be good, Sarah," Harry quickly said in response, his animated eyes, sanguine expression, and those few words all he could offer me at that moment. "Whatever happens. Years and years."

my part of the bargain

WE'VE DRIVEN OUT to Lewis on our way to the hospital on Tuesday morning. Oma's treasured cat needs to be fed and paid a bit of attention, and she has asked me to bring her Bible. The alpine peaks, stripped of snow this droughty summer, loom high above the dry land in the silky early light. The valley rolls south and west away from the mountains, its checkerboard of fields blanketed by fragrant and welcome dew—as close to rain as this season seems willing to offer.

At Oma's place, the flower beds are bright with color despite the drought, but the lawn has turned tawny, and it seems to me that the barns and sheds my grandfather built seventy years ago have slumped and twisted further in the summer's unrelenting sun. Harry offers to tend quickly to the chores inside the house, but although it takes time and substantial effort for me to join him, I insist on going inside, and, once I'm sitting in the sunny kitchen, I realize I've never been in this house when my grandmother wasn't here. Oma isn't sitting in her chair by the picture window; she isn't standing at the stove.

While Harry attends to the several tasks, I converse with Kitty, the cat standing in my lap and rubbing her head against my caressing hands. "We'll get her home as soon as we can," I say. "You be patient, and we'll bring her back."

"I think that's everything." Harry's quickly collected Oma's things and provided for the cat and is ready to go.

"Let's bring her walker, too. It's probably in her bedroom."

"Do you think she's going to need a walker any time soon?"

"She might," I say. "Isn't it strange for her not to be here?"

The surgery is scheduled for nine o'clock, but I hope to get to the hospital by seven, in time to visit with Oma before she is sedated, to read to her the psalms the ribbons in her Bible mark, to tell her how brave she is, and as we drive the highway that leads south to Cortez, I want to be sure we'll have plenty of time.

"We're fine," Harry assures me. "How are you doing?"

"Okay. I feel surprisingly okay. Maybe lack of sleep is the antidote to this stupid disease. Sensation is a little better in both my legs this morning."

"Is it?"

"Yeah. I think it is. What time is it?"

"It's six forty-five. We're really fine."

"Okay, but hurry," I say as we pass the graveled road that reaches westward, ultimately winding its way to the ruins at Tse Canyon. "Has missing work been a problem?"

"No. Not at all. Don't worry about that."

"I guess Alice can step in ably for you."

"She and Charlie."

We did not talk last night about the very big subject that we must soon find a way to address. On the drive home and in the hour before I was sound asleep, we passed the time with careful and quiet conversation about Oma, of course, about Teddy and Tom John and the several destinations he and I had reached, neither Harry nor I possessing the energy or the bravery to initiate the subject that hung in the thick air of the house like unwelcome perfume.

This morning, too, we've spoken only about logistical details so far, and I steer steadfastly clear of any more meaningful stuff until we pass the livestock auction, its hardpan parking lot empty except for a stock trailer missing a tire. "I do appreciate your willingness not to try to talk for a while," I tell Harry, turning to look at him, seeing in profile a face that's profoundly familiar yet also newly unknown to me. "I'm not sure I can successfully combine attention to Oma with this other thing."

"We'll talk. There'll be a good time before long. There's a million things I could say, or should...or maybe shouldn't," he says, staring straight ahead.

With those few words we make the kind of quick pact we've made a million times before, this time agreeing that Oma does indeed command our current attention, but also acknowledging that what Harry almost always needs to confront with tangled conversation I inherently prefer to address simply with patience— with avoidance, he would say. Yet I don't truly want to shun the subject of our marriage and what these last weeks have done to it. I simply want to see whether I begin to understand a thing or two, whether anything approaching clarity comes to me like the kind of grace they described to us in Sunday school so very long ago. God, how I would welcome that gift, I realize as we enter town and make our way to the hospital and work jointly but silently to maneuver me out of the car and into my rented chair.

Minutes later, as we leave the elevator, I see Dr. Theobold standing at a nurses' station writing orders in a patient's chart. Harry wheels me toward him and we catch his eye.

"Good. I'm glad you're here," he says, but he seems downcast. He closes the chart and walks over to us, his hands in his trousers' pockets. "Well, we're all set. But I wish I could say she was better. She's still full of infection; we're not making much headway. And this morning her urine output has slowed."

"How are her blood gases?" I ask, but the doctor only shakes his head because neither is that news good.

Barbara is in Oma's room already. So is my aunt Ruth, Oma's daughter, the member of our clan who is most openly emotive and who, I notice with the surprise that comes from infrequent contact, is beginning to grow old. Ruth warmly hugs both Harry and me and tells us in a whisper, "Your dad and Fran called from their motel. They'll be along in a little bit."

"How is she?" I want to know.

"She's comfortable, I think."

"How are you doing?"

"I'm fine, honey, I'm just fine," Ruth says, hugging me a second time.

At the bed, Barbara is brushing Oma's hair. Hearing my voice, Oma opens her eyes and tries to smile.

"Well, here's the big day," I say. "We got your things, and everything at your house is just fine. Kitty says to tell you to come home soon. We brought your walker too. We're going to have you walking these halls in a couple of days."

Oma nods but doesn't speak. I hand her Bible to Barbara, who begins to thumb its pages absently. Ruth joins us at the bed and takes her mother's hand.

"Shall we read to her?" Barbara asks.

"Will you, sweetheart?" asks Ruth.

"I want to show her something first," I say, turning in my chair to speak to Harry. "Would you bring the walker over here?"

I note that Harry immediately senses what I have in mind, and a thin smile of recognition slips onto his face as he lifts the walker across a corner of the bed and sets it in front of my chair.

"Oma. Oma, can you look at me for a minute?" I ask as I set the wheelchair's brakes. Ruth presses the button that raises the head of the bed, and Oma winces as it does, but her eyes don't falter. She trains them steadily on me and in turn I try to muster firm resolve. "Well, let's see here," I say before I take hold of the walker's handgrips and heave myself up onto my feet.

Ruth gasps. Barbara says, "Yes!" Harry laughs with pleasure from across the room.

A broad smile claiming my face now, I set my feet widely apart, then lift my hands away from the grips, balancing briefly on the legs I've lived without for more than a week now, legs I can't count on anymore but that, for only a moment at least, support me again, holding me proudly upright.

"My part of the bargain," I tell my grandmother. I grip the walker again, but stay on my feet, saying nothing more, my eyes meeting Oma's for another instant.

My grandmother slowly nods her head, then says "hooray" in a voice so faint I hardly hear it.

Ten minutes later, my father and Fran slip quietly into the room, hoping not to interrupt Barbara, who reads beside the bed. Ruth sits in a chair on its opposite side. Harry stands near the window; I sit in the wheelchair again, listening to my sister read the psalms in a voice that is lovely and strong. At eight o'clock, a nurse comes into the room to give Oma an injection, and before much more time has passed, two orderlies—one a Navajo who wears his hair wrapped at the back with a strip of cloth like Tom John often does—transfer Oma to a gurney. Once she's settled, lying flat, Ruth bends over to kiss her mother's cheek; the rest of us in turn take Oma's hand and tell her we'll see her soon. The young men wheel her through the doorway and down the long and quiet corridor.

her wonderful face

OMA PLANNED TO ride in an airplane. She planned to see
Colorado Springs and Denver with Ruth, then meet my father
and Fran at Stapleton Airport and fly with them to
Philadelphia. I hadn't managed to graduate from high school,
but it appeared that I was indeed going to be granted a degree
from Bryn Mawr, and I had asked my father early in my final
year whether, instead of a graduation gift, he and Fran would
bring Oma with them to the June commencement. Dad had
said he wasn't sure she would agree to go, but that he'd do his
best to convince her, and I had imagined escorting her on a
springtime tour of the Atlantic coast, astonishing her with the
myriad sights of Philadelphia, Washington, and New York—
Oma abroad in the world.

I drove up from Santa Fe to see her during my Christmas
break, expecting to have to do some resolute convincing myself,
but Oma utterly surprised me by announcing soon after I sat on
her living room sofa that my father had made the offer and she
had accepted with delight.

"Really? You're coming? Wow, you really are?"

"Well, I'm going to try to," Oma said. "I can't really believe it,
but if they let seventy-five-year-old ladies get on those airplanes,
I guess I will."

"Oh, it'll be great, Oma," I said, my enthusiasm hard to contain. "We'll show you all around. You'll just love it."

"Imagine," Oma said in response, and she started to chuckle.

But when I called her in April to begin to make specific arrangements, she had grown skeptical, sounding far from certain that she actually would come, telling me I'd have plenty to keep me busy—balancing my attention between my mother and my father and Fran—trying as best she could to talk herself out of the trip.

"Oma, I want you to come, for sure," I said into the receiver, sensing already that persuasion probably was futile. "It'll be so neat to have you here, and honestly, no trouble in the slightest. But it is up to you."

"Oh, sweetie, I've already had lots of fun just imagining it. That's been a pleasure already," she said, and she seemed to mean it. "But if I don't get there, I want you to think of me sitting here in my chair, so full of pride and beaming, the same as if I was sitting beside your dad."

"It won't be," I told her, my disappointment still evident in my voice when soon we said good-bye.

But I did try to envision her on the day, six weeks later, when I wore my mortarboard and gown and strode up to the dais to receive my degree, my acceptance into medical school secured, my plans made to move back to the West. I couldn't make out her wonderful face among the sea of faces I saw, but I could imagine her in her chair in Colorado.

perfect blessings

FOR FOUR DAYS, Oma has been in intensive care, too weak, too ill to be transferred elsewhere, too strong yet to slip away. Her heart stopped twice, but was revived, in the midst of Tuesday's lengthy surgery, and she remains horribly septic, the opportunistic infection spreading rapidly now. Her heartbeat is still erratic, her lungs are beginning to fill with fluid, and the respirator that kept her breathing during the operation hasn't yet been removed.

Old and anxious friends of hers and friends and colleagues of ours who call the hospital are being told that Mary Margaret Lewis's condition is guarded, which I'm sure sounds as if a brave watch is being kept against further trouble, but which skirts the truth: Oma is living her last hours, and one of us, at least, is with her continually now.

During times when I've been with her alone, twice she's raised her hand and touched the fat respirator that fills her gaping mouth and the nasogastric tube that's inserted into a nostril, pulling at them as if to remind me that prior to the surgery she made a very specific request. Twice I've told her I know she wants them removed, that I do as well, and the second time, I even describe to her the rather heated discussion I had with Dr. Theobold.

"She clearly told me on Saturday night, a week ago, that she didn't want her life prolonged in any way," I explained to him.

"I understand, Sarah," he said, "and I am sensitive to that, but as long as she's conscious and as lucid as she is, but still basically unimproved, I can't agree to it."

"But she can't even talk," I told him, my voice breaking as I tried to make my point. "Jesus, Pete, she just wants to say a few things before she dies. She's tripping the respirator on her own. Let's just see how she does without it."

Pete looked down at the polished toes of his shoes. "If you were in my position, Sarah, you know you'd be saying the same thing— that in her present condition it would be irresponsible to pull it. As soon as she's stronger, though, I promise we'll take her off."

"She's not going to get stronger."

"I don't know that. I don't know that at all."

"If you were in my shoes," I said, turning my chair away from him and giving up for the moment, "you'd want to grant your grandmother's wishes."

I tell Oma I do understand the dilemma Pete Theobold is in; I've often been in similar situations and I know how hateful they are. I promise her, however, that I will continue to try to convince him, that I'll do whatever I can. She looks at me with eyes that still seem sharply focused, eyes trying their best to speak, and she tugs again at the tubes.

We divide each day into three shifts—my father and Fran waiting in the family lounge adjacent to the ICU from eight in the morning until late in the afternoon, checking on Oma, talking briefly to her, holding her hand for five minutes every hour; Barbara and Ruth spell them in the afternoon and stay until midnight; Harry and I are with her, or nearby, from midnight until morning. We are all exhausted by now, each of us in an eerily placid emotional daze, but although the routine itself provides a kind of comfort for us, once each hour we are reminded that Oma is captive in a room where the lights never dim and where she has no notion whether it is day or night, her eyes trained only on the ceiling, her voice surrendered to the wheezing respirator, her valiant spirit still unable to let go of living.

But then Oma performs a miracle. She executes a simply and wonderfully miraculous act at the close of her life, one as remarkable as any of her profound accomplishments during the preceding ninety-three years—the lives she's created, the deaths she has endured, her faith, her curiosity, her laughter.

At 4:15 on Tuesday morning, almost a week since the surgery, an ICU nurse whom I've begun to like very much comes into the lounge where I lie on a long sofa and Harry sleeps slumped in an overstuffed chair. "Dr. MacLeish," she whispers, and I'm suddenly alert.

"Is she...?"

The nurse holds out her hand to calm me. "She's stable," she says. "But she's removed the respirator."

"What?"

"Somehow. I can't believe it, but she pulled it out. She got it completely out. I've already called Dr. Theobold. He said it isn't to go back in."

I nod appreciatively. "How is she breathing?"

"Her ventilation is poor. Real poor, but she *is* breathing."

In the moments it takes for Harry to telephone the others and for the nurse to help me maneuver into my chair, what at first seemed impossible begins to make obvious and perfect and overwhelming sense. Oma, I understand clearly now, has comprehended everything I've attempted to explain. She's understood that Dr. Theobold believes he can't in good conscience remove her from the respirator; she's known that I can't intercede, that none of us simply can demand that it be done. Only Oma herself can take complete control of these complex circumstances. And so, unbelievably but quite wonderfully, she has.

A strong and healthy middle-aged man would have a hard time drawing a respirator tube up through his own trachea, across his bruised larynx and out of his grateful mouth, but this astonishing task Oma has just accomplished. Hours before, I watched her struggle just to lift her frail hand to her face, but incredibly, and in a way that makes me want to believe in sublime and perfect blessings, she has summoned the strength to breathe on her own again, even if it hastens her end.

Beside her bed, I look at her for a long time but don't speak. I marvel at how beautiful she appears, how wise and extraordinary she is, and I'm overwhelmed for a moment by how much I'm going to miss her. As I watch, as I feel Harry's broad hand cupping my shoulder blade, Oma forms the word *good* with her lips and pushes it out with a tiny puff of breath.

I nod. "I'm so proud of you," I tell her, and then I begin to cry.

Ruth reads from the psalms again as Oma's breathing slows in the following hour. My father strokes her forehead with a hand that belongs to an aging man, and hand in hand with him, Fran and Barbara and Harry and I ring the head of her bed. We cluster ourselves around Oma to keep her with us a little while, and then at dawn she dies.

what i encountered at home

IT WAS THE time I experienced the end of innocence. It marked my transition from the simple certainties of childhood to the succeeding and lifelong years in which little is absolute and the best questions probably go unanswered. Yet in my memory, there was no single moment of epiphany, no watershed of insight, nothing that in itself signaled the sudden realization that this place, in fact, wasn't the center of the world.

From the time when I first became aware of my surroundings, vaguely conscious of the sustenance of family and the reassurance of landscape, it had seemed clear to me that the earth spun on an axis that sliced through the heart of the sere Four Corners country. The rivers whose headwaters trickled here finally gained strength and substance and flowed away to the peripheral places that I had heard about but only barely envisioned. The people who lived here—one sister and many hundreds of schoolmates, the parents who controlled life and set its specific agenda, the grandparents who were smarter somehow and knew that life kept its own chaotic kind of control—were people with splendid and animated faces, with distinctive habits and hearty laughs and wonderful stories to tell. They were people possessed of vital reality, unlike those in the rest of the world who simply took up space, or so it seemed.

But then, at about the time I began to temper my obsessive affection for Bill, my grandfather's horse, I started too to peer beyond Montezuma Valley and the mountains and canyons that enclosed it and sealed it off, and much of what lay beyond this center of things riveted my attention. Bob Dylan, the Beatles, Simon and Garfunkel, J. D. Salinger, and Sylvia Plath, the torrential images of television and the liberation of rock and roll—all were wonderfully invigorating, and all were elsewhere, and they began to matter more to me than what I encountered at home. There seemed to be this paradise called California, a place, or perhaps only an idea, called Carnaby Street, and both seemed inconceivably far from Cortez. In other parts of America, people were fighting and sometimes dying for social justice, and in a tiny country at the edge of the China Sea, something frightening and momentous was under way, yet people in Cortez seemed unconcerned.

The planet spun on an axis that had nothing to do with the place where I was standing, I discovered—one with no relationship to my particular vantage point, one unconcerned with who I was or where I'd lived my cloistered years. That realization—one every adolescent makes, I suppose—was overwhelming in many ways, scary, to be sure, but equally emancipating and full of euphoric possibility. Yet in my case, with it came not only the discovery that this meager piece of the far-flung American West was merely a place—one of many millions—but also the swelling recognition that it was, in fact, a haggard outpost. It was a barely settled and shoddily built locale in the meaningless back of beyond, and the few people who clung to it—who were born onto its hard soil or who came to it with complex aspirations—were people who lived far from the spirited mainstream, and who mattered, if they mattered at all, only privately and with little purpose.

The people who came here initially, who dug houses into the dirt and later built them under overhanging rock; the tribal people who came after them and who survived to present times; the first curious Europeans, then those who chose this place as a fresh, if forlorn, start: Hiram Lewis and his children abandoning

Kansas City; Hubbard and Margaret Spencer somehow hoping for better than what they'd scratched from Texas; the wry, redheaded Win and the wonderful Mary Margaret; David, Louise, Barbara, and Sarah Lewis—all of us, down the generations and through the several epochs, were people who amounted to little that I could plainly describe in a place that now seemed very distant from every other place extant.

across uneven ground

HARRY PUSHES MY chair down the rutted path that leads to the pond. I want him to roll the chair out onto the narrow pier as well, but he explains that it isn't me he'll worry about if I fall. It's the fact that the wheelchair is a rental.

I smile wanly at him. "So you're confident, are you, that I could manage to get myself out of the water?"

"I don't have the slightest doubt," he tells me, the compliment meant to encompass more than the way I would reach the shore.

"I *am* going to walk one of these days."

"I know you are."

"I mean soon. If I used Oma's walker, I bet I already could take a step or two."

"It's in the back of the car."

"Is it?"

"I didn't think anyone would mind you latching onto it."

"Good," I say. "I'll try when we get back to the house."

In the days since Oma's death, a number of things have needed to be done—many phone calls and a number of arrangements made, meetings with the mortician and the minister, queries about who can adopt a tabby cat and already the family's first tentative conversations about what will be done with Oma's property, a seventy-five-year-old house in need of some attention, a hundred and sixty acres of farm ground suffering some neglect. On Tuesday evening, although we both were exhausted, Harry and I shared a meal with Tom John, and my spirits stayed bright as I remembered how my grandmother always had been so curious about cities and terrain and regions she'd never seen, Tom John describing in turn the way he'd been charmed by how Arkansas, of all earthly places, had sounded fascinating to her. At midday on Wednesday, my mother and Lionel arrived, and although they refused to stay at our house, insisting this time on keeping out of our way, they agreed to join the rest of the family for an early supper at Barbara's house—the first time in nearly twenty years that my mother and father had been in the same place—and the encounter went surprisingly smoothly, the two of them treating each other cordially in deference to Oma's death.

I asked Harry to take me home soon after Rudy grilled hamburgers beside the back porch and served them at a picnic table with the obvious pride of the very-occasional cook—this subdued but nonetheless lighthearted occasion earning his best behavior— and I thanked him and Barbara for their hospitality, explaining to the rest of the clan that the lack of sleep finally had caught up with me. Yet once we were home—out in the quiet country again and peaceably on our own—the evening seemed inviting still and I wanted to go down to the pond for a bit instead of going inside. A hint of moisture hung in the motionless air; cumulus clouds overhead seemed to be sampling the entire spectrum of colors, and steadfast Teddy was full of energetic cheer.

Harry walks out to the end of the pier now, throws a stick into the roiled water for Teddy to retrieve, then comes back to me. "I'm glad there won't be any eulogies tomorrow," he tells me.

"Did you see the obituary in the paper?"

"Did they screw something up?"

"No, it was fine, but something about it seemed odd." I rest my forearms on the chair and lean back to see the sky. The clouds have begun to lose their luster. "She wouldn't have wanted any attention. What was there, if that much, would have suited her just fine. But I don't know. Those few pieces of information didn't sound like her at all."

"We know who she was."

"I know, and I know it doesn't matter. But when I read it I wanted to say, 'Yes, she *was* just a ranch wife somewhere out of the way, who raised a family and lived very quietly for an awful lot of years, but Jesus, she was extraordinary too.' It made me want to defend her."

"I'm not sure she needs defending." Harry sits on the matted grass, leaning back against the trunk of a cottonwood tree that is probably as old as Oma.

"God, if I could live with that kind of—I don't know—poise," I say. "That kind of acceptance of what my situation is, yet not get sullen or disgusted. She never went anywhere, never did anything, but there was always something she was captivated by."

Harry smiles. "You make her sound a little like a Tibetan monk."

I like that image. "A little old lady Methodist monk." Then I turn to look at Harry, my levity leaving me as quickly as it's come. "Do you know what it took for her to pull that respirator? I'm not at all sure I could have done it. It would have been a real effort for *you* to do it. It took strength she just didn't have. Even in that impossible situation, she still took control. She exercised her options."

"Which you didn't think either of you had."

"Me? I don't know. But if I do end up stuck in this chair or in the house, or stuck with you, for God's sake, maybe it doesn't have to seem so terrifying. Maybe I can still claim a little control. I don't know."

"You're stuck with me?" Harry is on his feet.

"Oma's sure kept us away from that subject, hasn't she?" My eyes meet his, but only for a moment.

"I don't want to be stuck with you," he responds. I've been home for most of a week, and Oma now has died, and Harry is trying at last to begin the conversation. "Would you believe me if I told you I *want* to be with you?"

I toss my hair back as if to sweep the subject into silence once again. When I turn to him I'm sure my face betrays the aching complication of it all. "Shouldn't we go experiment with that walker?" I say, snubbing Harry's attempt to take us where we have to go because it's a place to which I'm not yet ready to travel.

Harry acquiesces once more, says nothing more, and as he maneuvers the chair I can tell his silence bears no indignation. He can wait for our talking and our decisions—I feel him say directly, but he does so absent words. The sky is going gray now, and Teddy is dripping wet, and neither do I say anything more as Harry pushes me up the slope toward the house, across uneven ground.

distant and uncommon people

IN OMA'S YARD on occasional summer evenings, Barbara and I would squeeze together into the tire swing, and our grandfather would push us so high we nearly reached the looming limbs of that enormous cottonwood. We would walk with him down to the milking shed at dusk, watch as he pulled at his poor cows' swollen udders, and marvel at the pinging sound the milk made as it shot against the steel sides of the bucket. Then it was time for bed.

Oma would bring a coffee can for us to pee into in the night if we needed to, and the three of us would make our way up the narrow stairs that led to the attic bedroom. Once Barbara and I had settled the issue of whose side of the bed was whose and were calmly under the covers, Oma would turn out the light and acquiesce to our demands for a story—and almost always, we would want to hear the story about the cat.

When she was still a teenager but in charge of her younger brothers and sisters, twice a week Oma would drive them in the buckboard the three miles to the post office and general store at Lewis to buy the staples they needed and could afford and to check for infrequent mail. The postmistress, a woman who took a softhearted interest in these motherless Spencer children, always was cordial and usually had a new name to tell them—a name she'd noticed on the return address of a letter bound for one of her patrons, a name which—if they deemed it odd enough—the children would add to the string of names they'd already attached to the family cat. It wasn't too many trips to Lewis before their scrawny little tabby was called Percival Reggie Ambrose Frederick Cecil Algernon Van Heusen Archibald Grotepeter Coepeter Pangobales Okenpaw Judas Iscariot Spencer. The name "Judas Iscariot," Oma would confess each time at our urging, didn't come from the post office, however. It had been bestowed on the day the cat ate half the chicken she had plucked for supper.

Then we would demand to hear all about the people whom Oma had imagined were the owners of those amazing names. "Tell us about Percival," one of us ritually would insist.

"Well, Percival was a painter in the proud city of Paris," she would say, "and he was positively puzzled by how popular he was."

"And Reggie?"

"Reggie drove a rickshaw in raucous Rangoon, but it was a rickety rickshaw that the royalty wouldn't ride."

"Ambrose!" one of us would shout.

"Well, Anabelle Ambrose ate apples in Alabama, but all the apples she ever ate couldn't fill her ample appetite."

Each night we made it all the way to ignoble Judas Iscariot, and we ultimately knew the alliterated stories as well as Oma did, of course, but one night I remember asking her when she finished if she ever had sent letters of her own to these distant and uncommon people.

"Well, I believe I must have," she said. "I believe I wrote to each of them to say I'd be proud to make their acquaintance one fine day, and that I'd love to see the splendid sights wherever they happened to live."

"Did you meet any of them?" Barbara asked, as gullible as I was.

"Well, I don't guess I ever did," Oma said. "And, of course, I didn't get to visit all those places, but oh, that cat of ours sure had a proud and worldly name, didn't he?"

We agreed he surely did as Oma said good night, and even now, each time I'm at the ocean I still remember Okenpaw, who ate beside it and always ordered ordinary oysters.

to mark her passing

NONE OF OMA'S contemporaries from her earliest years at Lewis remains alive. The women who bring casseroles and rolls, a ham, vegetables from their gardens, and several cakes to her house today are the daughters—and even the granddaughters—of her first friends and neighbors, some of them in their seventies already, a few of them ill or feeble enough that it will not be many months before their own funeral dinners will be served. I know most of them, know their names at least, and since I can't be much help ferrying plates and platters from the kitchen to the cloth-draped dining room table, I sit in a chair near the back-porch door and greet the farm women as they arrive, introducing them to those of us they do not know, thanking them for their thoughtfulness and generosity, agreeing when they tell me with teary eyes that Oma was the sweetest thing they ever knew.

We returned to the house not long after noon. The service at the church was brief, and it was a joyous one in a way that surprised and pleased me. Then Oma's coffin was settled into the earth beside her husband's, their joint headstone in place for nearly thirty years now, lacking only the date that soon will be chiseled in to mark her passing. I hadn't been able to negotiate the concrete steps that led to the little clapboard church by myself, but Barbara's boys—both wearing ties and eager to be of help to their crippled aunt and ally—lifted me to the top of them, then I clutched Oma's walker and awkwardly shuffled the few feet to the pew at the front where the rest of the family was seated. At the cemetery, I had to resort to the wheelchair, afraid that the thick grass would catch my clumsy feet, but at Oma's house I reverted to the walker once again, the aluminum thing surrounding me like a fence.

As we are about to ask people to begin to fill their plates—the old oak table filled now with a splendid array of food—Alice and Tom John come to the back door and tentatively peer inside before I see them and wave them in. I've never seen Tom John in a suit before, and something about the way he wears it with a stiff white shirt and an oddly outdated tie makes him look as though he might earn his living baptizing sinners on the banks of languorous Southern rivers. Alice looks lovely, her hair pulled back and tied in a thick French braid. Tom John hugs me and holds me tight, momentarily lifting me out of my chair, then he tells me what a pretty place the cemetery was, saying he might even agree to die someday if we will lay him there.

I saw them together at the church, and waved from a car as we waited at the cemetery, but I hadn't been able to speak to Tom John until now. "I'm so pleased you came," I say, my eyes aimed at him.

"I wanted to," Alice says, aware that I didn't address my words to her, and there is something in the way she speaks that implies there is much she wants to try to say. "I didn't know her very well, but..."

I nod my head. Part of me wants to tell Alice I hope I never see her again after today. Another part wants her to know that I'm sure we share aching hearts, if nothing else. But instead of saying anything directly to her, I only motion toward the table and tell both her and Tom John to help themselves, saying Oma would have insisted that we all have lots to eat. I do mention as they start to make their way toward the crowded dining room I'd like them to stop by our house this evening. "We don't have anything planned and won't have much to serve you," I say, "but it seems like the kind of day to get together."

"I'd love to stop by," says Tom John, telling me that Harry already has issued the invitation. Alice purses her lips and nods in a way that seems to say she isn't sure.

how she could stay so silent

THOSE OF US at Oma's house are relaxed and at exhausted ease now, and we eat and talk long into the afternoon. Harry and Barbara's boys and a few others who own insatiable appetites do their best to empty the table, but by the time people begin to go, there still seems to be almost as much food as there was when the meal began, and Barbara, Ruth, and I do our best to send some of it along with everyone who's leaving.

But before too many people go out to their cars, my father stands in the archway between Oma's small living room and the dining room and, in the speaking voice he's mastered during a career spent in public schools, he thanks everyone for their many kindnesses, their friendship to Oma and her family, and their prayers. "It's been wonderful to have you fill the house this afternoon. I have to admit I don't look forward to tomorrow when it will seem so quiet. Barbara reminded me that in just a few more days, it would have been seventy-five years since Oma and my father were married and moved in here. Imagine." It's a word Oma herself always used. "Imagine," she would say, as if to exclaim, "isn't life the most amazing thing you've heard of."

My father says nothing more and soon the house is almost empty, and he and Aunt Ruth stand on the lawn beneath the cottonwoods and offer individual farewells. Barbara, Harry, and two women from the Lewis church clean the kitchen, the chair I've been sitting in now moved near the sink so I can dry a few dishes and feel like I'm being of use.

"The next question is," Barbara says, her arms deep in sudsy water, "who am I going to call every day from now on? I talked to Oma every morning, as soon as I'd gotten the boys pointed out the door."

"You can call me," I tell her.

"I guess it's just you and me now, isn't it?"

"Scary thought, huh?"

"We'll be okay," Barbara says, glancing at me with eyes that remind me of Oma's, strong and sharp and unafraid.

Later, I try to walk once more as Harry and I are preparing to leave, but my legs have had enough, it seems. They are weak again and uncooperative, and Harry has to fetch the wheelchair from the car. Barbara, Ruth, my father, and I agree we will return in the morning to begin to go through some things, then Harry wheels me down the ramp at the back of the house that was built for Oma years before. The afternoon heat has abated a bit by now, the heat's haze has settled, and the wide fields at Win and Mary Margaret Lewis's place stretch away beneath bright white and scudding clouds.

My mother and Lionel are at our house when we arrive, entertaining Teddy. I saw them at the cemetery, but they decided not to go to Oma's afterward, concerned again that they might intrude. Harry makes us drinks, we take them to the deck, which is shaded by pear trees, and I mention that we think Tom John and Alice will stop by as well.

"Lovely," my mother says. "But in that case, perhaps we'd better blurt out our news before they arrive."

"News?" Harry inquires.

"News," says Lionel, his face bright until something else concerns him. "I hope you don't think that today's an inappropriate day for us to tell you this, but, well, your mother and I have decided to be married."

"Yes?" Harry is enthusiastic. They nod, then look at each other with a kind of conspiratorial delight.

Harry says, "Hear, hear," and I give them quieter congratulations. I'm happy for them, and today is a fine day for the announcement, but for some reason, or for many of them, I can't muster true excitement.

"We want your sage advice," Lionel says, his words aimed at both of us. "We want our marriage to be as good as what you've got, so we want all your secrets."

But before either Harry or I can manage what will have to be an awkward and elliptical and strangely weighted response, Tom John comes out of the house. "Here you are," he says, and Alice is close behind him.

The six of us sit outside as the afternoon softens into evening, colors coming back into the summer landscape in the low and angled light, the house's veiling shadow spreading across the lawn to the pasture just beyond. My mother has met Alice and Tom John before, but they are new acquaintances to Lionel, and the four of them seem to enjoy each other's company, Tom John regaling them with stories about his excavations in the early days, tales about farmers who, when plied with whiskey, would unlock their cellar doors and show him dazzling pots and baskets that they'd illegally taken from public land, about a mule he'd bought in the summer of 1964 for packing, a critter who could break every hobble ever fashioned and who, Tom John claimed, could find his former pasture-mates from any distance in the dark.

"The image of you as a muleskinner is very entertaining," Alice tells him.

"I'll have you know that the mule is the state animal of Arkansas," Tom John responds in pretended pique. "Or if he isn't, he ought to be. They are complex steeds, it is true, but you've just got to treat them with clear and basic understanding of their particular worldview."

We laugh. Even earnest Lionel is tickled before he turns to me and asks, "And how are your horses, by the way?"

"Fat and lazy as usual, I'm afraid. And they act almost affronted when you have the gall to get up on their backs."

"They aren't exactly show animals," Harry explains. "The horseshoer kind of cringes when he sees them."

"Now," my mother scolds, "I think they're sweet. Shall we all go pay them a visit? I'm wearing decent shoes for it. How about the rest of you?"

I decline to go, decline to make Harry, or anyone else, push me through the sodden pasture, but from the deck I can watch the others wander far away—the stubborn horses still standing alongside the southern fence, neither making so much as a move to come toward them. Then I see someone turn back toward the house, and before she comes very close, I can see that it is Alice.

I tell her to help herself to another drink when she reaches the deck again, and as she comes back out from the kitchen with fresh glasses for both of us, she says what she's rehearsed in the moments she spent inside. "I wanted to tell you that I appreciated your being cordial to me today. I wasn't sure I should go, but..."

I say, "I was glad you were there."

Then suddenly, there are tears in Alice's expressive eyes. "I...I feel so terrible," she says. "I don't know what to say, except that. I have ruined something that was more important to me than you can know."

I turn to look toward the pasture again because I don't want to see her anguished face. I'm silent for a while, then I say what little there is for me to say. "While we were driving, Tom John and I, when neither of us was talking, sometimes I'd plan these perfect conversations I was going to have with Harry—how I'd brilliantly make him feel like the piece of shit that he is, and how I'd demonstrate my steely disgust and how I didn't need him and would not have him back. I imagined a conversation or two with you too, but it was harder to know what I wanted to say. I wanted to say something that really would hurt you—as eviscerating as I could make it—but with Oma, somehow the air went out of everything I thought I had to shout."

"I've wanted to try to give you an explanation, but...anything I think of sounds asinine."

"No. I really don't want to hear anything from you," I tell her, and that is one thing I'm still very sure of.

"I'm looking at options, work possibilities, in a few other places. A fresh start may be the one proactive thing I can do."

"I can't answer that one for you," I say, sounding more preachy than I mean to. Then finally, I look at Alice. Her eyes are puffy, her cheeks are flushed and moist, and in this instant she seems very much alone.

"Things can't be the same, can they?" she asks me.

I need a moment before I find a way to respond, and then I do by telling her a story. "Did I ever tell you about my grandfather? I must have told you this. Every so often he would just disappear. He'd be gone for a week or so on these terrible drinking binges. Oma never knew if he was in Cortez or Dolores or somewhere farther away, whether he was in jail or not. This happened maybe nine or ten times over all those years, but he would just abandon them. Then he'd finally come home and dry out and get back to his life. She hated it. She hated how he baled out of the work that had to be done, and she hated the drinking, and she believed it shamed the whole family.

"When I asked her once why she thought he did it, I assumed she'd say, 'Oh, honey, it must have been losing the little ones,' or that it was the hard times during the Depression, but she just said, 'Well, I guess it was because none of us is ever who we wish we were.' I asked her if she gave him any ultimatums. She said she was sure he knew that she'd have liked to kill him, but all she ever said out loud was that it was good to have him home."

The others have come through the fence's wire gate now and are making their way toward the deck. Alice can't see them from where she sits, and I wave at them to let her know they are nearing. She stands and turns to look in their direction—Harry and beloved Tom John rapt in conversation, their heads bent forward as they walk, behind them my mother arm-in-arm with the man she wants to marry.

"There's no moral to that story," I say to Alice, "except to say that now I think I understand how she could stay so silent."

the sorrow of archaeology

"SHE DIDN'T BEAR any children, evidently," Harry says as he and I drive in his truck toward Tse Canyon, the morning cool and still and splendid. "Alice's friend at UNM was pretty certain, I guess. She didn't think she'd reached puberty yet. And like you did, she thought the leg was congenital." I wonder whether he remembers giving me that information once before—by phone on the day Tom John and I were about to embark for Alaska.

Although only a few weeks have passed, it seems like such a long time since I encountered that ancient child, since I began to wonder what her life was like and worried about her death. The initial and uneasy shock of finding her bones beneath the ground, the sad evidence of her wasted leg, and the puzzling question about what might have caused that killing blow to her head unquestionably troubled me for a time. Somehow, her gray bones personalized those early people in a way I'd never imagined them before. The certain difficulty of her days and the presumably bleak circumstances at her end seemed to certify what Oma always had been sure of—that life's plights were visited on everyone, and that people had endured them for a very long time by now.

Yet in the days since Tom John and I ran away from trouble, since I returned to Cortez and watched my grandmother die with uncommon dignity and a spirit so brave it soared, I've been surprisingly at ease about the girl I disturbed at Tse Canyon, giving her only a little conscious thought, interring her again, I trust, into the unfathomable sweep of time and the tangled human record.

"Did the people at Mesa Verde have anything to say about the skull?" I ask, remembering how I briefly held her broken cranium like a mother cradling an infant child, remembering how my thoughts had leaped to what it might have been like to hold my own child in my arms, the daughter I'd hoped to name after Oma.

"They couldn't add anything. Definitely a blow from a heavy object, but other than that, I don't think we're going to figure out much more." Harry glances at me as though I will bear this as bad news.

"Sure," I tell him. Then after a bit I say, "Isn't it sad and sort of defeating that all you've got to go on are ceramics, and bone, and stones stacked up for houses? It seems like that's the sorrow of archaeology—that all it offers are hints and suppositions and good guesses. You try to figure out how people lived, and who they were, and what sense they had of themselves and the world they inhabited, but you've got so little to go on in the end."

"Look at the question of how we live today," Harry says in quiet response. "We have every tool imaginable and time is the present tense, but are we any better at understanding our own culture? Can we make better sense of our own lives than the life of the girl you found?"

"Maybe not," I say, taking his point, yet still feeling mournful about the fact that there's so little we really can know about what purposes our lives might have. "Maybe the end of it for me is just to wish her well. She was as inconsequential as the rest of us, obviously, but I hope that twelve years were enough for her to have a life before she died."

"I doubt she solved any eternal mysteries," says Harry.

I smile at him across the dusty seat, his tanned face darkened further by the shade of his archaic cowboy hat. "Actually, what I hope is that she got to be old enough to be a bit confused."

"You sound like maybe you still feel kind of connected to her."

"Not really. But I guess I can't help it in a way. She, Oma—me too, I'm beginning to wonder—have lived our entire lives right here. That's a pretty direct connection."

Harry shakes his head. "I'm about the smartest guy I know, but I'm not sure I'll ever understand why living here is such a difficult proposition for you."

"Neither will I," I say, then I laugh at myself in a way I wouldn't have a week ago. "Maybe it has to do with the question—the worry—of whether I'm really choosing how to spend those years, or just acquiescing. I'd love to have Oma's contentment, the peace she always possessed, but..." My words trail away, and I hear my father's voice, and Oma's too, in the way my words cannot describe my completed thought. Or is it that that particular thought—the question of my contentment—really does not begin or end?

No one is working at the site this Saturday. Harry needs to find the field book he lost track of during the preceding chaotic days, and Teddy and I have come along for the ride. The August sun is high in the sky by the time we get out of the pickup, but in the fragrant forest of piñon and juniper trees that encircles the head of the canyon, the air is cool and undisturbed still. Jays cackle at our intrusion, and I catch a glimpse of a big-eared doe as she bounds away from worry. The wheelchair has stayed at home, and Harry lifts the walker out of the bed of the truck for me as Teddy darts into the trees, certain the place is foul with rabbits. I can't take an extended hike yet, but my walking still is improving, and I reach the recently excavated kiva where Harry thinks he left his notebook not too long after he does, following him down the powdered-dirt path, remembering as I watch him disappear in front of me how his gait always seems to dance a little when he enters these scrawny woods.

"Well, that was easy," he announces from below me, standing on the kiva's packed-earth floor, holding up the yellow book that contains his arcane secrets.

"This is lovely," I say, surveying the tightly jointed masonry of the kiva's cylindrical red-rock wall.

"Isn't it? There were lots of ceramics on the floor of this one. Most had been broken when the roof beams fell, but there was this gorgeous little effigy of a magpie that was still intact."

"A magpie?"

"I think so—from the markings and the eyes."

"I'm going to miss being out here all the time," I tell him, my eyes scanning across the kiva to the canyon's slender cut.

"What do you mean?" My saying that seems to concern him.

"I think I'm going to retire from this rocky occupation."

Harry doesn't ask me more until he's climbed the aluminum ladder. "Stop digging out here?" he asks as he comes over to the shade I've found beneath a juniper—a twisted and grand old tree that looks like it might have been a sapling in the days when the people who built the kiva gathered a few possessions and walked away.

"Pete Theobold asked me the other day if I'd consider doing some fill-in work for him and his partners—vacation call and other occasional help, some GYN work with patients who'd be more comfortable seeing a woman."

"Are you up to it?"

"Oh, probably not, but if I keep getting stronger...Being at the hospital with Oma, I was reminded that medicine's the one thing I actually know a little something about. I can't pick up where I left off, or probably ever do too much, but maybe I could lend a hand occasionally."

Harry looks at me a little quizzically, trying to gain some sense of where this new initiative has come from, what has brought it to wavering life. He holds out his hands to help me to the ground, then sits beside me on the matted needles that litter the base of the tree. "Well, I guess I can try to replace you, although I suspect the attempt will be futile." He pauses. "Can I ask you something?"

"You can."

"How much does this have to do with us? With Alice?"

"All I can tell you," I say in quick response, "is that something about Pete's offer sounded good to me and seemed to make sense. But yes, Alice...I don't know. I don't know what's in store. Do you?" It's the first time since I've been back that I've asked him how he feels, about where he believes we go from here.

Harry looks away, intently watching something I can't see. But I can sense the swelling emotion inside him. I wait, scratching at the dry needles with a stick, and I can see that tears have clouded his eyes when he finally says, "The worst part was the fact that you forecasted it. I don't know why, but the fact that you assured me I'd do something like that someday, and then I . . . "

"Maybe I gave you permission."

"Don't be noble about—"

"I'm not being noble, Harry," I tell him, the words coming out of my mouth in an icy defense. "I'm being realistic." I let out a long sigh that is meant to tell him that I don't have readier answers than he does. "I remember when I was doing a neurology rotation in Denver during my residency, seeing MS patients among the other grim disorders. This neurologist who I liked a lot told us exactly what I told you. As far as he was concerned, it was such a certainty that you could almost demonstrate it clinically." I look at Harry, who is looking away. "He also said that nine times out of ten, despite the sense of betrayal and the terrible guilt, the spouse ends up bailing out. It just gets too hard finally, he said, and the spouse simply goes away."

Harry turns to me, his face blanched by what I've said, his eyes reflecting the cruel indictment I've seemed to issue. "So in our case you simply waited for that prediction to come true." His voice is quiet, careworn.

"And then it did, didn't it?" I ask him, as quietly and directly as I can.

"I still don't know what happened. I mean, yes, of course, I do." I haven't seen Harry cry in longer than I can remember, and his tears begin to draw me to him in a way I don't want to allow. "But how I let it happen, or why . . . the only explanation for why is that I'm a pretty disgusting human being."

"What's hardest for me," I tell him, my tears still staying at bay, my voice soft yet still distant, "isn't just this now. If that's really all it was—just one night of drunken fucking—I think it would be simple enough to shift and adjust and for me to reconsider some things. But what slices through me is the way in which this . . . illustrates—I guess that's a word I can use—what's been with you forever. Do you know what it's been like to sense your longing all these years? Longing that isn't directed toward me? Do you know what it's felt like for you to wish so strongly, but in vain, that I was someone else?"

"I love you. You know that." Harry's composed enough to argue now. "And you know, goddamn it, that what I've wanted both of us to do was to challenge ourselves, change our skins whenever we chose, to dig deep into things."

"Digging. You think you want to dig deep but that I insist on staying on the surface of things. That I'm shallow and you're so very deep. Well, fuck you. That simply isn't true." It feels so good to say this at long last, to tell him how ridiculous he is about what I want or don't, but this is normally a kind of confrontation I abhor, and already I'm searching for ways to bring it to a close. "You think I'm shallow, timid, stuck, and you don't really have a clue who I am, and that breaks my heart."

"Who are you?" he asks after a time. His faltering voice is full of collected anguish, and it may be the first time I've ever heard him sound as if he truly wants to know.

"One thing you don't understand is how much I wish I were like Oma," I tell him, my stick by now having dug something of a trench between my legs. "You think I'm afraid of change, but what I really want is something that feels like safety. I want to be completely secure, to be contented in this place and to feel *your* contentment with *me*. Instead, I've always felt the opposite of that—I've felt whatever it is that gnaws at you, and instead of feeling secure, I've always had to wonder when you'll finally be out the door." I toss the stick aside and stare at the hole I've made in the needled soil beneath the tree. "But now, it's all very different. I can't explain it, but the trip with Tom John and the way Oma died..." For the first time today, I want to cry as well, remembering the valiant way her long life came to a close. "She was stuck in the ICU with tubes down her throat and was simply going to have to wait. It looked like she was absolutely powerless, but the miracle was that she wasn't. *She* pulled the respirator; *she* stayed in charge. Do you have any idea how much that means to me? If she can do it on her deathbed, then surely I can maintain control as well—whether it's some sort of autonomy, given the body I now have, or whether it's life with you or without you. The deal is,

Harry, I'm not going to wait for what comes at me anymore, and you need to know that." I turn to look at him and on his tear-streaked face I can see something akin to comprehension.

"No, no, and certainly now you shouldn't wait," he says, and I think perhaps he really is my ally in this instant.

"I'm trying not to anticipate anything anymore," I continue, "not what my body has in store for me, and not what gnaws at you or what you need to make you happy. I'm not just going to wait and I'm not going to worry about why you've always wanted more than me and whether you're focused elsewhere. We both know chances are good that I'm going to have to sit in that chair again someday. And who knows if my arms are going to remain cooperative? And I realize that it may be much the best for you and me to be done."

"I think I understand that too," he says, sounding rueful still, expressing the anguish that certainly still binds us.

"If I wanted to make it easy for you, I honestly think what I should do is demand a divorce. Right now. Let you get on with other things with other people. Have children. But *I'm* going to decide—or *we* are together. I'm not going to simply sit back to see what you or God or anybody decides for me."

"Another possibility is that I may be the one out of the god-damn ten," he says, suddenly buoyant and sounding almost defiant now, the smile that stole my heart so long ago again spreading across his face.

"Harry…" I say as I shake my head, and speaking his name carries with it a hint of everything he means to me, yet it's also a spoken reference to the ways in which he stifles me and makes me feel I've somehow failed, the complex parts of him I love so much and never have liked at all.

"Yes," he says, "we'll decide together."

"And we will see some things very differently," I remind him as Teddy trots up to greet us, his hunt for rabbits evidently unsuccessful and already out of mind. "And this place that works so wonderfully for you may be one I flee from."

"Wherever you find what you really want," Harry says, and I think perhaps he actually has heard me.

I turn to him, and try my best to smile, then push him back onto the dry and dirt-caked and still-pungent needles, holding Harry MacLeish against this ruined ground, my head resting on his strong arm, my eyes focusing farther away on the bright smudge of green where the spring emerges from the rock—two tall cottonwoods and thick willows crowding around the sudden surprise of water—a small spring that once supported hundreds of people in this outpost village, but whose only task in present times is to trickle into the tiny creek that drops and angles away, and that patiently cuts Tse Canyon deeper into the country.

lean rewards

THE BROWN FLOOR of the valley that cradles our little farmstead sweeps northward in waves from the sheer cliffs of Mesa Verde. The valley where I've lived so long is bounded by the mesa and by mountains on three sides, and for ten thousand centuries, canyons have cut it away in the west. On top of a timbered hill in the valley's northern uplands, above the bend where the Dolores River makes a slow but determined turn and begins to carve its way to Utah, the mortared walls of an ancient village still stand, encountered by two Spanish Franciscan friars and members of their expedition on an August day in 1776—the first time evidence of a prehistoric culture was encountered here by Europeans. "There is everything that a good settlement needs as regards irrigable lands, pasturage, timber, and firewood," wrote Fray Silvestre Vélez de Escalante in his journal, conjecturing why those early people might have claimed this place, suggesting that others could come and claim it again.

But a century passed before immigrants began to arrive in any numbers. Pasture here was plentiful in the beginning, as Escalante had promised. The soil was rich in wind-blown pockets, and the river and the trickle of lesser creeks seemed to assure successful irrigation. It had the look of the kind of place where working folk could put down roots and prosper—and it

was obvious that sometime long ago, other people lived here in
large numbers. Yet those first inhabitants, the first people to
build houses here and stay, finally failed. These prehistoric people who did so much in so many ways also surely made some
dear mistakes. They thrived here once, but then, somehow, they
let their lives go bad.

The immigrants who arrived in the middle of the modern
nineteenth century were certain that a similar fate wouldn't—
couldn't—befall them. They had tools and talents the early people
hadn't possessed; America's westering spirit and the Homestead
Act surely were on their side, and they knew somewhere deep in
their bones that work was all they could count on. They succeeded in sending canals that brimmed with the river's water into
much of the thirsty valley, built haggard little supply towns, and
touted this place in pamphlets as a western American Eden. Yet
neither hyperbole nor mean and lifelong struggle ever resulted in
anything akin to collective wealth, nothing approaching ease, and
soon after the turn of the twentieth century, the defeat the early
people suffered was becoming easy to understand.

When Hubbard Spencer and his family arrived in Montezuma
Valley in the rainless summer of 1909, this outpost near the place
where the great new states of Utah and Colorado intersected with
the sprawling New Mexico and Arizona territories had begun to
look a lot more like heartache than like heaven, and the opportu-
nities it once seemed certain to nurture now seemed coldly elu-
sive. Hubbard Spencer hadn't said much as he first surveyed the
patch of ground the government would give him. It was thick with
scrub and stunted trees and its soil cried for moisture. The valley's
irrigation canals coursed nowhere near his property, and even if
he and his sons could manage to dig a lateral ditch, he had no
money to buy the water it would bring.

But going back to Texas was an option he didn't once consider. You could starve to death in Carter County, Texas, as easily as you could in crapped-out Colorado, and at least here you
could do so with some elbow room. The only alternative seemed
to be to grub the sagebrush and tear out a corner of the trees,
plow the plaintive ground, then plant and start to pray. Besides,

this country had fed folks once before, hadn't it? "By damn, these Moquis made the most of this place," he would tell his children at the dinner table in the first years after their mother had died. "It don't have to be the land of milk and honey to make it work. And it's all we got, at any rate."

All the Spencers had, in the end, was enough—at least it was to Oma's eyes. There never was much money, seldom new clothes or shoes, but the work got done, and the next meal somehow always was at hand, and Oma and her siblings grew into tentative adults. They found ground of their own to work in time; they married and raised families and encountered waves of trouble as well, much like those that had drowned their father's dreams. Hardship was a hearty weed whose roots reached deep into the valley's soil, and everyone had to contend with it to some degree. But neither Oma's family nor friends or neighbors ever completely called it quits, none of them moving on to some other touted agrarian paradise.

For most of us—for the children, grandchildren, and now great-grandchildren of that first generation of stubborn homesteaders, Montezuma Valley always has offered enough to get us by, if sometimes little by way of bonus. Survival itself seems the truest measure of success here, in the end, and at the close of too-short lives, I know that the people in Oma's family—*my* family— always have been confident that they've spent their days in excellent and open country, that they've had a fair run at life and have feasted on its lean rewards.

the words i hope i'll speak

THE SUMMER, AS it always does, is surrendering its tenure too soon, and already the distant peaks are powdered with autumn snow. The leaves of the cottonwood trees scattered across our farmstead have begun to go yellow, and the waist-high rabbit-brush is a cascade of orange color on the slope between the house and the pond where four of us casually stand, circling a small hole Harry has dug in the earth.

Earlier in the week, two Hopi men traveled to Cortez from Oraibi to collect the bones of the Puebloan girl I unearthed in June. Under the terms of a 1990 federal law, all human remains and funerary items excavated at archaeological sites or exposed in construction on federal lands now are returned to descendents for reburial. It is legislation Harry supported in testimony before a Congressional sub-committee in 1989, a law that is a practical and appropriate solution to a problem that vexed many Native Americans—and more than few archaeologists—for well over a century. The girl's cranium and ilium returned from Albuquerque by now, I prepared her remains at the field lab on Monday, wrapping each of her brown-stained bones in packing paper, then arranging them as best I could in a human shape inside an elongated cardboard box, which on Tuesday the Hopi men took with them to Arizona, the girl following her people south and west at last.

But I wanted to do more somehow, to conclude my time with her in something of a ritual way, and Harry, Tom John, and Alice have joined me on this beautiful Saturday afternoon for a burial service of sorts. The blanket fragments and the small gray bowl I found with the girl's remains have gone with her to the Hopi mesas, and when Harry finishes digging the hole he places in it a few Puebloan pottery sherds he has found lying here on our place over the years, as well as a handful of the soil from Tse Canyon that had blanketed the Puebloan girl for more than eight hundred years. I hand him two sagebrush sprigs, which he bends down to additionally offer into the earth, and Alice lights a sagebrush smudge as Tom John quietly recites the words of John Donne he has scribbled on a piece of lined paper: "If a clod be washed away by the sea, Europe is the less, as well as if a promontory were, as well as if a manor of thy friend's or of thine own were. Any man's death diminishes me, because I am involved in mankind . . ."

We stand in comfortable silence for a time, then I hand Harry something else to place in the ground that I take from the pocket of my sweater—folded white tissue paper tied with tan string. He looks querulously at me before he takes the object from me, then bends to the ground again, but I choose not to explain what the wrapping contains, deciding in that instant that I will not describe to them the single, pastel-yellow crocheted bootie I discovered a month ago in a drawer at Oma's house, a slip of paper on which she had written "Pair started for Sarah's little one" attached to it with a straight pin. Finally I say, "Thank you for joining me," and Harry fills the hole with soil—the sage and sherds and the bootie Oma once made for a baby who might have carried her name disappearing beneath the dirt.

Slowly, we make our way back to the house; the mood lightens, conversations commence again, and sitting on the deck in the warm afternoon sun a while later Alice mentions that her friend from Mérida has sent more details on the big project that was being planned when they were in Mexico City the year before. "Rosaria said this one's a three-year project, at least, and she's sure I can get a job, but—"

"You couldn't survive in that place, could you?" Tom John is concerned.

"Don't you think Cortez is a good apprenticeship for the rigors of the biggest city in the world?" she asks him.

"The filthiest. The poorest," he counters.

"Oh, but it's still wonderful in its own chaotic way," Harry says, and Alice offers nothing more, remaining intentionally vague, it seems to me, about whether she'll move away. This is the first time I've seen her in weeks, and the connective tissue that once bound us tightly together remains torn and unhealed.

"When I go, it'll be in the other direction," I say, too obviously shifting the subject away from Alice's plans. "I'm going back to the misty Northwest."

"You've been making plans without me?" Tom John teases.

"We really need to start planning our Inside Passage trip," I tell him. "No archaeology allowed. Just life at lazy leisure on a ship, seeing it all, having a fine time."

"Next time, I'm flying up there." Tom John is emphatic. "Weeks after the last little excursion, I swear I'm still seeing white lines in my fitful sleep."

"I'll pick you up at the Seattle airport," I tell him, "and I'll have a guest bedroom for you in my rain-weathered little house on Whidbey Island, and then off we'll go to Alaska."

Each of them returns a questioning glance at me, hoping to learn from my expression whether I really have begun to make such plans or if I'm teasing, but for the second time this afternoon, I choose not to offer information I might have, and I change the subject again by mentioning that in the hospital one evening when we were by ourselves, I confessed to Oma that I hadn't been detained in Denver. I explained to her that Tom John and I actually had taken a bit of a trip. I didn't tell her about the circumstances, but I described our travels for her in long detail— the Great Basin as big as an ocean, the Columbia's stately march to the Pacific, the stink and noise and splendid feel of Puget Sound, our voyage to Alaska, the one we almost made. "She was weak and couldn't ask much, but I could see it in her face as she listened. She could imagine every mile." Then I surprise myself by saying something else. "If I tried to tell you today I'd fall apart, but sometime...," I confess, my thoughts shifting to the thing that still seems so miraculous to me, to Oma's ultimate gift. "Sometime, I'll tell you about the morning she died." I glance at Harry and I can see a glint of acknowledgment in his eyes.

"What was the last thing she said?" Tom John's question is caring and unabashed.

"Good. The word 'good.'" I don't say anything else, and the others are quiet as well, and Tom John finally nods, as if to say... of course.

"Years ago in Chicago," he remembers, breaking a silence that might have continued for a time, "a dear friend of mine was dying long before he should have. Just a minute or so before he left us, he opened his eyes and whispered, 'Well, this is going to be interesting.'" Tom John doesn't know how to continue his story and his eyes flood with tears. "That seemed so... adventurous."

I nod this time, because they do seem to be the finest kind of final words, and because for this brief moment I simply cannot speak, realizing in a sudden rush of emotion that they are the words I hope I'll speak during each uncertain day ahead and then someday at the end.

In the week that follows the simple ritual and the afternoon hours—both welcome and profoundly complex—that I spend with the three of them, those farewell words of Tom John's friend stay with me constantly. They are linked somehow to Oma's act of heroism and her parting word, linked vitally to me as well. Because it *is* going to be interesting, isn't it?—regardless of whether I walk or am captive to a chair; whether I try to remain something of a doctor or go back to digging in the earth for remnants of a time before my time; whether I face the years alone and proud and at ease or in the comfortable company of Harry. At the end of a life that will seem too short no matter how long it lasts, it promises to be interesting—whether I've lived at large in the wondrous world or spent the rest of my days beneath the mesa, on old ground I'm lately trying to enjoy.

author's note

MANY COLLEAGUES WERE wonderfully helpful to me in the writing of this book, foremost among them my life-mate Lydia Nibley, who saw clearly into the story's caverns and lit a lamp to guide me toward them, helping me understand and articulate these lives in ways I otherwise could not. She deepens my work and my life in countless ways. David Lee, Dawn Marano, Lisa Lenard, and Katherine Coles also offered important insights, and I'm grateful to them for their lasting support.

This is a story about a particular time in a particularly dry but nonetheless fertile place. A number of people from that place have enriched it with their singular and invaluable viewpoints, and their lives of work. Some will deny that they played a part at all, but each of them did, in fact, in ways that were vital to me. To Robert Heyl, Joanie Luhman, Ruth Slickman, Emily Sutcliffe, John Sutcliffe, Mark Varien, and the late Ian Thompson, I am greatly indebted. I love them all; I love the place where they reside.